UPON US

CHRIS MOORE

Printed in the United States of America

First Printing, 2018

ISBN: 978-0-9861310-2-8

Beacon House LLC

Cover Photo Credit: Christopher Morrison

www.chrismoorewrites.com

 Created with Vellum

For Veronica

NOTE:

I came up with the idea behind this book while living in the mountains outside Denver around the time of 9/11/2001. In the bars, the classrooms, and lift lines of Breckenridge, I discovered how fashionable it had become to hate America, and to hate the normal family.

And not just any hatred, but a deep and frothing rage ready to burst out whenever a really controversial topic like marriage, laws, borders, or God were mentioned. I worked construction for a number of years after that, but began work on *UponUs* in earnest when I attended Columbia University and encountered the same kind of spiritual rage directed at Americana and anything that smacked of Christian religion. I also discovered this rage was typically linked with sexual depravity. But as I was writing the book and sharing it with friends, the hatred and violence at the heart of the left I was portraying in my novel just seemed like it couldn't be plausible.

Today we know how plausible it is, and we know that terror has become domestic like never before. There are a lot of people suffering for it.

From the shock troops like Black Lives matter and ANTIFA, to the bizarre nature of the sexual perversion in the public schools, Hollywood, the Catholic hierarchy, Washington, and in sex cults like NXIVM, the threat normal Americans face is now impossible to ignore.

UponUs digs into the roots of the current crisis beginning in the debauched 1960s and 70s. It is told from that American Christian point of view which is now under attack, and follows the catastrophe of the Sex Revolution up to today in the heart of a family and ends by showing the explosive and demonic outcome for all to see in the 24-hour news cycle.

In the words of gun industry legend Wildey Moore, a friend of mine: "Make America Great again! No. Make America Good Again."

We will all be called to account.

Chris Moore
Connecticut
Summer, 2018

"I am the spirit that negates."

Mephistopheles to Faust
Goethe's *Faust*

1

CHARLES MCKENNA

I run for my life—legs throb—chest burns. Wind drives through my clothes. I shield my eyes and continue forward.

I want to rest but can't. A man is hunting me. When I first ran from the roadside he was far behind. Now he's a hundred yards back and closing fast. With my every step he gains two and grunts as he charges closer. I hear him breathing; determined, then he shouts in pain. I turn and see him on the ground on his knees. The wind tears off his hat exposing red hair. But the fall has not weakened him—no—he is angry now, hateful, swearing, and determined.

He stands, and I continue on. The outline of the mountaintop is visible now about a fifty yards away. A stumpy bristlecone pine tree stands firm beside me as I pass. Just ahead, sharp granite crags form something like a small ravine, and I run into the opening as a wind blast funnels shards of sleet into my face. I too then slip on the ice and thrust my hand against the rocks to break my fall. The rock walls are closer here, and, in the murky light, I see the man under the moonlit white snow smiling. He moves faster now that I have fallen. Over his shoulder a flashlight shines in the darkness.

Someone else is following.

I run out of the ravine and reach the top where I sit on a flat boulder to catch my breath. Below, the highway is lit by the white and red dots of a gridlocked traffic jam. People are out of their cars with their phones in hand as fires burn all over the roadway. I look over the peak to the north and find that Interstate I-70 looks much the same as Loveland Pass but on a grander scale. I can see a helicopter circling near the Eisenhower Tunnel opening. Then a gunshot cracks and the wind goes silent. The man and his gun are close. He is strangely calm. Behind him, a two-person news team emerges from the rock walls. A cameraman is running with a reporter, his leash-like microphone cord in her hands.

But I don't have time to wonder about the news team, he's right on top of me now.

"I'm gonna' kill you, Charles" he says.

2

SARAH MCKENNA-HURST

The cell phone rings and rings and goes to voice mail. My dad has such an irritating voice mail message: "Yes—Charles McKenna—Leave a message—Beep."

I leave a message: "No longer your daughter—I moved to the coast." Click.

More than anything I'm irritated when people say they will do something and fail to follow through. My dad was supposed to call when he got mom from the airport in Denver, but he didn't.

I hadn't seen mom in years. From time to time we spoke on the phone, but other than infrequent phone conversations, she and I had no relationship—none—and I often felt an anger that if I had the chance, I would punish her by excluding her from my world.

Then the phone rang and I saw Mike's face on the screen. "I thought you couldn't talk 'till later." I said, picking up.

"Are you watching the news? Turn it on right now!"

"What? Why?"

The controller was near, and I pushed the button and sat on the couch. The screen came to life and hummed for a minute as the picture focused.

"Which channel?"

"Any channel? People are posting videos online. And there's helicopter footage. Something's happening at Eisenhower Tunnel. Something's happening everywhere."

The national news showed traffic backed up fifty miles in Colorado and people outside in the snow bundled up in winter clothes. I switched channels. Mobs of people were out in the streets of Los Angeles. I thought they rioted. In Washington the news was the same. In New York people walked across the George Washington Bridge wearing surgical masks and T-shirts on their faces.

"Turn to the local news on five . . . channel five!" Mike said.

I did.

A helicopter swept over Loveland Pass just twenty miles from here. Every inch of road was jammed with cars and trucks. A man turning his car in traffic got too close to the edge and slid down the frozen embankment into the pines. The camera swept upward. The word **"live"** scrolled across the top and bottom of the screen and people were talking over each other. Snow fell, and high on the mountain pass, a line of cars and trucks formed a roadblock. Police officers and others pointed guns at the mass of people in front of them.

The temperature outside was close to zero and there was a fire in the road. They stacked whole trees at the turnout for the scenic overlook and set them on fire. The fire looked weird because it had only just been lit, and the flames had not yet engulfed the whole pile, and the pile looked like a stack of freshly cut Christmas trees that would have been sold to some happy family if they hadn't been burned. The aerial footage moved up the mountain where people were running. One man had a rifle, someone else had a camera. Both were chasing the same person.

AMERICANA

3

CHARLES MCKENNA

Y ou don't think about your death till it's near and then long
forgotten images flash in your mind. I see the day I met my
ex-wife. It was summer then and winter now, but the same charge is
in the sky: the strong sense of momentum beyond control. That day
is especially on my mind.

I picture it.

I lived off Main Street in Breckenridge, Colorado. This is about
1973. I recently moved from the East Coast.

It was just before lunch. I was up on my roof with hammer and
nails fixing the shingles when I heard a rumble in the distance. At
first, I looked up at the mountains to see if a storm crept in to dump
rain and electricity over the valley. Instead, the sun shone bright in
the perfect blue sky, patches of snow sparkled on the mountainsides,
and a hawk swooped down from a gray tree by an abandoned
mining shack. The noise persisted; louder now, and deeper. I looked
down at the only road leading to town. There, a horde of motorcycles rolled at a constant speed toward me. This locust swarm now
passed the "Entering Breckenridge" sign and continued between the
old brick and wood buildings on Main Street. I watched them for a
moment in awe when the breeze carried exhaust fumes to my nose

at the same time a bike backfired like a pipe bomb. My hairs stood on end, and I stood with them on the roof watching the motorcycles approach in a relentless line.

Motorcycle hordes roamed the West then like buffalo before the fall. The gangs made their presence felt at festivals and country fairs. Their pictures on magazine covers and novels made money. Bikers were collective celebrities. Even a handful of bikes carried the sense of celebrity which the individual biker shared with intensity. I had never seen them before except in the media, and so I watched them now with a mixture of fear and excitement, noting their strangeness while weighing the genuine article against the version in the media. But these men looked worse than what I had thought. The combination of the decibel sound and gasoline smell added an exposed raw quality that was primitive.

The horde drove down Main Street past the old brick buildings with glass store fronts and false second stories. They turned left onto High Street where I stood on the shingles of my house holding a weather vain pointed north. They came toward me, and I nodded from off my low roof to the man in the lead, and he nodded back. The others behind him glared. Downhill from him, a man in a Viking helmet laughed on his motorcycle drinking a bottle of gin. The multitude passed me and turned left onto unpaved Ridge Street and on into a parking area for Shamus's bar. The bar was a large wooden shanty with a flagpole out front and a one eyed biker proprietor who was absent riding out a two-year jail sentence for narcotic's possession.

The bikers packed Shamus's dirt lot to excess and then log jammed back in front of my house and down into Main Street. The dirty tide was all me around now. I stared down at the frozen wave of nomads in disbelief. And then a biker at the head of a small pack within the larger horde yelled up at me. I hesitated to respond—too busy watching the group like they were a painting. Then he shouted again, "Hey you!" and louder and louder until the fourth time he screamed.

At that moment he became real. "What?" I said.

"We park in your driveway?"

It wasn't so much a question as it was a command that I heeded. I nodded yes, and with a finger he directed his bikers into my driveway. His group all wore the same insignia. They acted disciplined and chaotic and filthy. They stood in the middle of the horde, but made a unit all their own.

"You mind about the lawn?"

I shook my head no, and he pointed to the rest of his bikers who were waiting since the driveway was full. Men nodded and pulled through and parked by the porch on the lawn. The bikes rumbled and coughed. I looked down on them from my ledge of relative safety. They were predators, and I hesitated to come down. The mountains stood above us and a plume of black smoke rose from an abused motorcycle. A few buildings away from me, some brave locals ventured into the street.

After a minute and more shouts from the bikers, I set my tools to the side and got down from the roof. The aluminum ladder creaked. The man who asked to park in my driveway stood holding the bottom out of courtesy.

"We'll take good care of you," he said.

I thought about that but didn't respond.

Bikes all around me ran and the hard rumble of so many motorcycles in unison pounded my chest. One of the men closest to me had the word VETERAN carved in his bicep, and another had a list of names that ran down his chest, and yet another had the word RAPE and MOTHER tattooed in his forearm.

I heard more commotion in the street as the bikers surged to fill the void left when the bikers pulled into my driveway. When they couldn't go any farther because of the traffic, they killed their engines and leaned their bikes on kickstands.

I didn't know where I belonged. I was confused and awkward among them. The leader of the bikers who asked to park in my driveway looked at me. He knew I was unnerved, and sought to calm me.

"Name's Edzul by the way, you want a beer?"

I smiled.

He wasn't a big man, but he looked exactly like the type that even huge men don't fool with. He was in the prime of his life and enjoyed it as much as he knew how. Next to him stood his other bikers, but they didn't speak to me, just each other. Edzul grabbed beer from the styrofoam cooler on the back of a Harley and cracked it. He handed one to me and cracked another himself. Then there were shouts in the road, and bikers ran down hill to the women who followed in cars. "The women, the women," they shouted. "Don't forget the women."

Edzul smirked.

"Big entrance," I said.

"We didn't think you'd mind." He took the opportunity to engage me more. "Someone said they was making a run up the mountain and we tagged along. It's not organized or nothing. We wasn't even sure which town to go to till somebody said Brecken-ridge." Edzul paused and said, "What's the police like?"

"A Sheriff and a Deputy."

"We should be alright."

"This a rally?" I asked.

He thought about this for a second and said, "We thought it was going to be a small thing but when we got outside Denver, in Idaho Springs, we picked up so many bikers people watched like we was a parade. And when we came up Loveland, a few of these clowns looked like they was going over the edge."

I knew he was so talkative because he wanted to calm me and make me feel that as long as I was cool with him, they'd be cool with me. It was about respect because he didn't have to respect me.

I followed his conversation and said, "Tunnel will be open soon."

"Can't beat that Pass for views though, just maybe a guardrail here and there'd be nice," and he slapped me on the back and said, "But I'll be damned if it's not the most beautiful place on earth."

I smiled and sipped beer. I realized that he was genuinely and at least naturally likable. The mood slackened. Locals were out and relaxing. They sparked a joint and passed it around. Then the Sheriff in a squad car tapped his siren at the bottom of High Street.

His Deputy followed closely behind him in another squad car with his siren screeching. Everyone turned to see them.

Other town locals watched the police with disbelief, much the same as I watched the bikers a moment ago. First the bikers seemed a menace, but we found that to be otherwise, now the Sheriff and Deputy added another level of confusion. The crowd stood motionless wondering what the proper etiquette was; searching for a direction until one of the Bikers supplied it.

The Biker with the red Viking helmet and bottle of gin jumped onto the seat of his motorcycle waving his hands like a conductor. He was a lunatic. The crowd followed him and heads swayed with the rhythm of his hands while he grinned big and bright. He shouted and the crowd shouted with him. There would have been no problem, but he controlled the crowd, and he wanted a problem. But throughout this new commotion, the Bikers remained quiet; they simply watched him and the others like a military unit waiting for commands.

The man in the Viking helmet pointed to a local man who as if by order lobbed a beer can onto the Sheriff's hood. Schlitz splattered on the windshield and the can rattled onto the asphalt. Windshield wipes sloshed the beer off the glass.

"Take it easy Smiley," Edzul said to the Biker conducting the crowd.

Smiley sipped gin and laughed. Beneath his open black vest muscles constricted. His blond hair fell down past his shoulders. He turned back to the audience of angry locals and pointed to the Sheriff and addressed the locals: "This is your town . . . not theirs," he said.

The Sheriff was a World War II vet. His real name was Dodge, but even at bars Sheriff was what people called him back then. He was well respected in town, but today all history was forgotten.

Sheriff Dodge looked out his car window and drove through the crowd with a curious look on his face. The people here were already unruly, and he was eager to see what was going on, even eager to see what would happen. The day had become so unusual that some other power seemed in control, and even the Sheriff was interested to see how it would play out.

We wouldn't have long to wait. The crowd ahead no longer yielded for him to continue. The Deputy stopped thirty or so feet behind him stranded in a mob of men and motorcycles blushing like a virgin.

For a moment the crowd paused and watched. The Sheriff stood still and so did the Deputy. No one knew what to do. Then the Sheriff leaned out his window. "Afternoon," he said tipping his tan hat to the crowd. "You can't just leave your bikes here like that. Would you move out of the way?" He smiled a bit, but his body was rock rigid—his blue eyes so intense he looked ready to kill the Japanese again in a blood sand and sea foam invasion. Despite his man killing eyes he smiled like he would just assume shake hands and split beers as long as law and order were obeyed. But he saw himself as law and order, and no one was obeying.

Sheriff saw me and nodded. I wondered how he interpreted my presence. But before I could act, he shouted. "Move the bikes!" The crowd ignored him and he hit the siren. He shouldn't have. Aggression rose. The men in the street turned their backs to him and walked off toward the bar up hill; their bikes still in the street. Sheriff leaned on his horn in anger. He should have simply pretended that he wasn't an officer of the law and stayed put and kept quiet. But he couldn't. I wanted to tell him to go away, but I didn't. The thing was beyond me.

"You can't block the damned road! Move the bikes."

"Move em' yourself."

"I can get a Backhoe down here." He threatened.

"Get it."

Sheriff shook his head. Then he stood from the car stretching to let the men see his height. The baby faced Deputy in the car behind fumbled for his radio.

"You don't have to take this," Smiley said, "Who gave him his authority? We did. He's ours, the law is ours."

Then a local in a tasseled buckskin shirt jumped into Sheriff's face and shouted. The Sheriff didn't budge. He expected it as much as anyone, but he refused to turn. The man in buckskin stood nose-to-nose with him.

Smiley screamed, "You don't have to take it. Don't let that fascist pig tell you what to do!" waving his hands to an unheard rhythm. Life does not happen this way. But it was. In the air was a charge that could only discharge in a spark.

The man in buckskins raised his hands in aggression. It was like the frozen moment when a car tire abruptly punctures—but it's alright. Nothing's happened. The car continues down the highway in a straight line, but the right side just dropped a few inches and there's pressure in the steering wheel. But it hasn't happened yet; no over-reaction; no under-reaction, there's still time to think, time to react. But there is no time; the moment collapses and momentum takes over. The moment drives the driver.

It's so vivid. Sheriff Dodge reacts and catches the man twisting him to the ground in an awkward heap. He yelps, and Sheriff reaches for his handcuffs.

Smiley throws the bottle of gin into the top of Sheriff's head. The bottle cracks when it strikes, and ricochets up with blood. Sheriff stumbles back against the squad car and reaches for his gun. He's not fast enough and the crowd of bikers and locals surges in over him. They see red blood and react. Edzul shouts to stop them. No one but his men listen. In an instant, Sheriff is down. A man kicks his face smashing his dark ray bans to pieces. A piece of lens sticks straight from the man's boot. Men converge. Fists and feet pound. Men are so closely packed around him that Sheriff's no longer visible. Then a gap opens, and he lays in a puddle of blood, half conscious, bound by his own handcuffs. Men are over him. Some laugh, others walk to the bar.

As the first group rolls onto Sheriff, the remaining bikers and locals move en mass to attack the poor baby faced Deputy. For the most part, the Bikers stand still. The Deputy rolls up his window as fast as he can but they catch him. Men reach in and grab him. Others open the car door. They pull him halfway out the window. Some grip his heels while others hold his arms and pull back and forth. One side wins the tug of war, and the Deputy's belly breaks the partially raised window as they pull him forward and let him drop. He hits the ground screaming and grunting. Then they kick and punch him into unconsciousness, cheering and hooting when they are done.

The beatings happen instantly and simultaneously. The pack continues attacking their prey until Edzul's voice comes into focus. He has been screaming the whole time, but until now I didn't hear him.

He is livid. He motions to one of his Bikers who rips off a belt made of heavy motorcycle chain. The man whips one of the assailants in the back of the head to stop them from killing Sheriff. Blood splatters and the man drops like a shot. Another man turns and punches the Biker, which is a terrible mistake because a pack of them beat, stomp and chain whip him until he is featureless in the gutter. At that, the other bikers and locals step back from the Bikers and from the Sheriff and Deputy entirely. They received the message.

I have never seen so much violence before. Edzul is furious and shouting.

Some men lean over the Sheriff. He is breathing, but he's confused and hurt and bleeding. The Deputy is worse. He pukes in the street. Bikers keep him from standing up and falling down, which he would do. Sheriff holds his face and lays still as Edzul goes off on Smiley.

"Damn it. Why they Hell did you have to do that. What's wrong with you?"

"They did it on their own."

"You made it happen. You pushed 'em. Now clean it up. Clean it. Take that Sheriff somewhere's where he won't die, and he'll be safe from these lunatics. Get it. Just do it. Do it. And make sure they don't die damn it."

Smiley considers his options and decides to acquiesce. He's vile, his smile is vile, his clothes are vile, and he looks at me, proud of what he did, and then goes over to Sheriff with a man named Bronco and they help the Sheriff to his feet. Some others grab the Deputy.

"Did you find that fun?" Smiley says to the Sheriff. Others laugh, and the group walks away holding the Deputy with his feet dragging on the ground trailing blood. He is in and out of consciousness. Sheriff walks slow but stays on his feet. They head toward the jail. Smiley takes the keys from the Sheriff.

"This is my town now you know?" He says.

Sheriff doesn't pay attention, he just endures.

4

CHARLES MCKENNA

"Guess we're not in Kansas anymore," I say when it's over.

"Some get noble around a fight, but it don't last long." Edzul looks after Smiley and the men with him. "He's causing more problems than he should. Come on, lets us have that beer."

"What's going to happen to him?"

"Who? The Sheriff? You wanna find out? Just stay with me. The Sheriff will be fine if he keeps his mouth shut. Smiley's crazy, but not that much."

I follow him.

"By the way, I'm Charles," I say.

"Good to know you, Charles."

He takes my hand and crushes it. His eyes dart back and forth. He's not sure what to make of what just happened. He's still processing it all.

"You from Denver?" I ask to clear the air.

"Detroit originally. I lived in California a few years—I been looking at these mountains more and more lately."

"The big problems don't usually come here." I say, and Edzul smiles because we're in a big problem. "I wouldn't live anywhere else," I add.

He lights a cigarette. "Yup, plenty of open space to ride, but then you get snow. . ." Edzul cuts his sentence short and looks down the road.

About a hundred feet away two men with button up shirts walk out of a low slung clapboard building and head toward us. They have short-cropped hair and sinister looks. The few remaining Bikers watch them along with the others. Edzul stops. One of the two buttoned up men reaches in his pocket. He seems like a frat boy federal agent type. We both wonder what awful thing is going to happen now.

My nerves are raw and my hands are shaking. I watch the Bikers fidget; one scratches his beard and places his hand inside his dirty vest. We are unsure what the men want. They would be crazy to fight, but they appear ready. Edzul stands razor straight watching the hidden hand. When the man produces a large bag of mushrooms, everyone smiles. At that moment more locals come out of their homes and bring gifts of the same vein. I'm shaken, but the others, including just the regular locals could care less. Angie by the Rolling Stones plays from a car stereo and somehow it seems like everything will be ok, a sense that gains steam when a man passes Edzul a joint. He takes a few pulls and passes it on to an older local mountain man who passes it to me.

The freak parade moves in a rolling mass up High Street. There is a general consensus among the locals that freedom rolled into town. Woodstock recently happened, and when the violence of Altamont brought the death of the Woodstock notion no one seemed to notice; people still looked all over the country for their own sense of Woodstock, and the horde, regardless of violence, revived that sense of sovereignty here this day.

Miners had built Breckenridge in the 19th Century. They chased the silver and gold found in *them thar hills*, but when the minerals ran out, so did the miners. Only a few of them remained here in Breckenridge. And now, most of the locals emigrated from other states; many of them were running from something. To that effect, the Sheriff and his Deputy had only been window dressing.

With such a slim population, most other areas might have gotten rid of their Sheriff and simply increased the area of responsibility for another, but the County didn't want to lose more of its law enforcement officers, and, especially for political reasons, they kept a Sheriff and even added a Deputy in order that the state wouldn't reduce their funding. The Sheriff had no staff, of course, the County cut that back, and he and the Deputy spent their time bagging speeders when they weren't in the bar. But as long as there were ample tickets, no one complained. What all this meant was that no one outside Breckenridge would hear what happened here for at least twenty-four hours. As for a hospital for the wounded, the nearest was Denver.

I moved here because Breckenridge was a peaceful place, but without proper adult supervision, and no hope of its arrival, we were in for a long night. In some ways, people acted out what fantasies writers had written about the West and more. In the streets, bikers lit fires as if it were a camping trip and set up tents on the sidewalk. The smell of marijuana hung so heavy in the air that I wondered if someone wasn't burning bushels of it. Smoke hung thick like fog and dripped from the walls of the buildings. Ridge Street was paved with dirt. In spots, beer spilled making puddles of sticky mud that clung to people's shoes and boots. A man rode a llama out of his garage and parked in front of the bar. For some reason, Lamas are raised in Colorado. People congratulated him when he stepped down from his perch and laughed when the creature shit in the street. The people gave him a joint for his jest. Then the group moved when they caught a whiff of the stink.

People invited bikers into their homes and they took up positions on porches or on the side of the road in small groups getting high, popping pills, and drinking. I hoped the State Police would hurry up and arrive, but I knew that no one here cared enough to make that call. I certainly had no way to do it now.

Women were always scarce in the mountains, but today they materialized from the forests. Some girls were biker groupies or mammas who always followed bikers around. There were also local women, but the vast majority of girls came from Denver and had either heard there was a party from friends, or felt the bikes rumble past on the highway and followed to see if they could find a good time.

The summer of love morphed into the years of drugs-and-violence; lots of people hadn't noticed. Edzul had me under his wing, and the other men looked to me as though I were a personality. We entered the old bar, Shamus O'Toole's. The ceilings were low, blackened by smoke. The dirty wood bar sat opposite the door along the right hand wall. Music blared from black speakers mounted to the brown wall coverings. The place was packed with bikers and locals intermixed. But as we moved, they all gave way to Edzul. We got to the bar where room was made for us and began drinking. Someone passed me a joint. People talked and shouted and hooted. Someone screamed and a woman shrieked. I looked from the bar and saw an exposed, pink female nipple. A man put his tongue to it. She shrieked again.

Edzul put his hand on my shoulder. "You like?"

"Pretty wild"

"You want to say hello to her."

I looked to where the woman had been. She was gone. "She's gone," I said.

"There'll be another one."

Someone turned up the volume on the stereo until it cracked and broke and the speaker hissed. We turned our attention toward it and a woman presented herself before Edzul like a ghost with blue lips. She was jittery and her eyes blinked. She seemed like she had something to say but couldn't. Edzul laughed and turned back to the bar. "What you do keeps you in these mountains, Charles?" he said.

"Property's dirt cheap, so I bought a house. Now, I've noticed real estate around town picking up." I nodded to the men beside me.

"Yeah," Edzul said. "I might think about getting something here too. A couple houses look abandoned."

"The state used to burn some of them down for firefighter practice."

Edzul popped a Marlboro in his mouth from a soft pack. He lit the cigarette and inhaled deeply, drawing life from the tobacco. I handed him a joint but he declined, and I turned to my left to pass it when I met eyes with the most beautiful girl I had ever seen.

She was my future ex-wife, Joanne Hurst.

"You going to pass me that, or what?" she said as I hesitated.

She was wearing a green summer dress that flowed like water, and her hair draped her back like in those television conditioner commercials. She had a small oval face and perfect blue eyes. She was incomprehensible.

Edzul eyed her for a second until he realized she wasn't looking at him. He smiled and slapped my shoulder and turned back to the bar.

"Are you lost?" she asked me. Edzul laughed. I wanted to break the ice, but she did.

"You don't seem to belong," she said.

"That makes two of us then."

"I'm far from lost."

"Did you come in that car with the women?" I said.

"I live down the street."

"Really?"

"Yeah."

"I just never saw you is all."

"Well I'm here. I'm Joanne."

And Joanne was beautiful, blonde, tall and lean. I bought drinks and was captivated. All around bikers stood looking for any chance to get close, or to get me away. One of the bikers put his hand on my shoulder. It was a beastly, hairy, gnarly hand covered by scars.

"What are you?" she asked him, "An animal."

"This your woman?" he queried.

"Do I look like steak to you?" she said.

I handed her a beer and smiled.

"What happened to the Cops?" she asked. "Why aren't they here to bust this up?"

"They're locked up in a cell on Main." I said.

"That bastard Sheriff had it coming anyway, it's inevitable," she said, never breaking eye contact with me. She was young, I could guess, but something about her was outside her own age. She continued speaking, and I watched her pronunciation. Her lips were pink covering teeth that reflected light. We were close together in our own hollow of humans sitting on stools.

Joanne asked about how the Sheriff got locked up, but then Smiley jumped into the conversation. "We do what we can you know." He said out of nowhere.

"You do?" Joanne responded, somewhat surprised that he had joined us.

He shattered our moment and pierced the bubble. I was angry, and showed it in my face.

He then took her hand in his like a courtier. "I'm Smiley." He said, bowing.

"I'm Joan." She responded, and smiled to me. "Yes . . . Joan of Arc," she said with a grin.

"How about that? I'm in the presence of a fairy princess," Smiley said.

"That's right; now, what do you do Mr. Smiley?" Joan of Arc asked him mockingly.

"I came here to win the country. I'm AWOL, so I don't have any rights you know. I like the chaos; that's what I'm good at you know." She smiled, and so did he; noting how she dug what he said as much as he enjoyed saying it. "...Participate in this renaissance," he blurted. And either that was all he said, or I missed the rest of it. I watched him now trying to listen as the volume of the voices nearby picked up. He seemed like a boyish face draped in rags, and I was surprised that he not only didn't drool when he spoke, but that he appeared articulate (somewhat), almost elegant, and captured something with his tone and style that I could tell Joanne was in to.

"But do you care?" Joanne said.

"It's my job to care."

Edzul leaned into the conversation. "If you care so much Smiley then join the peace creeps on marches." I had lost the thread of their conversation.

"I can touch more this way."

Edzul looked angry. "Sell your cures somewhere else."

"I don't sell them."

"What kind of cures you selling, Smiley?" I asked, trying to catch up.

"Kinds? The kind that changes the way the world views."

"Makes 'em lay down faster," Edzul said angrily.

"Who's this?" Joanne said.

"That's Edzul."

"Like Edzul Ford?"

"No, like **ME**!" Edzul said.

"Nice to meet you mister Edzul."

"You got a smart mouth," he said.

Joanne looked back to Smiley. "He's not very friendly."

"No, he's not. But would you rather nicety or honesty."

"You agree with him?"

"Which?" He pressed the question.

"Honesty." She said.

"Good, that's real good." He said and smiled foully. Joanne turned away from him, and I regained her attention for a moment but Smiley pulled another joint from his pocket and passed it to me. "You smoke?" he said.

"I do."

"Well smoke."

"There's already one going around." I pointed to a brown paper joint someone had just lit.

"Not like this there isn't." He grinned, and then added in song, 'Makes you think all the worlds a sunny day.'"

I smoked and got stoned, and watched as Edzul walked away to a table of women, he was obviously sick of listening to Smiley. I remained where I was, intent on leaving the bar with Joanne.

When Edzul was out of earshot Joanne pointed at him and said, "I thought you were outlaws," with stress on the word *outlaw* like it was a joke.

"They've got different mentalities than you think," Smiley said gesturing to certain bikers around the barroom dressed similarly. "Edzul's mad a cop got beat up, he's mad 'cause he's just like a cop —same mentality, it's why he takes his uniform so seriously: he's just like the pig. He's an outlaw cause he didn't cut it in the system or didn't want to, but he has his own system—the same just outside— you dig, it's the way his mind's structured, he's not out of the law, not really, it's a parody, but a parallel, and he's the same for others, another state but no different, you see. What's the real outlaw think? We'll he's not that, he don't think enough to see it different."

"You're part of it too though." Joanne said.

"Good for my studies you could say."

"What are you? A student?"

"But I don't need a PhD to tell me what's what." He leaned on the bar. "I splash and watch the waves go out."

"You're crazy."

"But you don't actually think so; so what's that mean for you?"

He made me nauseous. I stopped listening, and now that he had Joanne's ear, I lost interest.

Bill, a friend of mine, walked up to the bar and said hello. His hair was short and red. I met him a few years back when I first moved to Colorado. He had just returned from active duty in Vietnam. Now he went back and forth, but he said he no longer saw combat. Something happened and now he worked a desk job or a plain-clothes position, but he was vague.

I said hello back to him and Smiley moved his hand to Joanne's wrist. Her expression didn't change. "What kind of truth you into?" Smiley asked her. I noticed that Bill was watching him.

"What kind of truth you got?" she said.

At that, Smiley produced a bottle of eye drops. "There's only one kind of truth."

Joanne took the bottle and inspected it. "What—is—this?" She enunciated.

"The eyes are the mouth of the mind."

For the first time, Joanne looked nervous. I wanted to stop her, but then I didn't think it my place. She was connected to his eyes in the same way I had been to hers. I clapped my hands together to break the spell.

"Just a drop'll do ya," he said and leaned in and grabbed the bottle from her hand. His mouth opened in a look of fulfilled desire.

She tilted her head back and he dropped a drop into her left eye. Then she blinked and blinked and blinked, and both eyes watered. "There's a cut of vodka there so it stings for a second and it's okay."

"No. I'm fine. It doesn't sting."

Smiley turned to me. "You want some?"

"No."

He observed Bill now, but didn't bother asking him.

Joanne looked at me then; her look was like the farewell from a departing train, but the moment passed, and Smiley asked if she was ok.

"The bar's just stuffy."

"We can go outside?"

She nodded and walked passed me. But she turned absently and said, "I'll be back with you later tonight." She seemed to ask my permission.

They walked out of the bar together, but as they did, she rubbed her hand down my arm, and as she passed Bill she said, "Oh, hi."

5

CHARLES MCKENNA

I drank beer and got bored and hot and waded through bikers standing everywhere around the bar. I looked for Edzul as I left but couldn't find him in the crowd. It was best I didn't see him. He was charismatically violent which is never a good combination, yet he was solid and almost friendly, and I felt that I should at least shake hands with him.

I walked through the barn doors of the bar and into the afternoon sunlight. For a moment I ignored everything except the mountains that rose steeply and walled the town on all sides. Rising from the forest on a mountaintop above, an immense mound of granite stood squat, ringed in circular striations like the stump of the tree of life. The gray stone was heaved out of the earth by force and searing pressure and during the ordeal had been bent so that its many layers formed lines turning on themselves. At the base of the granite on the mountain's peak, pines clung between pockets of stone where there was soil enough to sustain life. From a distance, those trees appeared to be new growth and branches sprouting from the gray stump's base. I could have spent an entire day looking at the mountains, and many times before I had, but today I wasn't lucky enough to have such peace. Men and women were out in the street dancing, talking, and laughing. Women were naked. Men were naked. Lighting fires must go hand in hand with freedom because there were more fires lit in the streets than at any campsite I've seen. Men drove over the fires with bikes, spinning their tires so that hot red ashes flew and filled the air like a thousand hellish fireflies. Wonderful, absurd and frightening, all of it exhilarating. I was repulsed while fascinated.

Joanne sat on the other side of the large pile of wood in the street beside Smiley on the hood of a car. I caught her glance but she didn't notice me. She had a distant, far away look to her eyes. Her pupils were huge. Men stood around holding beer cans and talking as if it were normal for the town to be under siege by lunatics. This morning I was at least intrigued by the commotion and carnival of the bikers. Now I was sick of the glorified Neanderthals and whatever Smiley was.

Joanne lay back on the hood of the big old car. I saw her kneecaps when her skirt gently moved with the breeze. Smiley sat scanning the men around the fire. His hands were bony and the skin that stretched over his knuckles was yellow; his eyes were a hollow pale perceptive blue, and his blond hair glistened with grease and sweat. He saw me look at him and smiled and looked down at Joanne. He leaned over her. His face was youthful, but his demeanor was eternal. He was disgusting.

Along with my stomach, I turned and walked back to my house for food. I heard the woosh of one of their fires ignite with gasoline as I walked. My body cast a shadow from the glow. The heat struck me in the back, but I didn't care for their fire and continued walking.

High Street was polluted with beer cans and straggling drug abusers moping around like lifeless zombies. "Hey man, hey," some tired-eyed ghoul said to me. His hands shook when he spoke, and I pushed him from my path.

"Thanks man, cool man," he said, and I continued walking.

Blood lay in puddles in front of my house, and the bikes had been moved to other locations around town. Someone had put the Sheriff's patrol car in neutral and let it roll backward into the

Deputies car which broke lose and rolled the rest of the way down High Street and across Main in through the glass front display of a newly opened real-estate office. The Deputy's car had entered the building and the small office inside was a mangle of strewn papers, file cabinets, debris, and shattered glass. Following behind the Deputy's car, the Sheriff's car crashed into the support for the porch roof which had partially collapsed onto the wooden boardwalk, but the car's red and blue lights still ran beneath the shattered wood and roofing to look as if a dilapidated shack collapsed onto a perverted Christmas tree.

I stepped into my driveway and looked into the gutter where the man had been chain whipped and beaten. He was gone. Either he staggered off to later die from a concussion, or some good soul drove him the two hours to Denver for medical treatment. Either way, he was gone from my curb, and I felt relieved.

I walked in through the front door of my house. I had left in such a hurry before that I now worried that it would be ransacked, but the house was untouched. At this I felt some relief. Once I got inside, I wanted to stay; I had had enough of the carnival, and since Joanne left, I didn't have much reason to hang around, and so I spent four or five hours in the house eating and then working on a porch that was half finished in my backyard trying to forget the wildlife outside.

I grew tired of the biker's takeover and of the behavior of those living in town. The antics were cumbersome. The end of the scene was long overdue but the end was not in sight. At one point I picked up my phone: no dial tone. Some jerk must have cut the only line out of town or a drunk took out a pole, either way, I wasn't going to be able to call anyone. Now I just wanted to ride out the night in my house with the normal silence and peace of the mountains, but the noise of the people in the streets drove me crazy. I couldn't get away from it, and I couldn't stay in my house anymore alone.

I went out into the street again. It was dark. The air was warm and moist, unusual for the mountains.

"I shouldn't be out here," I said, but I walked to the bar anyway. The night was alive. Out front in the dirt street a bonfire attracted a crowd. People stood around looking into the flames. There, I bumped into a man as I went. I apologized but he didn't care. He was too busy watching the fire burn.

Another man threw handfuls of human hair into the fire. He had shaved a passed out friend's head. The smell from the burning hair was awful. Some others egged him on in mummers, and I walked to the door of Shamus's still thinking I should return home.

Inside, the bar was mostly full, but the main party had moved off to parts unknown. The women had all gone elsewhere. Of the two females remaining inside, one looked near death, and the other worked the room. She looked at me for a moment but I looked away. Then there was a fight—which included a chain whipping. It ended when the unconscious victim was thrown out the front door. Truly, I was impressed. I hung around for a minute longer hoping to see a familiar face but no one was around. Edzul was off with his old lady. I was nervous. I looked for some local friends, but they were lost and mixed up in with the other vamps and creatures of the night, and so I left.

I walked back into the street by the bonfire again looking for what I didn't understand. The moon was up. The street was odd. The people were odd. Someone threw bullets into the flames, and the rounds popped and shot, and people ran for cover. The amusement had no end.

I headed toward Main Street, hoping there I would see some local friends and sit out the night in a quiet bar with them, but who knew, I wasn't even sure I would make it down the hill alive. I thought of Sheriff and what happened to him. I felt guilty and partially responsible, but it all happened so quickly, and the mob would have done the same to me. All the same, I headed toward the jail with the thought of somehow helping him on my mind.

I walked perpendicular to Main Street on Ridge Street, and groups of people walked passed me in rushes and waves as some maniac ran laps on a motorcycle up and down the street with his headlight out. It was dark and there were no streetlights then.

Some of the buildings gave off a soft yellow light from inside that lit the street here and there in alternate patches of light to dark.

Behind me the fire glowed red, I could hear Steely Dan's *Do It Again* on a radio somewhere. Then something popped inside the flames, and a man on a motorcycle emerged from a dark section of road into the red light of the fire. The bike's headlight was smashed and weeds and brush from the forest were jammed into the underbelly of the bike dragging behind him as he went. He must have been riding in the woods.

I pushed up against the building to let him pass. He paid no attention to me but roared by into the night. When he passed I heard a noise above. A car light partially fell on the balcony of the old hotel, and reveled Smiley leaning on the rail looking absently into the street. Then the light on him went out and he fell into dark silhouette. He hadn't noticed me, I thought, and so I walked away.

Rounding the corner, I bumped into Joanne. She was alone and radiant. She still had the sticky sweet smell of honey, and I forgot all about the Sheriff and Deputy down in the cell. Over my shoulder, I saw that Smiley no longer stood on the balcony, and at that I felt relieved and looked back at Joanne. She had a gravity that I could not avoid, but her hair was out of place, and her eyes had a far away focus that was different than I remembered.

She did not see me as I approached, and I walked to her and took her hand. She seemed to be looking for something. "I'm right here." I said.

"I've been looking all over for you," she replied casually.

In one flash moment I was happy and unhappy to see her. "Why? Did you lose Smiley?"

"Don't be jealous. He gave me some of his eye dropper that was all." The far away focus left her eyes and she smiled.

"Looked like he was giving you more than that."

"Oh, cut it out. I didn't know I'd trip so hard, but it was short," she looked around like someone was looking for her; I assumed paranoia was her reaction to drugs. Then she said, "I was out of it, but I wanted to see you. You've got such a . . . protected vibe. Now here you are. Where were you by the way?"

"Went home."

"Why?"

"Took a nap."

"You want to go back home again? I want to get inside," she said offhandedly.

"What do you mean?"

"This was fun for a while but now it's not, and, I don't know: *do you want me to beg*?"

"A little," I said. Her eyes cleared. I flattered myself to think I was the reason she so suddenly pulled out of the mental fog.

"Fine. *Please*, PLEASE can we go back to your house? I can't take this anymore." She was terribly beautiful. Her lips curled when she spoke.

"You still tripping now?"

"A little."

We went back to my house. At the doorway she put her hand to her head and stopped.

"What's the matter?"

"I feel dizzy."

She lost balance, and I grabbed her and carried her over the threshold. Inside she revived, and I put her to her feet and she sat on my red couch a few feet from the doorway across from an old black and white television.

"You all right?"

"It was just a second, but you're *so* strong," she mocked.

"It was nothing."

"Are you usually so chivalrous for nothing?"

But I didn't know how to respond and she had to say, "I'm only kidding," to reassure me.

She looked around the mostly bare room and smiled as I turned on the lamp and sat beside her under the light. When I did that, her pupils focused tight to the diameter of a pin giving her blue gray eyes the look of the infinite universe.

I rested my hand on her leg. It wasn't subtle, but she wasn't repulsed. Then I got brave or stupid and moved my hand upward to her chest. But it wasn't there a second before she slapped it away. "Did you think I was going to sleep with you?"

"I."

She stood from the couch. "Is that all you want from a woman? Is that how far your chivalry goes?"

"Not only." I stammered badly when I realized that she had many mirrored reflections of herself and to grab one was to be revealed, but where the central Joanne was, I was too far behind to perceive.

"You didn't seem like one of the animals before. Is that what you are?" She had me off balance and delighted applying pressure.

"You went off with one."

"That was different, and I saw all I needed of him? Anyway, I wanted to know what you are? Don't hesitate, tell me."

"That's a high question." I meant to say that she was high, but it came off that she was elevated on a throne and that's how she understood it and correspondingly presented herself, and, even though I had half complimented her with my slip, she wanted an answer to her high question.

"What are you? What do you think you are?"

I had to give an answer and, "A sincere man," was the best I could muster.

"Sincerity doesn't exist," she said quickly.

"I hope that's not true. You're still pretty high."

"Not high. But can you think of people who are sincere?"

"Artists. And . . . I hope priests."

She shifted her weight. She seemed upset. "Artists have no sincerity; trust me, that's their endearing quality, and priests are like artists without integrity."

"You're young to be jaded?"

"I went to Catholic schools. Father was protestant, which meant he didn't believe in anything but money, but mother was devout to an extent that's frightening and she forced me into all that stuff. Take it from me, you don't want to turn to a priest."

"God?

"Maybe you should shake hands with a tree."

"Maybe I do."

"At least your not stupid." She hesitated then said, "I'm happy I met you. Where are you from?"

"My brother was killed in the Tet Offensive, and my uncle helped me into Harvard." I said.

"A Harvard man?."

"Never graduated. Spent a few years doing pretty well, but I got off the East Coast and bummed around the country for a while."

"Was it amazing?"

"No."

"It never is."

"How old are you?" I asked.

"Does it matter?" She grabbed my collar and kissed me.

6

BILL SAXON

I met Charles in a bar in the mountains a year after I bought a house in town. The mountains are comforting, and I naturally gravitate to them. It seemed that Charles was here for the same reasons. He was a friend as much as anyone then. I met Joanne some time after that.

A horde of bikers rolled into town one summer afternoon and took over. When they came, I had just got back from hiking. I came out of the woods and onto the path that led to my road. When I reached the road, bikers were everywhere, and I slowed and watched them.

As I approached, I saw them pick Sheriff Dodge off the ground. He had been badly beaten and blood leaked from his head.

They were in front of Charles's house, and I followed Sheriff Dodge and his Deputy as they moved down hill toward Main Street. There was nothing I could do to help them; there were hundreds of bikers and locals mixed up in the disorder.

Down in front of the old jail, the Deputy was silent while Sheriff Dodge talked on his feet and bled out of anger as the bikers poked him and laughed on the front porch of the old jail. He gritted his teeth and puffed out his broad chest acting like the men around him were babies that could not hurt him, no matter if they actually did. A man with blond hair and a red Viking helmet spoke to him, and Dodge turned and said, "You're just a grinning idiot, did you know that?"

The biker pointed his horned helmet into Dodge's face and then grabbed him and threw him onto the porch. The boards rattled when Dodge landed. He lay there on the boards and then sat up and brushed dirt off his hip and looked up at the man who put him there. Despite the fact that his hands were bound in front of his body, he acted like he was comfortable. Then the biker pulled a knife and bent down and talked into Dodge's face. I couldn't hear what he said. All I heard was the mumbled cadence of words. I walked closer.

Dodge was angry. He eyed the biker with the helmet standing over him and then suddenly lunged upward planting his shoulder into the biker's chest. The biker sprawled onto the porch. The red Viking helmet bounced onto the black asphalt of Main Street as the others rushed forward and tackled Dodge. He fell easily. He had already been beaten badly.

The biker who was knocked down stood and watched Sheriff Dodge sink under the weight of the men. He noticed me watching and smiled big and bright; his teeth were overlarge, white and shiny in the sun. I took a step closer and he turned back to Dodge.

"I'm gonna' cut you for the spectators," he paused and looked at me again, "Now how's that sound?" He seemed to be talking to me.

He slashed Dodge's face and laughed and then looked at me with blood on his hands. The others laughed. Blood dripped from Dodge's face onto the dusty wood boards, but he did not make a sound. He was in obvious pain, but he did not allow them the satisfaction of hearing him express it. The Deputy whimpered and turned to hide his face.

Having done the Sheriff, the biker with the bloody knife walked to the Deputy and touched the cold steel to the back of the Deputy's white neck and held it there. The Deputy buckled and fell to the floor.

"America's finest," the biker said and the others laughed. Then they dragged Dodge and the Deputy into the old jail and shut the door.

After a minute they came out. The man who cut Dodge came first. He smiled at me looking spry and smarter than the fools that surrounded him. He was dangerous.

Two bikers sat down in chairs on the porch and cracked beers, and the rest of the bikers walked past the bloody floorboards where Dodge fell. They trod through the blood and left smeared, red foot prints in the street and then turned between the Sheriff' Station and another building onto a dirt path that led up to Shamus's bar on Ridge Street.

"You want your helmet Smiley?"

"Leave it."

I followed behind looking up hill at them. The clear blue sky seemed out of place above.

They went into Shamus's, and I followed. Inside the bar, I took a spot near the door and watched the bikers in their environment. Men packed the place to the rafters. Many were drunk or on their way; some were smiling and over happy, while a majority walked around or stood still with deep frowns sipping beer waiting for violence or some other spectacle only known to themselves to break out. Then there was shouting and the rush and push of bodies. Someone fell beside me. The living mass of people surged right. There was a fight. I looked where the commotion was. A lane opened, and a couple of biker women fought like men.

One of the women screamed at another womanish creature, then spit in her face and they grappled, fell to the floor and rolled around scratching each other on top of the cigarette butts and beer bottles, hissing as they rolled in the grime and filth. The men with frowns now laughed and formed a ring. I turned from the ordeal and walked to the other side of the room, off toward the bar, to escape the violent high of the crowd near the fight. At the bar, Charles stood and talked with a beautiful woman. I later learned she was Joanne. I watched them as Smiley walked up to Joanne and butted into the conversation. Smiley saw me and cocked his head to the side as if taunting me before he turned his attention back to her.

Soon he gave Joanne an eye drop of some narcotic, and they talked for a bit longer and walked away from the bar. They walked through the doors, and I turned back and leaned on the bar. I felt that Smiley should pay for what he had done: he had cut an innocent man's face.

Charles looked hurt that the woman he talked with left him for a maniac. He wanted to talk to me, but I wasn't in the mood, and I stood at the bar only for a while longer and left.

Outside, the street felt like an outdoor high school keg party. High powered and flamboyantly colored bikes and hotrods were parked against the building. Large motorcycles covered in intricate, bright colored designs and crusted with glowing jewel-like chrome gleamed under the high mountain sun. Men had their shirts off, and were lying in chairs in the street in the sun. Their naked whiteness burned red in the reduced atmosphere of high altitude, but they were too drunk to care. Empty beer cans were everywhere all around.

I looked for Smiley, but my attention was grabbed by what the pack of fools did in the street. One man lit a stack of pallets from the lumberyard as others stood around cheering. He doused the six-foot pile with gasoline from a red steel can and then stood back.

"Anyone have any last words before I burn the world down?"

"Burn it, light it, burn it."

He took a brass Zippo lighter from his pocket, walked about ten feet from the pile and tossed the lighter onto the stack. The fuel exploded into a blur of fire topped by a black ring of smoke. A wave of heat stuck me, and I turned my face.

"Holy shit," he said, "My eyebrows are gone."

The fireball incited the men, and they went scrambling for anything they could find to throw on top of the fire. A man picked up his girlfriend and threatened to throw her into the flame. She clawed his chest and pulled the gray and black hairs there squirming like a fish as her skirt pulled up and exposed her nakedness. Men screamed and so did she. "Put me down, put me down," she said.

"I'll have you burn like the witch you are, woman. Would you like to burn, would you like to be fuel for the fire?"

She cried, and struck him with a limp fist in the chest the way a wounded man will sometimes strike the ground.

"She should burn. She should burn for being the witch that she is."

"You wouldn't love her if she wasn't a witch, Marco," someone said.

Marco smiled like a delinquent boy and then let her go a few steps from the flames. "Run along woman. I'll find you later when I'm ready."

She crawled away, and then stood and ran out of sight. Her makeup ran, and her face turned a shade of white that reminded me of a dead man.

Charles was out of the bar now looking across the street. I followed his eyes and saw Joanne and Smiley leaning on the hood of a Pontiac. Smiley leaned over her with his hand on her leg and talked in her ear. He seemed demure to be a biker. I turned my attention back to Charles, who walked around the corner with his head down. He looked hurt.

Joanne lay promiscuously and a group of men were near all around, but Smiley was gone, and she lifted her head from the hood and looked to the others and began speaking words without meaning. She'd OD'd, or near to it, and the grimy next man came forward and she encouraged him in bizarrely seductive gibberish.

"Is that the woman you had your eye on?"

I turned and Smiley was behind me. He had walked across the street while I watched Joanne. Now he stood before me with some odd sense of accomplishment in his eyes. When I didn't answer he repeated himself, "Is that the woman you had your eye on?"

"You cut that Sheriff pretty badly," I said.

Smiley walked closer with his hands relaxed by his waist and his head cocked to the side. "It was all for your benefit," he said.

"You cut that Sheriff?" a man walking out of the bar said. "I told you to leave him be and just put him in the cell."

Smiley looked at me but spoke to the man, "It needed to be done, Edzul."

"You'll remember you did it," I said.

Edzul turned to me. "You been around soldier?"

The bikers looked at me but weren't particularly interested.

"You Edzul?" I said.

"We ain't friends." He paused and then said, "Walk away before you get into more than you can handle."

I wanted Smiley then, but I could wait. I couldn't win this now. I walked away.

7

CHARLES MCKENNA

"I love the mountains. I always have," she was saying. I had made her some dinner and she seemed to have recovered herself somewhat from the bizarre state I had found her in. "My father used to drive us to Tahoe for vacations. I always felt safe when we got into them. Safe," she repeated and seemed to shiver. "There was always something so beautiful and unspoiled." Her voice had a jaded edge and her eyes were still possessed.

"California?" I asked.

"We mostly lived in Hillsborough, outside San Fran, but my mother sent me to Catholic school in Monterey."

"I never made it out there."

"It's just so built up; houses go up as fast as weeds, and most weeds are prettier. But Colorado's not really like that, I mean, Denver, but that's a city, these mountains . . ." she trailed off, her mind elsewhere.

"It's the same thing on the East Coast. But I never pictured Catholics coming from San Francisco. I went to Catholic school too, but everyone was Catholic in Boston; Irish and Catholic," I said.

"Trust me, they're everywhere. Not the Irish, I mean, my mother wasn't, she was English and Scottish; parents might have come on the Mayflower for all I know, but she wasn't Catholic until she switched after she married my father. I think she liked Mary, and my father didn't like women so it was a way to get back at him for marrying her. You want some acid?" she asked with a jolt in the same jaded tone as before.

It took me a moment to register what she had said, but when I did I paused without answering. I had made it through college without a drop, but something in the way she presented it made me now want it.

"You want it. Don't lie. Everyone should. It's sanctified."

I didn't want it, or I did, but I wanted her, and this seemed a good way, though it seems so cheap of me in hindsight. I thought she knew it too. But she frightened me then by putting the paper under her own tongue and handing me another.

Her recklessness was outrageous, and I stood up, surprised that she would want more with what had already happened, but then I took the tab she gave anyhow, sheepishly, as if on a dare. Not long thereafter I began listening to her glossolalia, which made sense in some way as I got what I wanted and nothing I bargained for until I had to break away from her as she continued her madness all over my house and then in the window seat opposite my bed, carrying on like a cornered animal until the dawn broke when I saw the lights of a bright Fleur-de-lis slowly radiating Fibonacci spirals inward that collided to present oblong vesica piscis or Mandorla/almonds (I've had a long time to recall) out of which sprang bikers who I thought, at first, had broken into my home from the carnage in town, but were actually part of the thing. Some of them, about six in all, and two were nasty creatures who came toward me and got in my face, as though they were protecting her from me while the other grey, elven creatures held her hands with boney fingers and seemed to be leading her out my now open window. Although still seated, I thought she might fall and tried to get up to stop her, but the two prevented me moving and grew black with an almost geometric anger. They managed to pull some part of her through the window though, the taking of which left her translucent, and when they returned they seemed to be merging with me and her at the same time from across the room. She started talking again as the creatures receded in the pattern and a wavelength stretched from her endless stream of nonsense words like VR sand dunes. "Would you stop talking," I said politely. "Of course," I think she said, and even though it was late morning we were still in the same place. And while I wasn't hungry at all, I just had to leave. I told her I was going for breakfast to the Angel's Hollow which was beside Shamus's, and she asked to come along, a request I couldn't deny, and so we put our clothes on and left together, but we brought the bedroom with us. Or at least it felt that way since very little changed though we were apparently alone, but we were outside and that seemed better for now because of the mountains.

I remember she said, "the mountains are so safe." She wasn't wearing shoes.

It all happened something like that. I would swear forever afterward that things really had come into the room. There was nothing dreamlike about them. They were so individual and person like, and yet altogether strange and nightmarish.

8

BILL SAXON

Night came, and the bonfire burned.

I watched the flames from my porch. The smell of the fire came on the wind and smelled like pine tar and gasoline. The moon was up, Dodge and his Deputy remained locked away in their cell on Main Street, and my home no longer felt like a home. The town no longer felt comfortable but like a war, with warlike smells that were thick and hot.

I tried to call down to Denver but the phone lines were dead. I grew restless then on my porch and began to pace. Out back in my barn, I took a knife and rope from the steel munitions box and went inside and pulled my service pistol from the top shelf in the closet. When I put it there, I hadn't expected to need it domestically. There was a war that I had been part of, and a war against that war that ran on television, but the war that showed up here, tonight, was something different; I had only seen glimpses of it before. I disliked what I saw.

The gun in my hand was dirty, at least to my standards, and so I cleaned it on the porch and sat thinking with the unloaded gun in my hand. With my thumb, I cocked and released the hammer and then cocked it again. I filled the clip and played with the bullets, removing and inspecting them between my thumb and forefinger and holding them up to my eye and replacing them again. I loaded the gun and put it in my waistband, but I did not like how it felt there, and I went in and retrieved my green holster from the bureau. I felt better with the gun in the holster. I could relax on the porch, but sleep was out of the question.

The night seemed peaceful. The odor of gun oil soothed me, as did the sight of the dark shape of the mountains between the town and the stars.

When I first came to this area, the mountains took my breath away. I remained because of them. After my military career was nearly ruined and almost everything I valued was taken from me, the mountains were a cure.

But any peace I had was shattered when gunshots went off by the hotel on Main. Gunshots were soon followed by laughter. I was angry. They were soiling my harmony, and I walked off my porch to the back of the house. Between two cottages there was a walkway that led to the old alley path between buildings. The alley Smiley took earlier today. It was empty, and I walked to the jail, unsure of myself.

I removed my knife from its place and walked until I was near the street and ducked down and sat beneath the front porch. I had only a faint notion of what I would do. What I knew instead was determination.

I did not like the Sheriff or his doting Deputy, but they needed to be rescued. I had the training and the experience. To think of it then, that active place in my mind led me to remember my time. I was in charge of training a small group of Montangards outside Pleiku. One day, a group was on patrol when they were ambushed and killed. Several Americans died, and only one man, a New Yorker, survived alone. He understood that we had been set up.

The following dawn, as I sat unfolding who had betrayed us, explosions broke across the ridge line, and most of the village burned from the incendiary munitions the U.S. Air Force had dropped onto our position. This was at the moment the United States was reducing Special Warfare in favor of kill count statistics.

Afterward, if I was to continue life outside of Leavenworth then the government would have their talons dug deeply into my flesh. I was a puppet. But in Cambodia I wished I was never born.

Now I focused on the bikers. I lay beneath the jail's porch sweating. Above me a man snored and another talked to a woman. The wind changed and a rubbery smoke from the bonfire reached me. After a while, waiting and breathing smoke, contemplating my move, I watched the mountains. Even at night, the ski trails cut there made strange vertical light-green lines against the dark-green mountainside. I was unsure whether or not I liked the trails. The increased stream of tourists irritated me, and I thought about moving to Wyoming.

There were then footsteps above, and the woman walked onto the gravel walkway and into the paved street. She turned to blow a kiss, and then shook her way away.

"I'll be back," she said.

"I'll be waiting," the man said.

When she was far enough, I moved beside the porch stairs in the shadow of the building. The lights were all out in the Sheriff' station.

One of the men above walked to the steps and pissed onto the walkway. I put my knife away and shimmied closer. I could still hear the other man snoring at the end of the porch. The pissing man was oblivious. He turned back, and I jumped from the dirt and grabbed his mouth with one hand and severed his arteries with the knife. The spray of blood on the porch was audible but the other man wasn't aware of what it signified.

I grabbed him the same way. His chair leaned against the railing while he snored, and I ripped him over and killed him. The chair he had sat in crashed to the porch, and I waited to learn if anyone noticed, but they hadn't and so I walked onto the porch and entered the jail. The room was dimly lit and a biker sat at the desk opposite the door. Dodge and his Deputy sat together in the cell.

When I entered, the biker was asleep behind the desk to my right. But the noise I made on the way in woke him. The room was dark. The biker groggily stood up and called out a name I did not recognize. I removed a police baton from the wall and struck him in the face.

His body crumbled to the floor, and he bled. I took the keys from the table and opened the cell door. Dodge stood and came over to me, and the Deputy followed behind.

"Thanks."

We left the building and walked the dirt path. A shard of light came from the sun far off in the distance. Above, a man laughed, and we stood still and stayed to the shadow. Gravel crunched and footsteps came toward us. About fifty yards ahead, light from a house shined onto the path, and the footsteps got closer until Smiley emerged from the darkness, alone.

9

CHARLES MCKENNA

C ans and cigarette butts, and bottles of booze, and vomit
covered the streets in puddles of mud, and lawns had been
violated by spinning tires leaving furrows in the small patches as
though the earth had been turned over for something sown to grow.
Here and there windows were broken, but most of the storefronts
were untouched. Some men and women slept by their bikes. Joanne
pointed to one guy sleeping with his head on the handlebars of a
bike on a kickstand. His body draped down the length of the motorcycle and his feet hung to the ground.

A little farther up the street a man sleeping beside his bike on
the sidewalk lept to his feet. "You touchin' my bike," he slurred.

He was drunk and staggering; his dark hair was matted on one
side. He charged forward and I moved and struck him hard in the
center of the chest with my shoulder. His body folded making a
terrible noise as the air escaped his lungs, and he shot back into the
bike leaving faint trails in the air as he went. I hadn't hit anyone like
that since high school football and it felt good. The bike crashed to
the ground, and the sound echoed through the brisk morning
streets. Joanne covered her ears, and I apologized for making so

much noise. But she pointed back to the man who lay awkwardly on top of his toppled bike and vomited onto his handlebars.

"He'll be alright now," Joanne said with total assurance and I believed her. It seemed to me that he had expelled a great deal more than just vomit.

It was at that point I noticed how young the biker was; younger than most, which made me wonder if he was even old enough to have graduated high school. I felt bad at that point, and worse still when I realized that he was probably older than Joanne. I shuddered at that thought. But I couldn't worry about her youth for long as I saw a figure hanging several feet off the ground twisting in the wind. A man hung upside down on a rope; blood soaked hair hanging down from his scalp. We drew closer.

I had trouble believing what I was seeing. Joanne gave voice to this opinion, but it was really there.

Smiley's body hung upside down from a black nylon rope that ran through a pulley attached to the roof of the bar. Both his eyes were black and his nose was turned to the side, and he had a deep gash over his cheekbone. Blood drained from the wounds and ended in his hair where it dried and was now blackish. His hands were bound behind his back, and from the breeze, his body rotated and swung, which made him visible from all aspects. I walked closer and saw a deep puncture in his neck about two inches long starting in the center. The blood from that wound, dripped off his hair forming an archaic chainlike pattern on the ground in splatters and dots. I knew he was dead because he was ghastly pale.

"Is he real?!" Joanne said. "He looks like a Christ."

"I'm letting him down."

"No, don't."

I ignored her, and walked to the line tied to the flagpole on the edge of the building. As I approached his body, I smelled the distinct odor or urine, either from the perpetrator who had pissed on Smiley, or from Smiley pissing himself. When I got near, Smiley's body completed a full turn, and his shoulder was in front of me.

We were face to face, and he was upside down. His eyes were open, blue, beady and watching me. A black magpie flew from the wires above and landed near the shrubs beside Smiley. His eyes did not move, nor did they blink, but suddenly, as if prompted by the magpie, Smiley squirmed and oscillated on the line; his eyes flaring with hate as his nose dripped blood.

"You—You. Let me down. Untie me. I must go!!!"

"Go where?" I said. I couldn't believe he was alive.

"He did this to me. He made me." He was crazed and flailing about. I couldn't make sense of his babble.

"You need to go to the hospital Smiley, you lost a lot of blood," Joanne said from behind me.

"I don't need to go to no hospital. Just let me down." His voice cracked. I pulled at the knot, and when it came loose I struggled to keep him from crashing to the ground.

I managed to let him down gently, and Joanne lifted his head so that his shoulders came to rest on the rutted earth. When he came down he wormed around and crawled on his belly still ensnared in the rope.

"Stop moving so damn much," I said.

"Do you know what it's like?" he said.

"Do you want me to untie you or not you maniac?"

"You will untie me."

"Untie him, Charles."

I loosened the rope and he sprang to his feet and Joanne helped him with the rest. He was vicious. His lip was cut deep and opened like a curtain to reveal a fang. Joanne stood and looked at his blood smeared on her hands.

"Where'd all your friends go?" I asked.

"What friends?" he said.

He was deathly white. The long blond hair of his head matted in locks against his skull, and he franticly looked me up and down.

"Let me help you," Joanne said.

"You should have stayed with us last night. We just started having fun." She pulled away from him and he continued, "You're only on his arm now because he's safe, you said it."

"You're just a damned maniac." I said and stepped between them and nudged Smiley.

"I see," he said. "She shared the trip with you too."

"Go bleed on someone else." I shoved him and he walked away and down the steep hill leading to Main Street. Joanne just looked at me as if she was reconnecting to reality because it seemed like the whole experience might have been of a piece with everything else.

"That definitely happened," I said.

"I was afraid of that."

As if to make it even stranger, at least a hundred motorcycles or more fired up together down somewhere on Main Street in a great big roar.

"What's going to happen now," she asked?

"At this point, it could be anything."

As it turned out, they were all leaving. At least most of them were leaving as word had come that the State Police were making their way up to our neck of the woods.

"We should just go back to my house and come out after they sort it all out. Who knows what kind of trouble people are going to get in."

"Sure," she said smiling, "But why don't we just go back to my place?"

"That's acceptable to me." At that point I discovered why I had never met her before, because she lived across Main Street, toward the mountains, about three quarters of a mile away near the airport, in a house she had allowed her father to buy for her after he had located her again and only months before he died of cancer. Her mother had followed the old man to the grave within a year and Joanne had come to control a small part of a great fortune. This would have been just before we met. She had said her father would have written her out of the will entirely, but had relented at the last minute, and had left her an insultingly small portion for what was there, but enough to live on. It meant that our life would be very little complicated by interruptions from her family, at least living members that is.

10

CHARLES MCKENNA

"I want you to marry me," Joanne said.

"Are you pregnant?"

"What kind of thing is that to ask me? Of course I'm not pregnant."

We took our bicycles off Main Street and onto the dirt road that led into French Gulch, which was a narrower, higher elevation valley running perpendicular to Breckenridge. There, the topsoil had been washed away years ago by a mining outfit, and like Breckenridge's valley floor, all that remained was an expanse of round rocks through which a river flowed. At spots the river was visible, and at others it flowed through the rocks. Here and there, wherever the miners left a depression, stagnant and rusted pools of water dotted the valley floor.

We climbed beyond the point where the miners stopped, and nature remained untouched (except for the road). At the point where the mining outfit could progress no farther, they packed up their gear and abandoned the dredge boat with its paddle wheel where it now sat defunct and out of place in the Rockies.

We had followed the dirt road eastward beyond the dredge boat, up the side of a broad humpback mountain and came to a stop above the tree line where the mountain was bare and the view of the Rockies opened. It was here that Joanne asked me to marry her; surrounded by the brown gravel mountaintops, with lush summer green trees beneath, and the merciless sun beating in the sky.

"I want you to marry me."

"I want to marry you too," I replied, realizing how much I loved her, and how, like the mountains, I wanted her as my own private experience.

I took a knee, "Will you marry me?"

"Of course I will, if you get off your knee. You look silly." She smiled,

I stood, and she kissed me.

"I'll get you a ring tomorrow."

"I don't want one. I don't need a commercial object that tells me you're my husband, as long as you say you are."

"I am."

A few feet away, I caught sight of a lonely purple flower growing out of the gravel mountainside. I walked over and plucked the flower and returned to Joanne.

"Here's the symbol . . . I love you."

I grabbed Joanne and kissed her again, and we stood silent and embraced looking over Breckenridge in the valley below.

As we rode back through the valley, Joanne said, "I love this place, it's so wonderfully abnormal with all those piles of rock and that strange boat and the caves."

Down on Main Street, I made her stop at the Gold Pan to tell Bill and the Sheriff. It was five in the afternoon and they were sure to be in. The sun sat atop the jagged peaks of Breckenridge's Ten Mile Range in the west like an eye above the world.

The Gold Pan was an ancient establishment that had been in Breckenridge from early on. The building had the old type western windows that went from ceiling to a few feet from the floor, with woodwork beneath the glass painted a drab green, and a sign above in gold lettering. Along the walls inside were photos of the bar and town, crooked and cobwebbed. A few of the pictures showed the Gold Pan after a blizzard in the nineteenth century dropped snow enough that a series of tunnels needed to be dug to connect the buildings on Main Street: the bar was connected to the hotel that was connected to the post office that connected to the brothel and the mayor's office and so on.

The old brass railed mahogany bar sat to the right of the door, and on the stools sat two men who were usually there whenever they could be for dinner, Bill and Sheriff Dodge; although Dodge was no longer a Sheriff, now he collected a pension and plowed snow for the long winter while his wife worked at the ticket booth on the mountain.

"A special treat," Bill said when Joanne entered.

"We're getting married," she blurted.

Dodge stood, "I'll be damned, you finally got the courage to ask the woman. What's it been, five years?

"More than that," Joanne said.

"You're lucky she put up with you that long." Dodge tilted his glass back and took a swig of beer. The scar in his face had healed well over the years.

Andy the bartender leaned forward from behind the counter. "Your getting married?" He then shook my hand and reached behind the counter and produced a bottle of Champagne. "See the orange label," he held the bottle high above the bar, "That means it's the good stuff."

"No thank you," Bill said and waived away the bottle.

"When's the ceremony?" Dodge asked.

"Whenever she wants it, if she wants a ceremony."

Joanne walked to the bathroom at the back of the barroom while we sat at a round table a few steps from the bar and across from the black, cast-iron wood-burning stove in the corner.

Dodge talked while Bill was silent, which is how he was most of the time. He had a strong Roman nose, and his eyes were green. Sometimes his red hair, which he had grown since the war, hung low, other times he pulled it back. And though he sat in a bar for dinner nearly every night, he didn't drink alcohol. People sat next to him and drank beer and talked and talked, and he simply nodded and picked at his food, engaged but not talking. By 8:00 pm he always left the bar. When I often walked home at night, his light was never on past 9:30 pm.

He was an early riser. I saw him on my way to get coffee one morning; the sun rose and illuminated the mountainside west of town. That morning the valley sat under the shadow, and Bill walked from his side door to his Barn carrying a small, patterned piece of wood. I said hello, and he simply nodded and walked into the barn to begin the day. He hated to be bothered when he worked. He carved wood in the garage; Totem Poles big and small for gas stations or national parks or whoever wanted them; sometimes he spent a great deal of time painting his works, and other times he left them in "the Raw," as he called it. He would also carve blocks into unique, chaotic patterns of curving, undulating organic lines. When I asked him if his patterns meant anything, he told me, "It's about the goddess," but he smirked.

And after that, whenever I saw any of his work, I searched for meaning, but could never find any.

He owned a cottage off High Street, about a block farther away from Main Street than my place. He bought the cottage with money he saved from the service and then he buried himself there along with whatever lay buried in him from the war. He didn't talk about Vietnam, but when Dodge pressed him, Bill said that he spent most of his time in Cambodia.

"The war was in Nam," Dodge said.

"The war was there too."

"Well, we never should've lost that war," Dodge said.

"We used them and left them," he said.

That was the most I ever heard Bill say about himself, until recently, and he seemed angry that he had been pressed to reveal what little he had. But Andy broke the awkwardness with his own awkwardness, "Are you sure you're ready to be married?"

"The guy just got engaged. Do you think before you speak?" Dodge said.

"I know, but is Joanne okay with you?"

Dodge got angry. "Come on damn it."

"I'm just asking questions. Just forget it."

Joanne returned from the bathroom and picked up her glass of Champagne. "What?" She said when she looked at our faces.

"Andy was just being a fool."

"Really?"

Andy blushed and receded to the bar back where he wiped the counter, a position he often took after offending customers.

We left soon after and retrieved or bikes from the plank boardwalk.

It was then that I saw him. He wore a black spring jacket over blue jeans and his head was shaved but not bald. He had a small jaw and a light stance, and his eyes were a wild kind of Arian blue, almost hypnotizing; I hated those eyes on my wife.

I stepped down from my bike and went to him. Joanne noticed me headed for him. "Charles. What are you doing?"

"I'm sorry," the man said. "I know her." He paused and said, "and you too."

"You don't," I said.

"But I do. You don't remember?"

"Should I."

"Joanne," he said.

"Oh," she said, recalling him to memory.

"You should be behind bars," I said.

"I got out. I live in the valley now. I never got to thank you for what you did for me that night. Most people might've let me swing."

"Sure," I remembered him now.

"That night had a profound effect."

"I bet."

"Probably more than you can even imagine. It's nice to see you again . . . I don't think you ever told me your name."

"Charles."

"I'm glad to see you again, Charles," he said almost in a hiss, "And you always Joanne."

I hated the way he looked at her.

"You think I'm trouble, don't you Charles? But I'm not your devil."

He hadn't changed a bit. "Be no trouble elsewhere." I said.

"But I've carried my cross. Have you?" He searched my eyes and said, "Nice to see you again, Charles. Bye Joanne."

"Bye Stanley."

Then he left and I went back inside.

Dodge saw me enter and spoke up. "Back so soon?"

"Did you know Smiley's out of prison?"

"Yeah. He served five years for what he did to my face. That and going AWOL. He did his time in Leavenworth. And now he's a free man. I got the call from a friend a few months ago. He told me Stanley Joe White's out of prison and there's nothing you can do about it."

"He only served five years?"

"We got Judges that think the laws a day care center and there's no difference between cops and criminals; only cops get a pension. And lawyers is what lawyers have always been, so . . . you get what you get. I heard he got some type of religion while he was up there. Some new age beatnik crap."

"Beatnik's were last generation," Andy said.

"Whatever generation, Stanley Joe White was the head priest of his own church; he had a following of inmates and everything. Got so big, the state investigated. A guard followed him too, but he was queer as a three-dollar bill, confessed to killing and raping a couple inmates . . . said that Stanley Joe White was the second coming and the dark prince rolled in one. They made a story of it for a while last year."

"And they let Smiley out?"

"He served the time the judge gave him to serve."

Bill nodded and took a sip of water.

"I should have left him where I found him," I said.

Dodge looked curious, but didn't ask, but I could tell that Bill had discovered something he hadn't know before. It passed across his green eyes and was gone as quickly as it had come.

"I think he's up in some shack in French Gulch," Dodge was saying.

I patted Dodge on the back, nodded to Bill and left. Outside Joanne watched Smiley walk up the street.

"Did he talk to you?"

"He just said hello."

"He already said hello."

"He just got out of prison. He's not a bad man."

"The guy's a freak. I don't want him around."

"I know. He came to me when he got out, and he scares me; the way he stares at me."

"He came to you. You saw him before?"

"He scares me, Charles!"

We went home where Joanne hung the purple flower up to dry and then drove down to Denver to celebrate.

Sarah was born full nine months later.

YESTERDAY

11

SARAH MCKENNA-HURST

M y bedroom wasn't far enough away from them.

They would fight. Really, they bickered and argued.

They didn't yell very often. Actually, they almost never yelled when I was growing up, but the tension between them increased over the years and today was an explosion. Their voices carried through the floor so I could hear.

"You can't just put up developments wherever you want and expect there to be no backlash. The Eighties are the Twenties Charles; you'll come to see it."

"I work damn hard for what I have, you better hope there's no crash if you want to finish your PhD."

"Don't be an ass, I'd rather be dead than sit around and have you pay me to sleep with you."

"Our relationship's prostitution?" dad asked.

"The point is, we have plenty of money. There's no need to ruin French Gulch with those hideous houses."

"It's not just about the money—I build things. And it's not like other suburban developments either, we did our best, even with the stupid zoning laws, to lay it out like an old village."

"Just because you think you are supposed to build doesn't mean you get to ruin the Gulch with a Medieval dream."

"Ruin it. It's on a superfund site, Joanne for crying out loud. The entire valley was leveled by the mining company, and now it's a pile of rock and rusted equipment."

"We got engaged up there, Charles."

"We got engaged on a mining road on the side of the mountain not in the valley."

"I remember that day all the time."

I listened. I usually didn't, but there usually wasn't this much tension. They continued. I heard him walk away. But mom never backed away. "The mountains aren't the suburbs, Charles; they've never been and they never will be. Don't you remember why you came here or have you forgotten what you really are? Now you want to spoil it."

"Where do you think our money comes from?"

"If this were a hundred years ago, Charles, you'd be a miner or the owner of a mine. You're no different."

"Listen to me. Locals here can afford the houses I build. They have a center. They're not disjointed. They don't just have to live way out in the county. I won't stop Joanne."

"I'll stop you."

"You'll stop me? You'd rather impress your silly group than anything else. That's why no one cares what you have to say."

There was a crash from upstairs and a string of swears and then one of them burst into the garage. I heard the opener groan, and then mom's car pulled from the driveway.

After she left, dad banged around alone upstairs. "Is she insane?" he shouted to no one.

He came down the stairs to my room, hesitated at the door, and knocked.

"Can I come in?" he said.

"I don't want to hear about you and mom."

"And I don't want to talk about me and mom. I'm coming in." He opened the door and walked into my room.

"This is my room, dad, you have to knock."

"I did knock."

He looked upset, and his eyes were red. "I know you know we love you, but I want you to know so you don't forget, okay: we love you. I love you. And I love your mother, and I know she loves me. I'm sorry."

Dad was very upset. When he talked, his words came jumbled together, but I understood, and hugged him.

"Will you come upstairs?" he asked.

"You just don't want to be alone."

"No, I don't want to be alone, so will you keep me company; maybe we'll get some ice cream."

"I don't like ice cream, dad."

"Then we'll get whatever you want."

"Steak," I said.

I went upstairs. Against the wall opposite the stairs a vase full of plastic flowers and marbles lay smashed on the floor, some of the bits were embedded in the wall.

"I liked that vase dad."

"Sorry."

"Why'd you break it?"

"Your mother broke it."

"Is mom coming back?"

"Of course she is Sarah, we're just fighting. I love her."

He did love her, so did I, but I wondered if that was enough.

Our house was split-level, my room was in the basement, and the main floor was one open floor with a large vaulted ceiling and tall windows; mom and dad's room was a half floor up. The house had been built by some developer that mom knew in the 80s in the style of that time: the style that was angular and somewhat reminiscent of a chalet but ugly.

The developer had trouble selling the house, I wonder why, and mom made dad buy it and move in. I remember the argument they had over it a few years ago. She said the house was on the market for nearly half what it was worth and the family couldn't afford not to buy it. He bought it and she seemed happy.

Dad and I sat on the couch and turned on the TV.

"Your mother's been acting more . . ."

"What?" I said.

"She's more severe now, I don't know why."

He sat looking out the window. I watched him and then put my head on his shoulder. He hugged me. In a few minutes I was asleep.

When I awoke about an hour later he was gone, but he left a note on the coffee table printed in blue marker. The letter read:

Sorry Sarah, but you fell asleep, and you looked so peaceful that I didn't want to wake you. I went to the Gold Pan, and I should be back in a few hours.

6:20

IT WAS NOW 6:30, so he had really just left.

I wished that I had my license. Just over a year and I would, but not soon enough.

Breckenridge wasn't so bad by bike, but unfortunately the ski mountain had closed, and the summer crowd wouldn't arrive until it got hot down in Denver.

I just had to do something.

12

SARAH MCKENNA-HURST

I rode to Main Street to look for my dad at the Gold Pan. If he saw me, he would likely bring me in and all his friends would make a big deal out of me. Except, last time he brought me in the bar mom got all mad at him. She said she didn't want me introduced to the Saloon Culture; whatever that is.

I rode my bike out of the driveway. As I rode down hill, something caught my attention on a side street. Mom's BMW was parked in a driveway in front of a small Victorian cottage. She was in the driveway talking to a guy with long red hair pulled tight in a ponytail. I had seen my dad with him before, but I couldn't remember his name.

The man pointed to his barn, and they went inside. I wanted to know what they were talking about.

I left my bike on the street by the trashcans and walked to the window and listened. The glass was thin and old, and I heard, and saw and smelled everything.

"You've always listened, Bill."

He nodded. His barn was full of carved up logs and pieces of furniture. There was even a coat of arms painted green hung by the door at the front. Fluffy sawdust covered the floor, and I think a hang-glider dangled from the ceiling, but the heavy barn beams blocked my view. Opposite from me there was a narrow loft full of books, and to my right above the barn door was a huge American flag.

Bill sat in a chair, and mom stood erect in the middle of the room. She looked as if she owned the place.

" . . . he doesn't even give me . . ." She paused somewhere mid-sentence. "I don't need to tell you that."

He stood from his chair and walked over to his black workbench where he grabbed a glass jar with a fat cork full of green and red buds. The kids in my school already smoked pot.

"It's good," he said, "It grows up in the mineshafts."

"I know, above French Gulch, but I didn't know you still went up there. I thought you stayed away since Stanley came back," she said.

"He's something unique. He's got a few crazy hangers on, but they're under control, and what am I to do: the past is the past. You brought him here the first time."

"I know, I remember."

Bill sealed the paper joint. "He talks my language."

"I just didn't expect you to take to him so quickly."

"With the past?"

"No, I knew he'd forgive you of all people. I thought you were too distant for him to reach."

Bill smiled. Neither of them spoke. He ceremonially lit the joint, while mom stood and watched with a smirk.

Mom spoke, "I've felt so alone lately."

"We all feel alone."

"My marriage is what it is, and always has been."

"Did you come here to open up?"

"I'm not comfortable alone in a house where the man is oblivi-ous, he doesn't even know how I feel, and as long as he thinks I'm content he doesn't even ask; I just have to smile and give him a kiss and make him dinner and he's happy, but so much more goes on, and he has such a stupid contentment with the way things are. He just accepts the world at face value with naïve honesty, which is why I think I was with him, but it's worn me out, I can't stand how he is.

I thought he'd get it and maybe even get mad, but if somehow he thinks he's virtuous then everything's fine."

"I was there when you were engaged, you two were happy."

"He's easily amused. I think after my childhood, I was happy to feel safe, but that's not the same thing."

"I thought you were in love then?"

"Love's just what people say, it's a word. I'm sure he loved me, but life is more than that, and Charles just doesn't get it, and he never. And I don't think I ever . . . I mean—someone else may have, but he's so much like my father now, but a believer. I guess he always was."

"Shouldn't you talk with Stanley?"

"He's off preaching or whatever, he should be back. Maybe he is already, I don't know, he's hard to track. He won't be jealous."

Bill held the joint and offered it to mom. She looked at him and he turned his eyes away, and she took the offering, inhaled, closed her eyes and blew out smoke in plumes to her left, straight and to the right. She passed the joint back.

When they finished, mom sat on a maroon rug beside Bill's workbench. He stood and retrieved a freshly carved chair that hung on a drying rack. She saw the chair and smiled.

"I made this for you," he said.

"Thank you, but I don't think Charles's would like that," she said, but she wasn't looking at him. Instead she eyed his wood crafts-manship on the bench. "I like your work, it's natural. I like how the earth and sky seem one." She looked at him but he wasn't paying attention.

"Everything's always been ruined," he said from out of the blue.

"What's that mean?"

"This is what people do. They ruin—always have, they domi-nate to establish hierarchy and wreck everything if they can't have it their own way."

"You *have* been listening to Stanley, haven't you Bill?" she said and laughed.

Bill didn't see so amused.

At that point, my leg hurt, and so I moved to get a better position and knocked over a board that leaned against the barn. The board banged the wall, and Bill looked toward my window and then came at me. I crawled off into the driveway and got on my bike, horrified that he'd chase me out into the street. He didn't chase me though; in fact, he did worse and stayed behind with mom. God only knew what they did; God only knew what happened?

I didn't want to go home, and so I decided to check out the mineshaft they discussed.

13

SARAH MCKENNA-HURST

W hen I was a girl, I took a bike ride with mom through French Gulch and she pointed out the mine to me then. She seemed to have a strong attraction to the place. I remember she pointed to a trail that led to the mineshaft and said:

"Those mineshafts are unique because they follow ancient caves that were made when this valley was under water. The native people used to have rituals there. It was incredibly sacred to them."

"The Indians?"

"That's not their name, Sarah. They were Ute' ancestors whose culture stretched back to the Maya. They came to the mountains for safety. These caves became sacred to them because of the exposed veins of gold which would help them on the journeys. Their descendants were the last to lose their freedom to the land of the free."

She had pointed to the trail that led to the caves, and I remembered exactly where they were.

I rode over and through French Gulch where my dad talked about putting up houses. The sun was low on the sky, but high enough there was plenty of remaining day. The valley was awful and full of piled rock without soil or trees. And, here and there, rusted puddles of poison water sprung from the ground. Some said the water was still polluted by the arsenic the miners used to float gold above the sediment, but who knew. I wasn't planning on drinking it anyway.

Beyond this valley, the road climbed into the mountains, and I followed it, peddling my bike onto a small weather-worn path deeply rutted from runoff and age. After riding for a while I reached the base of the steep rocky hill. At intervals leading to the caves, small pyramids of stone stood on the side of the trail, supposedly put there by the Ute, and left by miners as trail markers.

The hill was too steep for me to ride, and I climbed on foot, pulling my bike beside me to the mineshaft at the top of the hill. In front of the shaft, a large pile of stone and debris remained from a landslide a few years back. Mom told me about how heavy rains caused the hill to give way and slide into the cave opening. It took the locals weeks to relocate the shaft and clear the mess.

I climbed over the pile. There were signs and razor wire near the entrance, but the razor wire was cut and pushed out of the way. The signs said "Danger" and "Caution" and "Risk of Explosion;" "Risk of Cave In."

The footing above the cave mouth was uncertain, covered in lose rock. I walked carefully. Below, I thought I saw a blue light but whatever it was it was gone. One thing was for sure, I could smell what they were growing. On top of that, there was a woodsy smell; like store bought mushrooms have sometimes. I moved to the wall at right for balance, eager to get down and inside. Over on the wall, I fumbled for something to hold, but there was only dirt, and then the rocks slipped beneath my feet. The hollow echo of nothing sounded back to me from below as the rocks cascaded away. I clawed the side of the cave, but could find nothing to grip and fell to my knee. When I fell, I grabbed onto a wire that stopped my fall. It was an extension cord, and as I attempted to pull myself back up, the plug pulled apart. I tumbled down the slope into the darkness. Rocks and dirt fell with me and we spilled down onto a cold smooth rock surface.

I was inside the ancient cave now. More rocks spilled down from above and barely missed hitting me. My knee was scrapped and I had an egg on my head, but really I was okay. The cave was damp. Light came from the opening above but that was all, and it didn't travel far. Deeper inside, the cave was black as ink. I sat and allowed my eyes time in adjust to the darkness.

After a minute, I saw a shape in the distance that seemed to be another rock pyramid; only tall as a man. The miners used it to mark their path. I wasn't afraid. Another minute and my eyes adjusted. On the walls, I noticed the faint shimmer of paint under the sun light from above. There were Indians being slaughtered by white men on pale horses, but some of the Indians seemed like white people themselves, they all seemed white, and all around the painting were crimson handprints and pink dots with mountains in the back. I wondered if the Utes painted this scene. If they had, some later person painted what looked like automobiles in the background.

While I observed the painting, a hollow echo of whispers came from inside the cave. I cast my eyes on the pyramid of stone that looked like it moved. My eyes adjusted more. My heart pounded. The pyramid was a man watching me. There were several people. The man walked toward me. His hands stretched out to grab me. I stood and scratched and clawed the rock and gravel entrance to get out, making it only a few feet before I slipped back down. When I sank to the cave floor every hair on my body stood. I imagined being tomahawked to death or stuck with an arrow like a deer.

The man came closer. He and the others moved in and out of the shafts of light as they came forward.

"You don't have to be frightened Sarah, I would never hurt you."

He was now beneath the shafts of light that fell from above outside. Only the top of his shoulders and head were in the light. The rest of him was hidden in the darkness. His head was shaved nearly clean, except for a growth of peach fuzz, and his eyes were wild blue. But not like regular people's blue eyes, his eyes were the color of the ocean if the ocean had flecks of gold.

Behind him in the shadow were two women who floated like ghosts in the shafts of light. One of them I recognized as mom's friend Gwen; my dad never got along with her; the other I didn't know. I turned my attention from them back to the man who was right on top of me. He offered his hand. It was small, delicate; almost feminine, but I noticed he had dirt beneath his nails.

"You don't remember me?" he said.

I shook my head.

"I'm Stanley White. Your mom never told you about me?"

I shook my head again.

"I didn't mean to frighten you Sarah, but you unplugged our lights. I couldn't see who you were."

His voice was soft and clam.

"You've grown so much, you're almost a woman now, you're almost ready; you've become such a beautiful full grown person. You have such a wonderful presence."

He looked at my knee. "You're hurt."

"I'm fine."

"I will bandage you."

"No, it's all right. My dad has bandages at the house." I didn't want him to touch me; his skin looked cold and scaly.

"You father?" He said. "I can fix you. I have food, would you like to eat?"

"I want to leave, I want to go, please; I want to go."

"You shouldn't be scared. I would never hurt you; I just haven't seen you in so long."

"Please I want to go. I want to go home. I want to go home."

He was angry from my tears and screams and moved closer. I ran to climb out. I scratched and clawed and fell to the floor at his feet, screaming and crying. Dirt showered down from above where I climbed. It was in my hair and mouth. I lay on the ground and more dirt fell. He walked slowly to me. The women followed. He stared at me. I couldn't move. I was horrified. I was an infant. And then I must have passed out or fainted or maybe that's how I got the lump because I woke up outside the cave beside my bike with a silver heart pendant around my neck. Inside the pendant was a picture of a baby, and the baby looked like me. My mom had the same picture in her office. I stood up. There was a note in my hand which had been scrawled on the back of an envelope.

Don't ever forget. I will never hurt you.

That was all the note said. I crumpled it up and threw it off into the trees. Then I felt my body in disgust to see if the freak violated me. I felt fine; at least nothing hurt or felt different than it should have.

A shudder came over me. I felt sick. They were watching me; out there in the trees somewhere. I got on my bike and rode down the gravel hill. My bike jumped around the trail hitting rocks and ruts, but after a few minutes I spilled off the trail onto the gravel road and peddled home as fast as humanly possible. When I got in the driveway, I threw my bike down in the bark mulch and ran up the stairs to get inside. When I came in, my dad was sitting on the couch watching the news on TV.

"What happened to you Sarah, where did you go?"

"I went for a bike ride."

"Did you fall?"

I didn't want him to know what happened, it was too strange, and he might overreact. "I fell on the dirt road, there was a rut that I didn't see, and I banged my head."

"I'll fix you up. You should leave a note next time you go out so I don't go crazy thinking someone kidnapped you."

He hugged me, and brought me to the bathroom where he bandaged my knee and washed my face. "Why are you so dirty?"

"Sorry."

When he finished he went back to watching the cable news on television, and I walked down the hall into mom's office. She was back now and sitting at her desk. I closed the door behind me. She didn't bother to turn to see who was there. I poked her and she was startled.

"Oh…Sarah…you scared me," she said.

I held out my hand and let the pendant with my picture dangle from its chain.

"Where did you get that?" She asked looking down at her own version of the photo draped over the corner of a picture frame.

"From that man, Stanley White?"

"Where is he?" she asked.

"Why does he have a picture of me as a baby?"

She thought for moment and said, "He's a drifter honey, he has a lot of people who want to hang around him, but he doesn't have any real love in his life, and when I showed him that picture years ago, he liked it and so I gave it to him."

"Don't lie to me mom."

"I don't lie to you. If he gave it to you, he must want you to know how important you are to him."

"That's so strange. That man is so strange," I hesitated for a moment. I wanted her to know that I saw her with Bill, but I was afraid: afraid she would be mad, and afraid she would tell me the truth, and I just couldn't bring myself to ask her why she said those things to Bill, and what that man Stanley meant to her. I wanted to, and all the questions hung loose on the tip of my tongue, but I couldn't say the things I felt, and knew and heard her say.

She sat in her chair and looked at me. I stood still, afraid of her and afraid of myself: the outside edges of my world that used to be so clear before were blurred. Before where there was a boundary, there was an open range of nothing that led onto an ocean of questions.

I turned from her and walked back with my dad to watch the news on television. She didn't say a word as I left.

14

CHARLES MCKENNA

Today was the first open house for my development and I wanted my wife to be there, but she was belligerent. It was months since we last argued. Since that time I went about my work without saying a word. I was certain she would appreciate the neighborhood when enough of it was up so she could understand, but she didn't. She barely spoke to me. She often mocked me. She even mocked the time I got out of bed. She said I was just *so* chipper *so* early that it made her sick. She often wouldn't let me sleep in my own bed. I didn't know if I should divorce her or not. I wondered why she didn't divorce me.

So when I asked her to see the development, she was less than thrilled.

"I'm not interested in seeing the development Charles, you know I'm not, just like I'm not interested in going bird hunting."

"I want you to see what I've built up there. I wish you wouldn't boycott me now."

"I've always boycotted you ruining French Gulch, I don't see any need to it."

"I'm taking Sarah down with me then. She wants to see what the finished houses will look like."

"You're not taking my daughter."

I walked toward her. "She's our daughter, and you are not going to stop me."

"Don't tempt me Charles."

"What the hell is your problem already? I built some houses, get over it. So the world doesn't look like you thought it would when you were young, what the hell else is new. I'm taking Sarah, and you're welcome to come."

Joanne didn't reply. Instead she closed her office door and went back to work on the paper she was writing on the doorway that psychedelic experiences could offer to the enlightenment of the human species, especially with the newer drugs that allowed one to go even further than ever before, where it was said that one could experience another place, a vaulted underground dome in fact, with creatures that gave one encouragement when they weren't giving one the finger. But this is only what I had heard from subjects in certain trials that had been conducted.

"Are you going to keep away from me forever?" I said through the door. She didn't answer.

Only the sound of her banging the keyboard came to me. In the last few months, as she had worked on her dissertation she had also begun spending more time with a new age group, known as the The Peoples Group, which she said had helped her to meditate and relax. I couldn't understand what she saw in them, or why she wasn't so relaxed.

I once entered her office when she was out and on her desk, beside an orange bottle of prescription pills I found a glossy brochure for The Peoples Group. The literature was very much *out there*, but it was all pretty much re-tread rhetoric: the white man is the patriarchal oppressor, he rapes the Earth (earth always capitalized) he enslaves the people, America is the most immoral country in history, but it didn't always used to be like this, there was a time when America was on the right track, but now it is horribly wrong—fire and brimstone, blah blah—and if you want to help spark the renaissance, send a check to the address at the bottom of the page or connect through our PayPal page. It takes money and support to spark the renaissance and evolve a blind society.

I asked her about the *church*, and she took issue with me using the word church because she said, "Religions were antiquated thought systems that we have to get beyond," and then she became unspeakably upset; she was literally livid with rage because she felt I did not show her religion enough respect. And I didn't, but I couldn't help it, it all sounded so foolish, and it was hard for me not to laugh.

I still loved her though, truly and deeply—almost hopelessly. But there was a bit of pity in it, and guilt. She was easy to fall in love with, there's no doubt, but she was also in great pain. I could see it so clearly. Where it came from, I couldn't be sure, but it ate her alive. In so many ways it made her void herself of her own love, while at the same time she could always pretend that I was the one doing it to her. Yet I felt it my responsibility to help her because I knew that's why she had married me, that the something inside her that could love, had sought help. The direction she was headed now only brought her misery, not because it separated her from me, but because it separated her from her own love even further. The remedy she sought was the very thing that poisoned her. But she had her own lights, and couldn't seem to stop following them into darkness no matter the pain it brought and that she despised the remedy because she could. Sometimes it seemed she had some other voice that pulled her, and the Joanne I knew and loved was a prisoner who was along for the ride.

"You can come out of there you know," I said and banged on the door. I didn't want to let this go.

"I'd rather be in this room while you're here."

"Oh come on, Joanne, get out of the room. I spent years on this project and I want you to at least see what it looks like damn it, now come on!"

I grabbed the handle and pushed the door open. She sat opposite the door and stared at me as if I had struck her in the face. The office was gloomy with leafs of paper strewn about. Two large maroon candles sat burning on the desk. The desk was dark brown mahogany and took up almost an entire wall. It must have cost a fortune, but she bought it herself, and men came and delivered it in the winter about six months ago. She didn't even think to ask for my help.

"I don't want you in here Charles. This is my space."

I stepped inside the room and shut the door. "I want you to come with us, like a family. So you can see what the houses look like. You won't feel so mad if you see what I've done—how well designed even the streets are."

"Get out Charles. You act like you're some divine building and loan and I can't stand it."

"What the hell's the matter with you!"

"I don't care about your buildings Charles, I don't."

"This is what I do, this is what I'm good at. I'm part of the growth. I can look back and see what I built and feel proud. The development is more than just money to me, the houses are like monuments."

"To your vanity. I'm surprised you didn't put up a statue of yourself." She looked at me with bleak eyes. "I can't even stand to look at you anymore. It's not such a wonderful life Charles; no matter how you pretend"

"You're extreme."

"No. I can't, I can't stand it, I can't stand you, and the little boys like you. All you spoiled little boys who want whatever you want, whenever you want it with your fat little fingers."

"Can't you just deal with things as they are? Can't you be rational?"

She shuffled some papers to the side of her desk and then stood up and faced me. She was so angry that her face was near purple, and veins pushed out of her neck. For a moment she turned hateful attention toward me, and then she looked back at the desk and picked up the Rocky Mountain Post from off a side table and flung it at my face. I caught the paper mid flight and slapped it off to my side.

"Don't throw things at me Joanne."

"Or what? Do you see what the paper says today? Have you

been watching the news? Do you care at all what goes on outside your selfish world?" She stormed forward. "The President has troops in Africa and they call it peacekeeping. I'm glad those helicopters got hit. At least the government used to invent better reasons for war. And the press is afraid to report the real story because they've been ruined with money."

"Maybe your medication is a little too strong."

"Don't try to write me off as being crazy or drugged. I won't allow you to marginalize me."

"If the shoe fits."

"Get out Charles."

"Maybe you'd be okay with what I did for a living if I set up a non-profit. I'll call it Humans-R-Us, and we'll have a beautiful mission statement. We'll say we save people; we don't even actually have to do anything; just talk the right shit, then you'll be alright with the money. . . At least I'm honest in what I do."

"Shut up Charles."

"I know I'm not selfless . . ."

"We don't make sense anymore Charles. And you know it. We never did. I've always just looked out for Sarah, and you were the most stable man I could find. Now I'm only here because it would be a disaster if we had split custody and you had a free influence on her. At least now I mediate your poison."

"Then divorce me. You asked me to marry you, now ask me to divorce you."

"Don't tempt me Charles."

"Either way, I'm going to the site with Sarah. I hope you figure it out before I get back." I walked to the door but turned, "I'm worried about you Joanne. I think that you may need more help than you think."

"How sweet, you want to protect me. It's not an option."

I closed the door and stood in the hallway. I wanted to go back in, but I decided against further confrontation—to move her would take an exorcist anyhow. I continually told myself that if she needed space to save our marriage, then I would give it to her. Given time I hoped she would realize how important what we had together was.

But in an honest part of my mind I knew our marriage was held together only by the habit and fear.

I walked into the basement to get Sarah from her room. I reached the bottom of the stairs and knocked.

"If you and mom are just going to fight, I don't want to go anywhere. That's all you do is fight, and I can't stand it, dad."

"Your mother isn't coming with us."

I opened the door. Sarah stood from her bed and shut off the television. Her eyes had bags from crying. When she stood, I went over and hugged her. She pulled away and smiled, and then we walked out into the driveway.

I turned back to look at the house. Joanne stood in her office and watched us through the window. She saw me and walked away. I turned my back and stepped into my white GMC pickup. Sarah was already inside.

I pulled down the driveway. Traffic was re-routed off Main Street and onto our street which made pulling onto the road difficult. Early September is usually slow, but this week there was a festival in town that pulled thousands of people from Denver. The festival celebrated some Viking god, Ullr, or another, and was designed to help local business until ski season arrived.

The sky was perfectly blue for as far as the eye could see, and winter was right around the corner. We pulled onto the street and followed the flow of traffic parallel to Main Street and then took a right onto French Creek Road and drove up toward the development. The main settlement of Breckenridge largely ended at this point.

After we pulled onto French Creek Road, we passed a group of women on an afternoon walk. I waved to them, a few waved back. Smiley was among them; same baldhead with blond fuzz. I slowed beside the group and looked out the passenger window to see him again, but the other people blocked him from view. Sarah got annoyed.

"Why are you going so slow?"

"I thought I recognized someone, but I didn't."

"Who?" She looked over her shoulder, and then was silent.

I accelerated.

Lodge pole pine trees, and a few aspen trees filled the forest around us. The lodge poles grew like weeds. They choked out the light and killed smaller trees that fell to the ground in a rat's nest of flammable debris. The tree choked forest stood on both sides of the road here but as we drove a little farther, the forest opened and the valley floor was devoid of topsoil and no longer capable of sustaining life. At the turn of the century, the trees had all been cut and the soil washed down river by a mining company's dredge boat. What they left behind was a valley about one quarter mile wide and four miles long, completely devoid of topsoil, but surrounded by hills of lodge pole pine on two sides.

We rounded a bend by a large crystal blue pond at the edge of the road. As we came around the pond the development became visible.

"Wow, dad, this is what you've built up here."

"I told you what we were doing."

"I just never knew how big it was actually going to be."

"Right now we only have one house finished; the others are in various stages of completion."

She pointed to the development. "What are all the gray squares in the ground?"

"Foundations. We have forty in the ground so when winter comes, the framers can keep building, and hopefully, I won't go totally bankrupt."

"You won't. They'll sell, they're beautiful; they look like the old houses people used to live in."

"I hope you're not the only one that feels that way."

"I can't be. Anyway, it looks like so much fun what you're doing. You plan the places people live; I'd love to do that."

"It's not so romantic."

15

SARAH MCKENNA-HURST

"I can't believe all this is yours dad?"

Dad had a serious face as he looked out the window at his development.

"I didn't bang the nails, but I arraigned the financing and the permits and helped design the property. The hardest part was fighting the town and whoever else."

"Mom doesn't like the houses."

"Your mother and I just disagree.

"I hope you stop disagreeing."

Dad smiled. "Everything will be fine."

He pulled his truck beside an unfinished house on the block and got out. I opened my door and jumped down onto the freshly paved surface and followed him.

"Get back in the truck Sarah."

"Why?"

"Just get back in the truck, there's too much here that can hurt you, okay."

He came over to where I stood. "You'll have your license soon enough, and you won't need me driving you around." Seeing that I wasn't pleased, he added, "When we go to the model home you can get out there. I just have to check something."

He walked away, but I was upset. I looked down at my feet and refused to look up, as if in some way my posture could bother him.

When I did, he stood in the rock and gravel front yard with his feet wide apart and a broad smile across his face. A skeleton of a house stood before him, and beside him were several piles of lumber. The frames were taller than everything in the valley, except for the power lines and mountains in the background.

The carpenters had finished for the day. They moved around packing up their tools. Dad said, "hello," and the skinnier carpenter in jeans shorts nodded back, while the heavier one looked over dad's shoulder to me.

He saw where the carpenter was looking and took a few steps toward him, staring at the man until he looked away. Suddenly someone shouted at the two young carpenters from up on the roof:

"Damn it. You boys packin' up already? I pay you till four. It's ten of, and your tools are on the truck. Don't expect to get paid a full day."

The older man was in better shape than either of the younger men. He shimmied down the steep roof to the top rung of the ladder, and turned and came down to the second floor. "And you took forty minutes for lunch."

With those words, he came down the interior stairs to ground level. Neither of the workers said anything to him. He was shirtless and tan with a few tattoos and had his black and grey hair tied in a ponytail with a pair of black glasses on his head and an old tool belt over his shoulder. Dad watched him and smiled when he walked down the plank that was used as a front stair.

"How's it going Edzul?"

Edzul spit in the dirt and said, "It's going. If we can finish this house before Thursday, we'll be on schedule. Then I won't have to worry next week when I head to Lake Powell."

"Watch you don't get stuck in the mud down there," dad said.

"Water level's up this year. I got a sixty-foot houseboat rented for the week, should be nice."

"Maybe you should speak to my wife. I've been trying to take the family down for years now. I just can't get it to fly."

"Good luck to ya' on that one."

"You taking your motorcycle down," dad asked.

"Hmmmmm, prob'ly not. I just go to Sturgis now. I prob'ly won't make that this year. I like my truck and air-conditioning."

"It's not like it used to be."

"What is?" Edzul said, "Time moves. We either move or die. That's the way."

"So you don't see any of your old . . . ahh . . . family?"

"I still got my colors."

The two old timers reminiscing was somewhere between cute and absurd, but I hung on every word. I wanted to unravel the story of my dad's past and it seemed like Edzul held keys.

They stood around for a minute, but the time-out ended and dad asked, "You think you'll be done for Thursday?"

"I don't see a problem with it as long as the boys show up and work like they're supposed to." Edzul said, shouting the last two words over his shoulder toward his young men. He then looked at me. "Is that your daughter?" he asked.

"Yeah, that's Sarah."

"She's lucky she didn't get your side of the shallow gene pool. Hi Sarah, I'm Edzul." He seemed nice enough, and he walked nobly.

"Hi."

"If you'll be finished by Thursday that's all I needed to know. You need more lumber?"

"First list I gave you's good. Anyway, if I do, I'll go down the yard and pick it up on your account."

"You might be in for a surprise." Dad paused and said, "You coming to the open house over at number nine."

"You finally got it open? You guys moved fast."

"Had to. We need to start selling these things or it's over. There'll be food over there if you want," he said climbing back into the truck. Edzul nodded back, and we drove up the road.

Dad waved and then pointed out some things to me. "Right here will be a row of five houses surrounding a central green."

"It's nice."

"Thanks." He pointed again, "This is where the river used to flow—through all the rock here." And he waved his hand indicating the general course of the river after it had been dredged and scattered throughout the valley's river rock rather than in a single flow. We managed to channel it over there, by where the poles are driven in the ground. The town planner said it could never be done."

"Now it's a pretty water feature."

"I think the buyers will like it."

We parked in front of the model home a few houses away. The model looked like a farmhouse with large green gables and white trim and a front porch with red boards.

"What's the porch made of?" I asked.

"Redwood."

"Isn't that endangered."

"Well, not endangered, but prices are going up."

My dad rubbed his foot on the decking. "It's a beautiful wood, and holds up if people keep it finished."

A flag jutted off the porch and the railings were festooned with red, white and blue fabric banners behind which tables had been set up with flyers and brochures for potential customers. We walked onto the oak floors and dad introduced me to a woman named Courtney. She set food on tables and greeted people as they walked into the house.

"Hi, Sarah. Nice to meet you," she said. Then she turned her attention to my dad. "Her mother didn't want to come? Oh. Well."

She looked at me and turned back to dad who looked nervous. "You have nothing to worry about. It's a great day for an open house. A lot of the trade people are coming, and some of the local building inspectors and even some of the town council is coming through." She looked to me. "They want to see what they voted for. There should be more actual customers tomorrow. I pushed to have the opening in the afternoon on a weekend, but your dad didn't want to listen to me." She smiled and offered me little appetizers on navy blue rectangular plates. "You like the plates?"

"I do," I said.

"Your dad hated them, but he eventually let me decide. He knew I was right."

Dad opened some cherry cabinets and then inspected the faucet. "The house came out great Courtney, better than I expected."

"You expect everything to go to hell."

Now he picked at a blemish in the countertop. "Anyway, the house is terrific, I think people may even want to buy one."

She leaned on the counter. "Don't be hanging around here acting all pressurized on me," she said, "We can't sell houses that way."

I smiled. She seemed like a nice lady, and I usually didn't like other women. Mom would hate her.

We stayed for an hour, and at around five o'clock dad came and got me from the living room where I watched TV. We left. People had been in and out all afternoon, and dad smiled.

"I think we sold six maybe seven houses today," he said to me.

"That's great, right."

"Yeah. We need to close on at least five to keep the banks and the workers happy."

We walked to his truck and drove out of the neighborhood. As we passed the last row of grey foundations, dad pulled to the side of the road by the pond where a man with a red ponytail built a sign. I wasn't interested in the man or his sign, and instead I looked out at the mountains.

The mountains changed with the time of day, and as the sun lowered now, the light yellowed and turned the brown of the high peaks gold, and made the gray of the granite there sparkle. The same brush of light painted everything. The pond beside the road was Caribbean blue, and the clumps of tall grass growing among the rocks were amber and crisp. The sun's light was heavy, almost so heavy it could be touched, or scooped like golden iridescent water.

While I sat enjoying the texture of the light and what it did to the world, my dad and the longhaired man obliviously talked about nothing.

"I thought this sign was going up yesterday? You missed the open house," dad said.

"It was, but I didn't finish it on time, and the stain just dried an hour ago."

"All right, Bill."

With those words, I realized who the man was and breathed heavily. Bill looked at me. I was terrified that he knew I spied on him that day and would tell dad.

"Is that Sarah?" he asked.

"Yes," dad said.

"It's been awhile since I saw her. I think the last time was when you brought her into the bar. Right Sarah? She's really grown up." He looked at me.

They quickly turned their attention from me, but from time to time Bill's eyes returned, making me worry that he knew.

Bill had installed a large sign with the words "FRENCH GULCH" etched into a piece of wood that was carved to look like the bark of a tree with cars on a road and houses in the background. At the top of the sign the pattern of bark changed to look like snow capped mountains. In the golden summer light the sign breathed, almost as if there was movement beneath the surface that the eye could not detect. I wanted to see more of his sign. It had meaning. I stared at it, and Bill observed me.

"I'm going to head out," dad said. "Will you be here much longer?"

"No. Signs already finished."

"It looks good, Bill. You should head up the hill and grab some food at the party. Courtney's still up there."

"No thanks, really, I've got something else I'm going to do."

"See you at the Gold Pan then."

We pulled away, and Bill watched me.

"I've seen that man before," I said.

"That's Bill, he's a friend of mine."

"No. I mean, I've seen him with mom."

"What?"

"When you and mom fought last spring, and I fell asleep on you and then you left."

"I remember."

"I took my bike for a ride and saw mom's car parked in front of that man's house. They talked inside his barn. I looked at them through the glass."

"Your mom and Bill have known each other a long time, Sarah."

"They talked about you."

"What did they say?"

"Mom was mad at you, and the man told her it was okay."

"And what's that mean?"

"I didn't know."

"You shouldn't peek in windows."

"I don't like that man."

My dad looked at me and took a deep breath. "We've known Bill a long time, he's a little different, but everybody is."

"I know, but something about him, I just don't like him. He hugged mom."

"Did they do more than that? Is that what you're getting at? Did your mother do more?"

"No . . . I don't think so. I didn't stay the whole time."

"Then let it go."

"They smoked pot."

"Let it go, Sarah."

"Is mom going to leave us dad?"

"No." He said, but judging by his tone, I don't think he believed it.

I waited until he cooled off and said, "Don't tell her I told you?"

"I won't."

I had an urge to tell him about the locket and the cave, but he was already angry and I didn't want to upset him more. I didn't say another word. Dad pulled the truck to a stop at the house and waved for me to get out without speaking. I followed his hand gesture and closed the door as I went. He turned the truck around and then drove away, but as he reached the end of the driveway he rolled the window down and waved goodbye. It made me smile.

The house stood tall and sharply angled with large glass surfaces that reflected the daylight. Mom's Beamer was still here, and a light was on upstairs in her office window. She was probably working on her dissertation. I hoped she would finish, and that finally having accomplished her goal, she could be happy.

16

SARAH MCKENNA-HURST

I walked up the stairway to my house. Mom made noise above, and I stood and listened for a second. She talked to someone on the phone, but I couldn't hear what she said, and I didn't feel like going in doors now anyhow and so I turned back and went into the garage and took out my bike. I wanted to get a better look at the sign, and I wanted to walk around the unfinished houses without dad telling me to get back in the truck.

I rode up French Creek Road and followed that up to the gravel piles by the pond where the road went from gravel to the fresh pavement leading to dad's houses. The place where Bill had installed the sign earlier that day.

It was an odd sign, about six or seven feet wide and at least as tall. At the bottom, cars headed away from a set of homes and up a road toward the words and the mountains. Just above the cars, the letters that made up the name were tinted a fiery red with touches of yellow and orange. The parts of the sign around the letters had been carved in such a way as to resemble the bark of the local pine trees, smooth and dark with snake like qualities. The carving looked real enough that I touched it to see if he had glued bark onto the sign for the effect, but he hadn't.

Near the top, the carvings changed. There was a buffer zone where the carving and colors became blurry and uniform. The tree bark morphed into mountaintops and above that was a touch of gray sky at the top of the sign.

My bike lay in the dirt near the edge of the road and as I went to grab it a man in a red Jeep almost ran me over. When he rounded the bend, he was going so fast that his Jeep drifted sidewise, but at the last moment the driver gained control and passed by in a cloud of dust.

The Jeep disappeared down the road, and I picked my bike out of the gravel and peddled to the development, heart racing. The open house was long since over, which more or less gave me free run of the jobsite, and I was determined to explore.

I rode to the first house my dad had taken me to and stood where he stood a few hours prior. His footprints were still in the gravel as a matter of fact, and I was surprised to see them so clearly. They actually made me miss him; as though I might not see him again, left only with the impressions of places he'd once been. The houses increased this sense as they were lonely themselves and stood in precarious skeletal states that depended on effort to complete. If my father never returned, then they would remain like this as monuments to the loss. But this was silly of me, I thought, and decided to go inside the house. The first thing I noticed, however, as I stepped forward was a board with a nail sticking out of it. My dad's voice rang through my head at that point. I pictured him standing next to me telling me how dangerous the jobsite was. My mom was another story all together, if she heard I was here alone she would lose her mind.

I would be more careful, I decided, and watched the ground closely as I went. Off to the right, orange spray paint marked where the walkway would eventually be laid, and beside that, a stubby blue pipe stood from the ground with a round cover on it, which I thought was the water shutoff for the house but I guess it could have had something to do with the sewer.

The board that was used as a ramp to enter the front door rested against this blue pipe, which prevented the board sliding out.

I could only imagine what mom would have said if she saw me using this ramp, but I stepped on it nonetheless, and bounced on it a moment for fun. That's when I noticed a strange smell on the breeze, but I passed it aside and continued up the plank. Half way up, I used the spring from the board to bounce me into the house. It flung me right through the door in fact, and I landed on the plywood floor, which to my surprise was as slippery as if it had been covered in grease. I immediately slid and fell to my side where I noticed the plywood was wet. It was covered by water, but not water at all: gasoline. The whole floor was saturated with it and dripping down the stairs, as if it had just rained fossil fuel from the perfect mountain sky.

I was covered in it, and my clothes were ruined. Even my hair had gasoline in it. I noticed a generator in the other room, and thought that might have been the cause, until I heard noise in front of me; at the back of the house I saw a blond man holding a flame in his hand. He looked like a strange monk, the Hindu or Buddhist type or whatever, with short hair.

He did not see me.

"NO!" I cried.

But he did not hear me.

I turned to run and slipped in the fuel and fell. My knees and palms were wet. Smoke poured over my head then, and there was a loud flash and the sound of rushing air and heat. Then hands grabbed me hard around the waist and lifted me off the floor. A man held me like a football and jumped through the open doorway into the gravel yard outside.

When he jumped, the flash of rushing flames reached us, and the parts of him that touched me caught fire. I screamed when I felt my hair ignite, and he dropped me on the ground and grabbed and ripped off my clothes patting me to douse the flames. I couldn't see him because I had closed my eyes, but I heard him scream as his own hands burned. I opened my eyes for a second and saw Bill using his own shirt to smother the burning parts of my arms and legs. I noticed I was naked then and wanted to be embarrassed, I wanted to cover myself so he couldn't see me, but I couldn't. I couldn't do a thing but scream. Though even with the pain, I caught sight of the blond man running up the hillside across the street. We looked at each other, and it was then that I noticed the fire he'd lit was massive and had crossed the street and was chasing him. And then I don't remember . . .

17

CHARLES MCKENNA

The Gold Pan was dead. Even Andy wasn't smiling, and he's usually nothing but smiles behind the bar telling stupid jokes that no one laughs at but him. He served me a beer. I relaxed and drank and tried to think about what I was going to do with my wife. Thinking of my trouble led me to think of my houses and what would happen if they didn't sell. Relaxation felt like a far off memory now. I took a sip of beer. The beer was flat, which seemed about right.

"Hank been in today?" I asked.

"No." Andy slouched when he spoke.

There were other men in the bar, but no one I wanted to talk with. I usually didn't talk with too many outside my circle—I liked what I knew, and what I understood—and these men were enough in the periphery that they didn't count. The beer was still flat when I took another sip. I didn't deserve to have good beer.

"Your beer's flat," I said.

"It's a new keg."

"Flat, nonetheless."

The other men sat deep in the bar and argued with each other while I tapped the hard wood surface in front of me for amusement.

Andy wiped his forehead with a bar rag and poured himself a flat beer from the keg.

"You got crackers and cheese today?" I asked.

"A fire."

"I just want crackers."

"There's a fire over there. I can see the black smoke over the trees." Andy took a sip of the beer. "This *is* flat."

I looked to where Andy pointed and saw a plume of dense smoke mushrooming behind the hilltop on the other side of the street. My neighborhood was on fire. I knew it. Nothing else in that direction could put up black smoke like that. One of the backhoes must have been on fire, I thought, and I ran out the door and turned to Andy. "Call the fire department, French Gulch is on fire."

The GMC was parked on the street. I jumped in and sped to the traffic light on Main Street. As almost seemed natural under the circumstances, the traffic light was red and I had to wait. I couldn't. I mashed the accelerator. The truck lurched forward and the tires squealed as I fish tailed through the hard left hand turn. The car coming opposite swerved and stopped, and the woman inside shouted words that I couldn't hear but could read on her lips.

The development was just up the road. I ran every stop sign I came to. Within sixty seconds I rounded the bend by Bill's sign. At this point, where the road turned from gravel to asphalt, I saw one of my houses almost entirely engulfed in red shafts of flame. The thick smell of an industrial fire penetrated my truck. The fire quickly spread. The predominate wind in the area moved from south to north across French Gulch and drove the flames over the road and onto the south facing hillside. The wind also funneled up valley from Breckenridge. Near the houses, where the two winds met, the fire swirled like a tornado.

The fully framed house that I was in earlier today was on fire and so were the frames beside it. Under the wind, the flares from the first house arched over the road and kissed the hillside, where the perpetually dry trees exploded in a crackle.

I sped up and drove under the arch of fire over the road; fire broke off my windshield. I was in a red tunnel, and for the flash of an instant, it looked like I was in hell.

As soon as I parked my truck, I noticed Sarah's bike in the dirt beside my front tire. A shock of terror shot through my body then. Beyond the bike and up against the house, Bill's red Jeep was engulfed by flame. He stood about fifty feet from that, shirtless, some of his hair was blackened, and his hands covered in pink blisters and black singes. Sarah lay at his feet wrapped in a shirt. Her hair had burned off, and the part of her arm that hung from the shirt was burned as well. I ran to her.

"Don't touch her," Bill said, "She's burned pretty badly. I called and the paramedics are coming."

I bent down and removed the shirt from her head. Her scalp was burned but her beautiful face was completely untouched; while her hands, arms and legs were in extreme condition.

"Sarah, Sarah, I'm here. Sarah, I'm here."

She responded in a whimper and her eyes opened and closed involuntarily.

"I waited for you daddy," she said absently. Her words crushed me.

"I'm here now. You're alright, you're safe, I'm here."

I shook; tears blurred my vision, and my voice wavered with sadness and uncontrollable hatred. How could this house have burned so quickly? I turned to Bill and asked him:

"What happened? How could the house go up like that?"

He didn't speak. His eyes were distant, and shifting. I wanted to strike his face. Then he said, "Saw someone running out of the back door; up the hill. Then the place went up."

He met my eyes. I scrutinized him.

"Someone lit it?" He nodded.

"I saw Sarah playing on the front plank when I came around the corner. When I saw what he was doing, I drove straight over the gravel and grabbed her. But she had gas on her." Then he paused as he remembered things he knew I didn't need to hear; like the sound of her voice as she screamed, or the smell of her flesh cooking, but I could see them in his eyes. I looked off to where he pointed and traced the line of his truck with my eyes. Just then I realized that the smell I smelled was gasoline. Why did Sarah have gas on her, I thought.

"She fell inside the house," he anticipating my question, "and she must've gotten it on her then."

"Lucky you were there." I said, "You say the man who did this ran off into the hillside?"

"Yes."

I watched the fire run up hill spreading fast as it went. The entire hillside was one inferno, boiling and throbbing up toward the ridge like a glowing ember. I wondered where the man was in the fire. And then I saw him as a he entered a clearing in the trees near the ridge. I hoped he burned to death.

Just then a cruiser pulled onto the gravel front yard alongside my truck. Hank, a cop friend got out and ran beside me.

"What the hell happened, Charles?" he said.

"My daughter is burnt. Where's the ambulance?"

"Right around the bend. Who lit the fire?" He asked.

I pointed to just below the ridge. "Some son of a bitch doused the place with gasoline and took off up the hill."

"He better go for the gold." Hank said grabbing the radio on his chest. "We have a suspect on foot, headed north through the trees off French Creek Road, by the new subdivision. Yes, French Gulch."

He turned to me. "Do you know who it was?"

"Bill saw him. I have no idea."

"No." Bill said.

I held Sarah's wrist where her skin was untouched by flame. Her eyes opened from time to time and once she smiled.

"Where's the ambulance!" I said.

"It will be here," Hank said. "Be patient."

Sarah tried to roll over, but the burnt flesh on her shoulder touched the rocky ground, and she squirmed and moaned in agony. I gritted my teeth and talked to her, but she was in so much pain.

"Please dad, please dad, please dad."

Oh, God. She called my name. I was powerless to help, and every call for my help was like a blow to my soul. I shivered with grief. Hank put his hand on my shoulder. My knees turned rubbery, and I sank lower into a crouched position.

A minute passed, the fire fighters arrived and were running hoses down to the pond where the fire hydrant stood so they could spray the charred foundations of my houses with water. The ambulance would be a little longer. Only a few minutes elapsed from the time I arrived until now, but that time was eternity. Sarah lay dying in the gravel before me, and the siren from the ambulance was barely audible and at least another minute off. I could not move an inch to help my moaning daughter, and I could not speed the arrival of the ambulance. I just kneeled and gripped her perfect wrist tightly in my hand and wept. Every time she called my name, I shook with grief. I felt dizzy and sick, and suddenly two ambulances pulled onto the gravel.

The emergency workers jumped from the back of their trucks and ran to us. They spoke, but I couldn't hear. Hank made everything work and directed the emergency workers while I remained kneeling. As some of the paramedics converged on Bill, I heard Hank say to him:

"Sure was lucky you were here to pull her out of that fire."

"I was just coming back from fishing."

Then the paramedics shouted. One of them dragged a stretcher over to Bill and asked him questions. Someone said my name, but they spoke too softly and my heartbeat sounded louder than their voice. They yelled at me, and I watched Sarah as she was placed on a white sheet on a silver stretcher. A man laid a plastic breathing mask over her mouth and they put her inside the ambulance. Bill then lay down on another stretcher, and they took him away. Someone shouted my name and like a brick through a window, the world realized itself again in my ears and suddenly I could hear.

"Charles," Hank said.

"Yeah."

"You all right?"

"Yeah."

"Sarah's going to Denver by helicopter from the county medical center here. There's room for one more in the chopper. You can go if you want."

"Will she live?"

"The paramedic's think so."

"I'll get Joanne, and we'll take the truck."

A Ford F-250 pulled onto the site, and Sheriff Dodge jumped out of the truck. He wore a camouflaged baseball cap and tan denim pants over boots with a t-shirt tucked in. He nodded as he walked toward me. He was no longer a Sheriff, but whenever something big happened around town, he always made sure to show. Since his wife died, he didn't have anything else to do. Ever since that day he seemed to be slowly declining. He even had a pacemaker installed in his chest to keep him running.

He said something, but I wasn't listening to him. Instead his face invoked memories, and I traced the remnant of the scar that Smiley put there.

18

CHARLES MCKENNA

I had to tell Joanne that the daughter we made together was burned. I thought, 'Sarah is burned—Joanne is her mother— My neighborhood is burned.'

"You alright?" Dodge asked.

"No, I'm not."

"Where you headed, Charles?"

"I've got to tell Joanne."

"I can take you if you want."

"I'll be fine."

He looked at me and knew there was no point asking further questions. No man could help me now. My daughter was burned at the hands of the unspeakable, and I had to inform her mother, my wife, the unspeakable.

In my truck I cleared the windshield of the grey and black soot that turned to a kind of paste under the wipers. The glass was still covered in streaks as I headed down the road and passed a convoy of firefighters heading to pre-empt the wildfire that had already begun.

Ahead, Bill's three-dimensional sign stood sentinel at the bottom of the subdivision where the road turned from the fresh pavement of my development to the old gravel surface that had been in use since the miners first laid road. I watched it as it grew near.

The letters etched in fiery red advertised "French Gulch", though in former days part of this area had been officially known as "Slave Gulch": named after Barney Ford, an escaped slave and self-made man that came here and mined the valley. Because he was black, he couldn't officially stake a mining claim in his own name, and at his lawyer's request he had the claim filed under the lawyer's name. But when Barney stuck gold, his faithful attorney legally stole his mine. Despite the setback, Mr. Ford moved on to become a successful hotelier and restaurateur in Denver. Nevertheless, the name "Slave Gulch" stuck, but now, after what happened, by what name would the valley be known: "Fools Bluff" or "Fire Gulch." This valley was the place of broken dreams forever. Maybe Indians were buried here and the naked, painted, screaming, angry ghosts were alive to ruin any man, white or black, that dared make his fortune.

By fraud or by fire, but by which didn't matter, this valley brought loss. Mr. Ford lost his Gulch when a legal swindler hustled him, and now my development was gone and my daughter burned by a fire that was set by God knows who or how many. Only the mining company that raped and scraped this valley naked got off without a hitch, although who knows if they got off easy at all. The men who did the mining barely had a life expectancy of thirty, and the company pulled out in such a hurry, leaving behind piles of equipment, that they seemed forced to go. The company's owner probably choked on his caviar back in Connecticut or took a bullet in the head from an anarchist.

The Gulch now seemed to have a mystical cursed quality and that filthy sign summed up the indescribable idea behind my fear. A lawyer had burned Barney Ford, the miners slashed and burned the valley, and now the unspeakable burned my work and dreams to the ground.

Then I saw fresh graffiti on the sign. Florescent green spray-paint letters read "PEOPLES GROUP."

I veered the car to the side of the road and crashed through it.

The sign was made of heavy wood and was a solid piece of work, and when I crashed into it, it didn't just shatter as I had hoped, instead the supports collapsed and I literally drove over and pushed the sign ahead of me with the trucks bumper. The sign skidded across the road and slid down the embankment into the pond. As I drove away, I saw the sign bob like a giant surfboard in my rear view mirror.

Soon I was at my house. I felt a sense of chill cover my body as I entered the driveway. The house loomed large and angular, and I looked up at the window where Joanne stood earlier.

When I entered her office, Joanne turned in her chair with a smile. "Why do you refuse to knock, honey?"

I shouted: "Sarah's been burned."

"What . . . What was she . . . that can't be, that just can't be. I thought she was with you."

"She was in the development and someone set fire to it."

"No."

"She'll be fine, She's been taken down to Denver."

Joanne turned pale and ugly. Her beauty drained away, and she quivered with rage self-pity, but she didn't say anything else. I walked to her and put my hand to her back. "She'll be alright, we just have to drive to Denver."

"But why did you build those houses there, why? I told you not to."

I didn't reply to that, instead I said, "Get up, lets go!"

"I won't go with you. You did this."

"Like hell I did. Now get up!"

I took Joanne's small hand in mine and pulled her from her chair. She gave way and followed me out the door to the truck.

We made the two-hour drive to the airport in silence in only an hour.

19

SARAH MCKENNA-HURST

Rubber and blur

My vision was nothing but a blur—and my bones felt like rubber, and I was drunk with a drip in my arm that was controlled by a button that I pushed when it hurt. But the pain was still there. The pain was always there; no matter if I pushed the button until the nurses came to tell me that I couldn't have any more morphine, or if a lay and tried to ignore it, the pain never went away. It just sat in the back of my mind like an over-looming cloud of bad weather. The pain was dull and low and itchy to excruciation, turning off and on and growing in waves at a depth that reached the marrow of my marrow.

I would cry. I cried and I cried, and sometimes the tears fell out my eyes uncontrollably, at others I shook like infants who cry for milk, yet without making sound. The cry was internal and so deep and personal that only *the me* on the inside felt it.

The suit I had been given at birth was damaged, and I couldn't have another.

When I shivered from the pain, hands always emerged from the darkness beyond the bed to hold the parts of me that were not toast. The hands were soft. The hands were love, and they calmed me and reached all the way inside the person that lived beyond my bodysuit and told me that I was all right; that the burns and the pain and the humiliation were all right. I could not always hear what she said when she touched me, mostly I just drifted off to the land within my mind and lay on the shores of opiate induced delusion until the pain that loomed high above ruined my paradise. Then I'd return to the world and grope the bed for the button.

My eyes worked, they were just blurry, and for the first part of the eternity I spent in the bed in the room in the hospital, I didn't use them.

I first used my eyes when I screamed in pain and the hands came to rescue me again, and then I heard her words in my ears. I opened my eyes and there was mom—my very own.

The doctor told my mom that I could regenerate skin. That in many of my burnt areas I would re-grow it and that's what caused the pain, the re-growing of skin. I was healing and the pain was a good sign. But my scalp hurt also. And that was because my hair grew in spots and touched the blisters that pussed and festered on my scalp and so the growing of hair caused me much discomfort.

Dad came often and we talked. Sometimes I was asleep when he came, and he sat by my bedside until I awoke, and then he kissed my cheek and touched my wrist.

"I'm here Sarah," dad said. "You're okay. You'll pull through this, you just have to fight. You've never had trouble fighting, so I know you're ready for this. There isn't a doubt in my mind that whatever goal you set yourself you'll achieve. But this is it, it's time to fight."

He loved me, he really did, but there was never a question. When I got well enough to hold a conversation he asked me:

"Do you remember what happened? Can you remember anything?"

"Some parts of it. I remember being pulled out, and I remember the man running up the hill, and he watched me, he stopped and he watched me, he just stood there when the forest fire came and he looked at me."

"You don't have to worry about him," dad said, "He'll be in jail for a long time, and he can never hurt you again. The man's just a freak."

"I don't think he wanted to hurt me, I think he was sad that it happened."

"He didn't mean to hurt you honey, he just tried to burn down your father's neighborhood." My mother added.

Dad looked up at her and then back to me, "He can't hurt either of us now," he said and added, "Do you remember who saved you, do you remember Bill pulling you from the fire?"

I couldn't because it was so fuzzy. I only saw bits and pieces. We talked about the pieces of image I remembered and then dad left to go back to the mountains for work.

When he was gone, mom returned to the bedside and gave me a kiss.

"He can't even stay with you," she said. "He always has to go back to that development; back to Courtney. He spends more time with her." She took a breath and touched my hand, "I love you," she said.

"Will he be back soon?"

"Do you know how much I love you?"

"Yes."

Then she asked me questions about Bill. "Would you like to meet him?"

"Who."

"Bill. He saved you. He was coming back from fishing the beaver ponds, and he saw that man lighting the fire. He drove his Jeep right up onto the gravel, and he ran into the flames and pulled you out. He's your angel."

"The man with the red truck?"

"That's right."

"He didn't fish for very long."

"What?"

I didn't bother to answer. I knew that Stanley was caught alone walking on the highway just over the hill from the fire. At the trial Stanley said that he didn't want his shack in the Gulch taken away.

He was just a poor man who no one would protect and he acted all alone. He said he had no connection to the Peoples Group.

My mom broke into my stream of thought and said, "Bill wants to see you. He would like to come."

20

SARAH MCKENNA-HURST

B efore I knew anything, because I didn't know much of anything then, the man was on his way. Bill, he made me shiver, there was something about him that I didn't like; I never had. He spent time with my mom, and he made the sign for French Gulch, but he saved me, and I still didn't want to see him.

Now I remember him bursting into the house and pulling me from the flames. I remember him screaming from the flames on me that burned him, and he stripped me and put me out, but still I didn't like him.

Bill was on his way though. In a few days he would be here. Mom called him and made the arrangements and he was on his way. Then, suddenly, one day when I was asleep, I felt a hand gently touch my wrist and mom woke me. "Honey, he's here."

Bill walked over to my bed; he wore baggy khakis and low hiking boots with a green button up shirt that hung over his pants, and his long red hair was pulled back into a knot behind his head. He looked strong and alive and relaxed. I was afraid when he walked in. Little shots of fear coursed through my blood. I moved back in the bed when I saw him, but I smiled anyway. I had to pretend that he was so important because he had saved me and I couldn't pretend otherwise. He had been hurt in the fire, and now he was here.

"Hello," he said when he leaned down to look into my face.

"Hello," I said, but I wanted to tell him to get away from me, and to get away from mom, but I was quiet.

There wasn't much that Bill and I could say to one another really; he saved me, but what did he want from me? After our introduction all we did was look dumbly at one another and blink. I blinked several times, then I yawned. Mom couldn't stand the tension. She fidgeted and swayed and then broke out and said:

"Bill was burned very badly when he saved you, honey. His hands and wrists and even part of his hair was burned."

Bill held up his hands and then smiled like I was his child. "You'll get out of this and be fine Sarah," he said, "Don't worry. Just think that now you can see with new eyes."

"We have a lot to learn from children," mom said.

He paused for a moment and mined my eyes for understanding. "I don't know if she's said it to you, but your mother's told me that the fire was your moment in time; the one you'll never forget. We all have moments where we see the world for the first time. You can break from being a mechanical little girl and choose to see the world the way it is."

He seemed to believe what he said. He conveyed his truth with dull enthusiasm, like a surgeon for surgery, which I found most frightening. I wondered what he really meant, and how much he and mom shared and agreed.

When he finished talking, I didn't reply. I just continued as I was, but what was I to say? Thank you. Or, wow? Mostly I thought he was weird. He wanted to help me though, and his words, in a way, gave comfort. I felt I understood him when he talked about my chance to start over and do what I was afraid to do.

Like at school, I always did well, even exceptionally well, but I was never the most popular and social girl, nor did I ever want to be. What I did want was Mike Reilly; a boy from my homeroom. I liked him because he was an East Coast boy. Mike Reilly, all the popular girls always tried to get him interested in them and their materialism, but he never went for them. He didn't care that they were popular between themselves. He wasn't afraid of them either, he just wasn't into them and didn't bother with those girls.

There was something in the way that Mike looked at me that I knew he could love me—more than that, I could make him love me (but that was part of it), but that we had some understanding that existed without effort. I knew that we had this connection for some time, but I was frozen stiff by fear. I never had the courage to make conversation with him. With my new lease on life, I decided going out with him would be the first order of business.

Bill tried to look into me and understand if I knew what he talked about.

"You know what I mean, don't you?" he said to me.

I didn't say anything and he went on:

"You don't have to say anything, just know people are here for you and care about you and understand you. The group has put together a donation for you." Mom looked at him and he continued, "Your mother knows more than you give her credit for, or than most children give parents credit for. She has wisdom. I don't want to push you. You should rest. You look tired. Get well."

Mom walked to the doorway with him and they talked. The pain increased, and I could hardly stand it. All his talk about rebirth and searching my eyes to see if I understood gave me a headache, and I wanted it to end. I pushed the button on my drip. Pushing it was my protest to him. He probably would've told me to endure the pain, but I didn't care. In rebellion, I pushed the button once— twice and held off at three. I had three pushes and could use it, but I didn't need to go over board, at least not right now. If he came back suddenly and preached again, which it seemed he was on the verge of doing, then I would certainly dose myself and drift off into la la land, where apparently he spent plenty of time with my mother.

The drip then sent me spiraling into a dead sleep where not even dreams existed. I found myself without knowing, and I was at peace until noises interrupted me and invaded my wonderful silent world.

The noises turned to voices, and the voices turned to mom and Bill talking somewhere distant and muffled, but close enough that I could understand. Where were they? I had no idea how much time had passed. I opened my eyes to find them, but they weren't in the room, and they weren't in the hall. I pulled back the screen beside me but found the bed empty. Then I noticed a door to my left slightly ajar.

My room was connected to the one beside it, and the room next door must have been empty because my mom and Bill were using it to talk. They talked in the hush hush sort of way that does nothing but make other people listen closer, which, of course, is what I did. At first it was difficult to hear what mom said.

The door between rooms was open only a crack, and mom talked in a strained whisper. I put my hand to my ear so I could pick up their words better. A nurse shuffled her feet in the hallway, and her movement disrupted my surveillance. I could have thrown something at her. After the nurse finished trouncing about, I heard my mom say, "I've heard it before, but I can't get it across to her."

"There's places to go. I wouldn't give up."

"I can't just pick up and go."

"I don't think it's intended for you to pick up and go, we all have connections that keep us. I haven't been out of the hills in a while. I wasn't prepared for what the city looks like now."

"But I want to talk. I like to hear you talk. I need to know what you think."

"I'm not complicated."

"Don't say that."

"What would you like me to say?"

"Say you'll visit her again."

"Don't think she wants me to."

"I don't see you anymore."

He paused. "I want to head out and get back to Summit County before the commute starts."

"You should then," she said quickly.

I heard nothing more and mom came straight through the door. I closed my eyes. There was no way I wanted her knowing I listened. She paused at my bedside and then kissed my forehead and sat in the corner and read a book.

I waited a minute before I ended the charade and opened my eyes. Mom immediately noticed and came to my bed.

"Hi honey," she said. "Have you been awake long?"

"No, in and out a few minutes."

"I must've woke you when I came in and kissed you."

"That's okay mom."

"You could've been a little nicer to Bill you know. He came all the way down to see you, and you barely said a word."

"Come on mom."

"No I won't. He saved your life. Don't you know what that means? Don't you? He's important to you now."

"Then maybe I should fuck him." I didn't mean to be so harsh, but once it was out I couldn't back down.

"Don't say something so disgusting."

"You should fuck him then. Get over it."

"You've had too much of that drip. Bill pulled you out of a fire, honey—a fire. You would be dead if it weren't for him."

"He was there so fast he might have lit the fire; who knows."

"He didn't light that fire, the other man did."

"Your friend Stanley, or is he Smiley like dad calls him."

"Stop it Sarah, you sound like Charles."

"You mean like dad, mom?"

"Don't look at me like that Sarah, I'm your mother. You don't understand. I love Bill, but it's not sexual. He loves me. We are true friends in symbiosis."

"What?"

I looked away and pushed the button on my drip. She kept talking, but I didn't want to hear her anymore.

21

SARAH MCKENNA-HURST

A month passed after the day with Bill before I was allowed to leave the hospital. By then, my hair had begun growing back in strands of blond angel hair and baby peach fuzz that was strangely new to me. My scalp was burned and scabbed in places, but mostly the hair had caught fire, and the skin was only singed. I would eventually grow a full head of hair again. Just like new. I could even walk around now, though the burns on my thighs and knees were severe and would never heal properly.

I underwent countless procedures to graft skin on different parts of my body, some took, and others I don't talk about. There had also been burning on my bum and on portions of my back, but that would mostly all heal to look like nothing happened.

Of all the places I had been burned, my hands worried me most because they were visible. The backs of my hands were without scar, but the palms were obliterated where the gasoline soaked in. My palms looked so awful that I cried whenever I caught glimpses of the burnt morsels that used to be so pretty pink. Every time I turned the page of a book, my hands glared back at me like they were neon. My heart sank down deep and low. No man or boy would ever want me. I was, and would forever be, disfigured. No matter how well I healed, I would always show signs of my trauma, and what type of man would accept it, what type would not look to other women for what he was repulsed by in me? He would surely leave me to fall in love with the dainty handed girl without graft marks on her thighs. I resolved myself not to care, and I resolved that when I walked through the doors of the hospital I would never look back, and never think about anything other than achieving my goals, disfigured or not.

The day came for me to leave, and dad came down from the mountains to pick me up. Mom was already there when he asked to drive me back to Breckenridge.

"You haven't even seen fit to be by your daughter's bedside," mom said. "Instead, you're up there chasing money and whatever else it is that you do with your time." Dad seemed angry but didn't say so. He just sighed and mom continued, "Why do you think that gives you the right to take her back?"

"You're being unfair. Of course I wanted to be here. I don't think Sarah questions that, but I couldn't. Everything came apart with the fire that Smiley lit. And what is that anyway, people tell me he founded The Cult Group you belong to, and you're still a member of it?"

"Not for a long time, Charles. Don't try to make it seem like I've neglected *my* daughter. I was here with her day and night."

I couldn't take their fighting. "Stop fighting," I said, "I don't want to hear you fight, I can't take it, please."

They stopped their argument and looked at me.

"Mom, I haven't seen dad in a while, and I would really like to drive up with him. We could always take the same car."

"No, we can't, we brought different cars, but that's fine if you don't want to go, I understand."

"It's not like that mom."

"No, I understand."

"Please mom."

I cried and she left the room angry. Dad drove me back to Breckenridge.

22

BILL SAXON

When I was you, I was a product, a product of my government and a product of my society: the death trip, the kill or be killed, winner take all, survival of the fittest, rape the earth, and plow-the-land-until-it-is dust-and-reduce wages-until-there-are-none mentality. Total war. Wage total war. Even words are war. Words kill.

We don't free the oppressed, we oppress the free.

I would have been better if I had been raised on an island. By the time I was out of Cambodia and released from my obligations it was ten or fifteen years before I was disentangled. You can't just walk away, and I was observed to be sure I stayed on the reservation in Breckenridge. But there was one moment for me that grew in importance over time and became like an obsession.

I broke Dodge and his Deputy out of the jail and took them up the dirt path beside the building. It was dark. The Deputy was afraid. The moon was out, and light was beginning to show from the east. The bikers had gone indoors, but I could still smell the fire burning at Shamus's.

"Won't they find us," Deputy Hank said.

Dodge grabbed him by the collar, "Shut the fuck up and walk!"

"Stay in the shadow," I said.

Ahead light fell from a backyard. The gravel crunched above, and Smiley presented himself beneath it. His blue eyes penetrated the night.

"You should come out of the shadow," he said.

I slipped my knife from its place.

We could have walked away without incident. There was an opening between buildings and we could have been in my house before he realized, but I wanted to murder him. One lunge and I was on top of him with the knife. My first stab grazed off his cheek. I withdrew and grabbed his wrist. The knife had a thin line of blood along its cutting edge. He took two long steps backward into the darkness, and I followed, holding his wrist and punctured his neck like a balloon. He gurgled, and I grabbed his collar and let him down softly to the ground.

"My house is around the corner. Go there." I pointed to Dodge and he followed my command. The Deputy followed him.

I turned back to Smiley; he was staring at me and I watched him as he seemed to die. After that I walked to my front porch and took the rope I had left there and returned to his body. I was surprised to find that he was still breathing, but very faintly. I then slung him over my shoulder and carried his sleight body uphill to the bar. Shamus's was empty when we arrived, and the moon was low. The coals of the dwindling bonfire burned red. I set him down beside it.

There was a pulley on the gable above the front door of Shamus's bar that was used to hoist provisions into the attic. On the pulley was a guide rope tied to a cleat on an empty flagpole a few feet away. I used the guide rope and pulled my nylon rope up through the pulley. I cut the excess and used it to bind Smiley's arms and legs. Then I attached him to the rope on the pulley. I wanted him to be a message to the other gratuitous idiots on Harley Davidson's.

While I bound him hand and foot, Smiley strangely watched me and did not resist. He was alive all the while. I hoisted him. His dead weight was heavy, but I was possessed. The scaffold above creaked as he rose.

I felt better after that. It was like I had killed the thing I hated most, and I could kill it again if I needed. But as it turned out, I had killed the wrong thing. I was disturbed by my trip to the big city. I can only imagine how I would have felt if I visited New York or L.A. But I think I feel worse having seen how Denver spoiled. Denver used to have character. Now it is a patchwork quilt of ramrod cinderblock carwashes, funeral homes, and strip joints. I guess tits, cars and death are the American dream. I saw the whole thing: the sprawling idiot suburbs, the foothills ruined by McMansions, and the endless parade of mini vans. Daisy cutters would make an improvement. They're all bloody vegetables. And like cancer, they spread without radiation.

Joanne dragged me from the mountains to come down to the rampant sprawl of suburban orgy and see Sarah in the hospital. I felt partially responsible for what happened to her, or I would never have come.

She looked better than I guessed after pulling her from the fire. That day, part of me hesitated to help, instead I watched her go into the house, but I did not move. If I had gone in when I saw her enter, I might have saved my Jeep, but I did not. She might not have been burned at all, same with me, but I had to think about saving her. I saved her because she was Joanne's. I could not live with myself if I let their child die.

I might have felt different about saving her after I came back from Denver today. She was a special girl, we had hopes for her, but she didn't seem to care and followed her father's beat. Not only was she frigid toward me and ungrateful to her mother, but the absolute state of that city made me sick to my stomach. The whole thing enraged me. I knew I had to talk with Stanley. I needed perspective. But he was in jail again, and would probably be there until he was an old man. It wouldn't be possible for me to make contact right now.

Years ago he changed my life. He had a following of people then: mostly local women, but others also. I could not understand what attracted them, yet because of our history, I thought of him often. A few months after he was released from jail, Smiley stopped by my barn. He was with Joanne, or Joanne was with him, and they came unannounced. At the time, I still worked for Uncle Sam.

Smiley walked through the doors and Joanne followed. His eyes looked exactly the same as the night I strung him up.

Joanne said. "He wanted to see you, Bill, he said that he didn't mean you harm."

I didn't have time to respond before Stanley said,

"Of course I don't, you gave me the greatest trip ever, and I thank you for the opportunity to take the journey. You sent me to the other side, over the rainbow, all the way there where the spirits have shapes and talk to you, and I can tell you that you don't have to die to go there too. I found the way. All those years I wanted back, and told people what else there was out there too. But I wanted to show them what they could see, but nothing ever did it, not the psilocybin not the LCD, but this, this," Stanley said pointing to a clay chillum packed with perfect clear white crystals, "this is the magic molecule, the spirit drug. If you want to see what I saw, and I think you do, then you'll take three pulls. It's only fifteen minutes for a lifetime across the Styx."

I knew things about some of the substances that came into this country that made me abhor their use, but he was right when he said the I wanted to know where he had gone. I had watched the lights blink out of his eyes. I knew I had sent him away. I had done it before. But as the lights tripped off, I was curious about where he was going and for the first time thought it was more than nowhere. But how he knew that I wanted to know where he went as he died, was beyond me.

23

___

CHARLES MCKENNA

The highway rolled beneath my truck.

Ahead a hill climbed from the red moonscape, and from its crest waves of heat rose like bent mirrors. We'd been driving for hours out of Colorado and into the strange sculpted sandstone world of northeastern Utah.

In front of my truck was a rolling red region that received less than six inches of rain per year; such rainfall produced almost no plant or tree and hardly a living creature for hundreds of miles, yet never can this red desolate world be called nothing. Only with an east coast bias can I think of the landscape here as nothing. Where in the forests of New England you find green trees and streams, here in northeastern Utah you find the stumps and stems of eroded hillsides carved out of red stone by wind and by water—by God himself. The rock formations all around were amazing; created by an absence of stone that washed away. In effect, the rock formations were the remnant of what once was.

To the right of the highway, stood orange and purple stone pillars. I was driving eighty miles an hour, and watching the stone pillars pass by my window. My truck drifted until the tires hit the grooved pavement and there was a sudden noise. I pulled the truck back straight. Joanne didn't bother to look up.

"Maybe you can keep it on the road, you do have a family along with you."

I smiled in embarrassment and anger and continued watching the landscape. The incident made me no less meditative, and the world around me seemed meaningful. I was sensitive. Even the stones had importance and seemed the medium of communication for the higher power, as if the coincidences of nature meant something. These feelings were not superstition; rather, nature was capable of being both coincidental and significant, and could in effect speak to a man or mean nothing at all.

"When are we going to eat?" Sarah asked from the back of the truck. She had been sleeping, but driving over the grooved pavement woke her. Joanne simply looked at me. I adjusted the mirror and looked at Sarah. "I'll stop at the next place I see."

"Good," Sarah said.

Forty minutes passed before we came to a roadside village comprised of a few low-slung adobe shacks and shanties with a cross before the church building. The village lay several hundred feet from the highway in a depression between two broken tabletop rock formations. Green trees flanked the dusty roadside and a few of the houses had bushes in their yards. One hundred feet beyond the cross and church were gas pumps and a restaurant with a shaded dining area nestled against an orange cliff. The restaurant's wooden sign was planted in the red dusty front yard and read "El Cuervo."

"Is this really where you're taking us, dad?" Sarah said from behind me.

"Why, what's wrong with this place?"

"Don't drink the water," Sarah said.

"It's not bad, honey. The water's fine, we're not actually in Mexico, and I bet they make great food here."

"Yeah, I'm sure they're four star . . . oh my God, these people don't even have cars, they've got a mule tied out front. That man. Is he coming over to the truck? Lock the doors, lock the doors, dad."

"Stop it Sarah," her mother said.

I rolled down the window for the man who approached us. He wore black jeans and boots and a navy button up shirt that was crisply tucked into his pants with dark sunglasses on his heavily wrinkled and reddened face that appeared much the same color as the tabletop mesa beside us.

"Hello," he said as he got near.

"How are you?" I said.

"Hola senor," Sarah said from the backseat. The man didn't hear her. Joanne leaned over the seat and glared as Sarah giggled.

"Would you like lunch? My wife will be out shortly to take your orders, or would you like to sit inside?"

"No that's fine," I said, "We'll eat outside."

The man walked into the building.

"Oh great, I love bugs in my food dad," Sarah said.

"Would you stop it, Sarah," her mother said, "Would you stop being such a little brat."

Sara was quiet. I pulled the truck passed the gas pumps and looked for a place to park where the boat behind my truck wouldn't block any cars coming in. The boat was twenty-four feet long; not big in the scheme of things, but trailing behind a truck, a twenty-four-foot boat felt like an ocean liner. I dropped the girls off and pulled into the street so that I could back in perpendicular to the pumps and as far away from any traffic as I could get.

"Tell me when I'm close to that tree," I said.

"Oh come on; just park the thing; it's not like anyone's coming in here," Sarah said. Joanne walked over to a picnic table and sat in the shade of the trees and cliff.

"Just tell me when I'm too close, Sarah."

"Fine . . . you're too close."

I stopped the truck, and Sarah went and found the bathroom and I went around to see if the boat was properly lashed to the trailer. As I did I saw Sarah find her mother at the picnic table, and then I joined them.

"This really is God's country," I said and then sat.

"It's amazing what time and water can do to a landscape," Joanne said.

"Coming to a place like this really shows me reason for faith," I said.

"It's really very spiritual."

"Oh please," Sarah said, "Can we just order, I thought the bathroom was bad?"

At that moment a squat Mexican, almost Mayan looking woman walked from the brown adobe building to our table and distributed menus.

"Hi, I am Lenora, can I get you some water?"

"No. No. No," Sarah said.

"No water?" Lenora said.

"Yes, bring us some water please," I said. "My daughter's only kidding."

Lenora walked back into the building and Joanne got angry. "This is Utah, not Mexico, and anyways that's an awful myth about Mexico's water that people say just to be hurtful. What's wrong with you Sarah?"

Before Sarah could respond to her mother, Lenora was back with the three waters. "Hi, here you are."

We ordered and sat quietly and waited for our food. There was tension between Sarah and Joanne that grew in the last several months and especially since Sarah fully recovered and became fiercely independent.

The food came and we ate. I listened to the wind in the tees, and Joanne picked at the greens that Lenora brought her. I watched both of my girls but did not dare insert myself in their argument.

Joanne chewed with precision and premeditation while Sarah was calm and carefree. There was a rustle in the tree above and a night black Raven dropped like a stone onto the table. It hit and knocked Joanne's water into her lap.

"*Kraa Kraa.*"

Joanne sprang sideways, and the Raven clicked its claws and cocked its head. Then it jumped forward onto Joanne's plate. In its talons it grasped some food and flew onto a perch on the cliff behind us. Joanne turned pale; at first with fright and then with anger, as another Raven from the tree branch above made a repeated *kraa kraa kraa* call that sounded like insidious laughter. Sarah burst out. I couldn't help it and also laughed.

"You have to admit it's funny, mom."

"So funny. I can't believe you would laugh at your own mother Sarah."

"Oh, it's not like that."

Joanne walked to the truck. We finished our meals. Then I paid and we walked over and climbed into the truck. Inside the cabin Joanne was angry and silent. Sarah smiled and looked out the window. I thought the whole thing was silly and pulled forward to the pumps to gas up. I filled both the truck and the boat and then got back in the driver's seat.

"You smell like that poison, don't you think you could have washed your hands?"

"I love the smell of gasoline. It's a good smell."

"That doesn't mean it's perfume, Charles."

"I'm not washing my hands."

We pulled back onto the dusty road.

"Thank God we're leaving this place," Sarah said.

"Why, what's wrong with it?" I said. "They're a family establishment."

"Family business?" Joanne laughed mockingly. "He's the food pimp and she's his worker."

"Gee, I didn't even think it was that bad mom. The Ravens really got to you."

"They're stupid birds."

"They're monogamous anyway," I said.

24

CHARLES MCKENNA

Within a few hours of El Cuervo, we reached the shores of Lake Powell at Bullfrog Marina in the northern reaches of the sprawling reservoir. The marina was little more than a massive asphalt parking lot and cheap buildings in the middle of a red rocky oasis.

On the waterfront there were a series of cinderblock buildings painted white close on thirty or so interconnected docks and a boat ramp. The boat ramp was a concrete ramp one hundred feet wide and almost infinitely long, as it needed to go far into the reservoir to account for water fluctuation.

I backed the truck down the boat ramp to the water's edge where we launched the boat without argument (which is almost unheard of with a wife and teenager) and then I parked the truck in a space with faded white lines by an asphalt curb stop that was baked into a shriveled piece of charcoal.

"It took seventeen years for this lake to fill," I said to Sarah as we walked over to the rental area.

"And I wonder how many years it will take to fix the damage the dam caused?" Joanne said. "This is so much fun."

"You're not going to start that are you? We're here on vacation for God's sake."

She shot me a look and then walked out alone into the forest of floating docks. Sarah shrugged.

I responded to her glance, "We'll get the houseboat and then we'll get your mother."

Sarah and I walked into the boat rental office to confirm our reservation with the crusty looking white man at the desk. The interior of the office was dimly lit and stunk of cat urine and decades of chain smoked cigarettes. The man standing behind the counter was skinny, but pot bellied, and his eyes shifted nervously when I spoke.

"How are you?" I said.

"No one would care if I complained."

"You're right. I've got a boat rented under McKenna."

"The American Pioneer 76?" he said.

"That's the one," I smiled and Sarah rolled her eyes.

"I need to copy your driver's license."

I showed him my Colorado driver's license and he handed me the keys to the houseboat. "Only in America," I said. "I can't believe you don't need a boating license to drive this thing."

The man walked us to our houseboat, the American Pioneer 76'. Its actual size was daunting. The houseboat was painted white with black tinted windows, and had two furnished levels above water plus a top third deck and sleeping quarters below water level. The top deck was a covered terrace with an additional steering wheel beside a water slide and Jacuzzi.

We boarded. The cabin was a cool 68 degrees.

The man showed us the ship's various rooms and brought us onto the bridge to explain the controls. He gave us his *houseboating 101* course, and for the most part, we paid attention, but there were so many buttons and knobs and levers that it was difficult to remember them all.

"And the bow thruster's the most important on this rig," he said.

"Yeah, yeah, thanks, we got it."

"You sure?"

"We can handle it." I wondered if he himself remembered all the controls.

He left. Sarah and I walked over to the ramp and got into the speedboat. I fired up the motor and drove over to the houseboat. It took a few minutes to hook the speedboat to the back so we could tow it around the lake. With that finished, I walked Sarah over to the waverunner dock and she rode the rented waverunner back to the houseboat while I walked beside her on the dock.

"The water looks amazing."

"It's so warm dad." Her feet were wet. She wore sleeves to the elbows and shorts past the knees. Sweat formed on her forehead and she plunged her hand into the lake and spread water on her head.

"We could get two more wave runners. You think we should? there's three of us," I said.

"I think we'll be all right, we can always come back and get one."

"Right you are."

I jumped onto the houseboat's large rear platform and tried to understand the control panel there. Sarah pulled the waverunner up beside me.

"How do you work the waverunner garage?"

"It is not a garage. Let me see it dad."

"I got it."

I fiddled with the control panel. Waves lapped against the boat and water came onto the platform where I stood. My shoes were wet. I pushed another button to make the ramp open but nothing happened.

"This stupid thing doesn't work."

"Just hold the waverunner dad, and I'll figure it out."

I continued pressing buttons. "Damn it." I banged the control panel with my palm.

"No wonder your laptop doesn't work."

"What?"

"Dad! Let me do it!"

Sarah jumped onto the houseboat. She observed the control panel for a moment. "The directions are right there on the panel."

Then she turned a knob, pressed a button and the ramp dropped into the water. She grabbed a cable and hooked it to the front of the waverunner. She turned and pushed some other buttons, and the waverunner was hoisted aboard, and the ramp closed up.

Sarah flashed a toothy grin. "See how easy that was?"

"Just get on the boat wonder child."

I untied the houseboat and we walked up the stairs and through the tinted glass doors into the spacious living room. To our left there were two large black leather couches and a coffee table, and across from that was the entertainment center. The walls and ceiling were wood paneled red mahogany, and off in the corner was a bar. We walked through the entertainment room and into the kitchen that was divided by a granite counter top. In the corner of the kitchen there was a stairwell and a bathroom, beyond that was a spacious dining room that led onto the bridge that housed the large steering wheel and control panel. The keys were in the ignition and I pushed the gold "ON" button and the motor came to life.

Sarah and I pulled The American Pioneer 76' out of its initial docked location without incident, while our flotilla dragged behind us. I had Sarah grab me a beer from the refrigerator, and I cracked it open and drank it down to quench my thirst. We traveled slowly down the channel. I increased speed and then turned the overlarge chrome steering wheel and smiled at my daughter. Our boat turned left around the main aisle of docks where the gas pumps were housed. As we rounded the corner, another large vessel, the Intrepid Sleek 70' with gilded stripes, barreled fast upon us.

"Bow thruster, where'd he say the bow thruster was, Sarah?"

"I don't know, dad."

"Weren't you listening?"

I quickly scanned the cluttered instrument panel for the bow thruster. The Intrepid Sleek 70' bore down on us and blew its horn. We were on its side of the channel. I was going a little fast for the channel, and boats of such size don't maneuver easily. We were about to crash. Sarah stood beside me scanning the NASA like panel. Then I found the knob marked bow thruster in gold lettering and turned it to the right. Our boat followed abruptly, and we narrowly avoided collision. We passed the Intrepid sleek 70' and a drunk from the top deck held up his can of Budweiser and yelled out, "Hey buddy, nice driving." Their boat moved beyond us in the channel and the guy kept shouting and sipping beer. "Alright, alright," he said as he moved to the rhythm of some music pumping his fist. A browned woman walked up behind him. Some of her hair was braided the way American girls on vacation in the Caribbean get it done. She danced in a stiff way as their yacht rounded the channel bend. The words "strummin my six string," carried over to me on the breeze. Before I could give this any thought Sarah laughed.

"We should re-name the boat the Exxon Valdez," she said.

"Let's find your mother."

I pulled into the lake and we sailed passed the docks. Sarah stood on the top deck to get a better view.

When we found Joanne, she was sitting at the end of one of the docks feeding a writhing school of golden scaly carp that lived on tourist bread. As we approached I blew the horn. It seemed like a good idea at the time. But when it sounded, it was much louder than I thought. It was so loud that the dishes in our cabinets rattled, and my heart increased its pace.

Joanne nearly jumped into the lake when the trumpet sounded. Sarah giggled, and so did I, but Joanne was livid. She shook her fist and shouted. Then she recognized who was driving the boat and turned and walked toward shore.

"Is she leaving?" Sarah asked.

Joanne changed her mind mid flight and turned and walked back to the end of the dock where I parked the behemoth American Pioneer 76'. Her face flushed red, and her hands clenched into fists.

As we slowly closed the gap with the dock, I pulled open a large tinted window and said, "I didn't know the horn was so loud."

She was angry. "I was sitting peacefully watching this stupid monster yacht approach, wondering what type of idiot needed such a thing for camping, and of course, it was you. And then you just had to blow the horn. It sounded like a train at a crossing. This is not a vacation for me: it's a test of my patience."

"I wanted to do something special; it's the first time Sarah's been out since she got out of the hospital. I thought getting the big one would be fun."

"I can't believe you rented this boat for three people. It's a complete waste. I can't believe this whole place."

"Just get on the boat, alright, you can yell all you want when you get in here."

"I will not."

"Get on the boat!"

Sarah put out the plank and waved, trying to coax her mother to get onto our houseboat. Finally, Joanne relented and walked onto the houseboat. She did not say a word. She went straight down to one of the berths and locked the door. Sarah and I remained up top and pulled the boat out of the bay and into the canyons.

The water was pristine and the red cliff sides were beautiful. The world turned, and the sun hung low on the sky while the rock walls changed color from red to brown to gold. Stretches of cliff appeared to show a gasoline like rainbow. We searched for a proper isolated place to land our boat and anchor for the night. We settled on a cove a half-hour from the marina that I had marked on the chart, but traditional lake terminology does not work to explain Lake Powell. The stretch of water we pulled into was not a cove at all, but a box canyon, flooded when the dam had been built.

I saw the opening in the sheer cliff walls and pointed the boat toward it. The six-hundred-foot red cliff sides were just far enough apart for us to fit through. Sarah yelled down from the top, "You won't make it dad." But I knew we would. In a few places I scrapped the walls but the bow thrusters came in handy in such instances.

We traveled a thousand feet or more, and were just about to reverse back out and search for another camping spot when the walls suddenly opened into a vaulted amphitheatre hundreds of feet tall and wide. The area looked like the inside of a dusty red balloon half filled with water. Directly up against the amphitheatre wall lay a sliver of beach about one hundred feet long and thirty feet wide. This was why I had come here. I was happy I actually found it.

The first mate and I (as Sara had now become) navigated the boat onto the beach beneath the shadow of the great rock and as the boat landed on shore, Sarah ran down and dropped the large front plank.

"Land ho captain."

She pulled steel pins and a hammer from their cubbies with a grin on her face and then skipped onto shore and hammered the large pins into the sand and soil to keep us from drifting.

"A hurricane couldn't budge this boat," I said.

"Don't tempt it daddy. Can we start a fire?"

I cringed, but didn't allow her to see my reaction. Just the word "fire" out of her mouth was eerie. Last winter, I did my best to refrain from lighting fires or using the word "fire" altogether, but Sarah developed a love for it, and about mid-February she asked me to light one for her, which I promptly did, and she spent the night staring into the flames as if they held secrets. Man never lost the affinity for fire—the campfire was the precursor to television—but Sarah never had an appreciation for it until after she had been burned, and then any one I lit was like the center of her world.

"Sure we can start a fire," I said.

"I'll go find kindling."

"There's probably not much for wood, I don't see any trees."

"I saw some sticks on the beach, and on the cliffs there's some dead bushes that will be perfect. Just bring out the wood that you bought at the dock."

I went along with what she said.

"Can I light the fire tonight?" she said.

"If you want."

Earlier, at her behest, I bought wood at the dock. I went to the rear of the boat now and grabbed it. On my way back to the front, I walked down the stairs and stood by the bedroom door where Joanne locked herself. I wanted to knock, but she was talking with someone. She must have been on her phone. I checked my own cell phone and saw that there was no service; I wondered what carrier she had. Then I walked back up the stairs and onto the beach.

On the beach, I dug a small hole for the fire and thought about my wife. I hoped she would get over her anger and come out and join us. I had plenty of money to rent the boat. Houses in French Gulch were the hottest things on the market now, it wasn't anywhere near a waste for me to get this thing, but she would never see it that way.

25

CHARLES MCKENNA

I stood at the edge of the fire pit and watched Sarah light pieces of newspaper with a book of matches. The newspaper ignited and the flames kissed the burn scars on the palm of her hand. Sarah let her hand linger in the flame for a second longer than she should have. After she pulled it away, she examined her hand and then looked at me and smiled.

"My hand is awful," she said.

"That's not true."

"My hand is awful, and it doesn't feel pain as quickly as it should."

"Do you want me to light the fire?"

"No dad, I got it."

When she did finally have the fire lit, I walked over and sat barefoot in a chair and dug my feet in the sand. It felt cool and dry. The odd yellow light of the fire sent bizarre shadows onto the walls of the red amphitheatre that surrounded us. Our shadows projected onto the walls in massive proportion. Sarah pointed the farce out to me. She made hand puppets. I laughed, and curled my arms like a body builder. "I am iron man."

Aside from our shadows, flickers of flame light illuminated parts of the walls so they appeared to sparkle like a thousand red rubies. Off in the distance a coyote howled and moaned in the night. The smoke from our fire whirled around on the winds and smelled aromatic and spicy. There was something special about the wood Sarah gathered, maybe the way it was seasoned by sun and sand.

Certain aspects of our campsite were frightening and even had a spectral, ghost like quality. There was the sound of constant dripping that echoed off the walls and reverberated within the amphitheatre in a melodic phantom rhythm.

There was an odd echo in the distance. I pictured full dressed Indians long since killed by white men storming about the red alien land with hatchets honed by the bones of dead Caucasians. When this last bit of poetry slipped into my mind, I had all I could do to keep from relaying it to Sarah as a good old ghost story and scaring the hell out of her.

Sarah and I settled into the night. She sat across from me, and after we passed the initial elation and fright brought on by our curious location, we kept silent and watched the fire. When I was a boy, it was my father who remained the silent party at night, but here and now both my daughter and I were silent contemplating those things seen and unseen. I thought of my wife. I wondered whether I could blame her or not, maybe she was brain washed. But it always felt like there had been something else along with her. Ever since the night we first met. I could never shake the feeling that she had caught something that night; that they had given it to her with the drugs, or that they opened her up to something that took the invitation. I had taken my own experience seriously and thought that those things remained with her, but that they hadn't fully taken her. I also felt that love would win in the end.

As the fire grew small, and the circle of light shrunk the amphitheatre to a large room, Joanne walked down the plank and planted her foot on the beach. Her white canvas shoe sunk into the red sand at waters edge. She removed her foot and walked onto the beach. In the low light cast by the fire her shadow projected out onto the opposite wall and appeared to dwarf the immense houseboat.

"I'm taking our boat and going home."

"What do you mean?" I said, confused.

"You can't go home mom, we've got a fire going," Sarah said.

"I'm sorry honey, but I have to leave. Your father and I have something to talk about. Would you please go inside the boat and close the sliding door?"

Sarah hesitated. The look of anger in her mother's eyes immediately killed any instinct to resist her mother's will, and Sarah walked off the beach and into the houseboat.

When Sarah got inside, Joanne said. "You're a fool, and I want a divorce. I don't want to be separated; I know I don't love you. I really don't think I ever loved you. It's as simple as that. I thought you were safe, but I can't put up with this farce."

There was nothing I could say, but she continued, "I can't stand you. I would have left a year ago, but Sarah needed someone to take care of her. Now she wants to be just like you. She loves her *daddy*."

"What's that mean? We're supposed to meet Edzul tomorrow back at the marina." My words had no meaning. I knew it.

"Just shut up. Like I want to see that idiot. You're so out of control, driving around a reservoir that'll be a uranium laced silt dump in a hundred years on a carnival cruise ship for three people."

"You agreed to come."

"I never, ever wanted to come here, EVER, but I'm glad now that I've seen what an ass you are with your boat sucking gas and polluting the water that millions rely on rolling around in air-conditioned, white trash luxury, and you think this is the greatest thing you've done since high school football. I can't stand you. I can't, I just can't play the marriage game any more. Not this way, not when you have Sarah in training." She paused and trembled while she glared at me. The fire was dying and the shadows grew smaller and smaller, soon there would be no fire and no shadow at all.

"Where are the keys to the boat?"

"Joanne, we're in the middle of the desert, where the hell do you think you're going? It's dark out?"

"The boat has GPS. I'll go back to the marina and find a ride, and if I can't find a ride out, then there's a motel in town I can stay at. Don't follow me Charles, okay, just let me go. I'll leave the boat at the marina, you can pick it up tomorrow."

I got angry and said, "Why don't you call whoever you were talking to in the cabin and have them come get you?"

"Do you still feel like you have to control me? My phone doesn't even work."

"I think you're off the deep end and the prescriptions don't work."

"You were someone different when I married you, and I thought my baby would have a safe environment to grow up in. I thought you would give it to us, but you poisoned her, you poisoned Sarah. I hoped that maybe after she had the accident that she would see through you, but she can't, she's enchanted. She wants the same simple path you chose. But you live in folklore. Our arrangement is over. Do you here me, it's over."

"You can't take her now, she won't leave with you tonight."

"I know she won't leave with me tonight, but she's my daughter, Charles. She's mine. I'll teach her what you are."

"What if she comes to know what you are? What then? when she knows that you left us for hocus pocus. This is all for you anyway; all this Peoples Group brainwash . . . have fun."

"I've given my life for my daughter. Everything I've done has been for Sarah, all of it was for her, but I lost her, I lost her to you."

"How can you lose her to her own father?"

"You're not her father, you're an ass."

"Joanne, you're the one that wants to enchant her. I never tried to enchant her, I was just her father."

She took a deep breath and said, "You won't win."

"The keys are in the boat, Joanne."

When the sound of the boat disappeared, Sarah walked out of the sliding door.

"Dad," she said, "Is mom really gone?"

But I couldn't say a word. Sarah walked out, sat by the fire and cried; neither of us spoke.

26

CHARLES MCKENNA

In the morning, we took the houseboat to the marina to find the boat Joanne took, but it wasn't there. We drove around all day and took our houseboat to another spot and went to sleep. Next morning we looked for the speedboat again but couldn't find it.

"Let's return the houseboat and go home."

Sarah nodded in agreement. I no longer cared for my speedboat or where it was, I lost my wife.

At the marina, Sarah and I dropped off The American Pioneer 76'. I couldn't get my deposit back because I returned the boat early.

I took my time unhitching the boat trailer in the parking lot while Sarah sat in the air-conditioned truck with the engine running. The temperature was one hundred and eleven degrees with no humidity. The sweat from my body evaporated before it stained my clothes. The trailer came away from the truck easily, and I pushed it to the side of the dusty red lot. A lizard ran for its life under the trailer's tire.

We pulled away from the lake at noon and were well into our trip when the sun turned the ground purple.

But we weren't headed home.

"Dad, where are you headed?"

I wanted to eat dinner in Santa Fe, New Mexico. I dreaded seeing the awful mountain world of Breckenridge without my wife. That world lost all meaning for me, and the mountains were so cold without meaning. With a wife, I had direction, I had family and I had purpose, but now without her (and that she was gone there was no question) without her I was anyone else living in a resort town. The hills and valleys are for civilization. The mountains are against man. And a resort town is cold and materialistic.

I ached for a better existence and pined with nostalgia for the small treed lane I grew up on in Massachusetts. The world was safe back home. But, believing that I was better back in Boston was just as foolish as thinking I had nothing in my life. I turned to my daughter beside me and realized that she was all the family I needed. I dreaded that Joanne would take her from me. I loved Sarah.

I had good memories of Santa Fe that didn't involve Joanne, which is why I wanted to go. On my first trip across country in college, my friends and I stopped in for a few nights. I never forget how charming a village it was. The adobe houses and tree-lined streets all nestled into the hills and mountains with streams, and breezes, and outdoor café's, and patios paved in terra cotta bound by mud walls and tiled with blue friezes. I wanted to be there.

"I'd like to go to Santa Fe, if you don't mind," I said.

"What's in Santa Fe?" Sarah asked.

"What's at home?"

"Okay," she said, "It will be fun, I've always heard good things about Santa Fe." She could see my pain.

We drove east through the dessert. The sky was blue and endless without cloud, and the ground was a sea of red and burnt orange that lulled my mind into thought and contemplation. I fought hard not to think of Joanne. She was lost, and I couldn't help it, and that was the worst part. She wounded me long ago. I never recovered.

We passed the intersection of some highway and a sign advertised the White Sands National Monument. It struck me odd that White Sands was now a national monument and valued as a treasure. In 1945, The Trinity Site at White Sands, New Mexico was the first place a nuclear explosion ever occurred ushering in the nuclear age. From then on, people feared the nuclear apocalypse. I drove passed and said nothing.

In a few hours we reached Santa Fe and rented a room with two beds in a whitewashed two-story adobe hotel. The shutters, beams and doors were stained in a deep purple brown. The room we were given was on the second floor with French doors that opened onto a patio railed with wrought iron. Inside, the room was white with deep window wells, two ornate pine beds and by the corner a purple tapestry hung from the wall.

After Sarah and I settled in, we went to town and surveyed the hundreds of art studios and galleries that lined every street and corner.

"Let's have coffee," Sarah said.

"I didn't know you drank coffee?"

"You have to start sometime."

"Then today isn't the day."

"*Dad.* I drink coffee all the time on Main Street at the espresso bar. Don't you think I'm old to be telling me I can't drink coffee?"

"I'm a throwback."

We walked into the thistle of streets below and found a small café with old plank floors and a huge copper machine that made coffee or espresso or something along those lines. We sat.

"Just a coffee."

"I want a cappuccino," Sarah said. "It's really pretty here dad. There's so much culture here. Most places look like truck stops."

The coffee came, and Sarah took a sip. "We don't have a culture like other places do," she said.

"Culture now's mostly behind closed doors in families. Beyond that, it's easy for a lot of things to make no sense."

"Aren't movies culture?

"No."

We left the café and on our way to dinner Sarah said. "I don't want to have Mexican food again; I hate Mexican food dad."

"This is Santa Fe you know?"

"I know, I like the town, but I can't stand the food, the *refried* this and the *mariachi* that. There's plenty of places in Breck that have Mexican, I'm just not into it."

Instead of Mexican, we had overpriced French food at a Bistro. Sarah seemed happy. But she looked so much like her mother that at times I looked away from her and out into the street. When we left, I got angry with the waiter for how he acted toward me. I left him a nickel for a tip, and Sarah laughed. Then we walked through the galleries and down into the Governor's Palace where poor Native Americans sold rugs and other ware. Sarah found a purple and red Navajo rug in a triangle pattern like a kaleidoscope.

"I like this, dad, it looks like the one in our room." She held up the rug and inspected it and then suddenly grinned.

"What," I said.

"Made in Bangladesh."

She held her head back and laughed. Then she said, "Mom would just hate that." When the words fell off her tongue she had the look of someone who has done something awful and knows it. "She's really leaving you?"

"She was serious."

"But what's it mean?"

"We'll find out."

We went back to the room and Sarah checked the tapestry to find where it had been made.

"What's the label say?" I asked

"Doesn't say anything. It might actually be authentic."

We talked for a little while. I remember she talked of business hopes, and I said something silly like, "If you don't learn to sprout legs then you'll be drift wood forever." I felt like it meant something. Sarah laughed and asked how driftwood sprouted legs, but she was tired and fell asleep quickly. I had trouble falling asleep, but after a few glasses of scotch and water I slept like a baby.

Early in the morning, before the sun rose, Sarah hit me with a pillow and told me to "STOP SNORING."

After that, sleep was out of the question, and I sat on the patio and looked into the park across the street. A few hours passed and the sun rose and lit the patio in pleasant morning light. After a quick breakfast in the lobby, we packed our things and headed north back to Colorado. I could only hide for so long.

We drove up through the hills and into the mountains north of Santa Fe. At its southern border Santa Fe changed from fertile valley to desert, but heading north the highway followed the valley until it climbed the rolling hillsides and farther still into the deep mountains.

We headed over a mountain pass with a scenic overlook and then down into the high plains that were covered by a labyrinth of cedar trees, none more than fifteen feet high. The forest lasted a hundred miles and forever. I imagined what it would have been like for the traveler on horseback a hundred years ago in an endless landscape of repeated forms.

Out of the labyrinth we drove. The road was as straight as an arrow and rose and fell and rose and fell with the countless hilltops and low spots. The road then took a long sweeping right hand northerly turn and suddenly out of the flat landscape ahead appeared the near vertical Sangre De Cristo Mountain range of Southern Colorado.

The name in Spanish meant Blood of Christ and was supposedly named after the red glow that appears near the peaks at sunset. As we drove parallel to the mountains and north beyond the sand dunes at the southern end of the range, and saw why they had been named this way: near the bottom of the steep mountains a purple hue of vegetation was visible. The mountains looked like they were cut and bleeding.

I pointed this out.

"They do look like they're bleeding dad," Sarah said.

"It's beautiful here."

27

CHARLES MCKENNA

I was alone. Sarah was out driving her friends and going to school, and I was alone and supposed to be on vacation but going insane with nothing but time on my hands. I was glad that Sarah wasn't devastated; though it was possible she was in shock.

We came home on Monday. By Wednesday I had thrown myself into work to hide from life. My phone was surprisingly quiet for a Wednesday afternoon. People thought I was still on vacation. I didn't bother to tell them otherwise, if I needed to speak to someone, I called them. Other than that, I didn't announce my return. At around noon that day my phone rang.

"Hello."

"Charlie." Edzul's raspy voice came through the receiver.

"How are you?" I said.

"I've got your boat."

"How?"

"Joanne came by my campsite the other night, late; don't know how she found it. She got a ride back up with some guys. She left the boat with me and pointed out the ravine you camped in, but you were gone the next day."

"Yeah, we left that spot early Saturday. Did she say anything else?"

"She was real upset, mostly sat by herself and watched the campfire. I told her she should go back to you, but she didn't want to hear it. She kept saying: 'She couldn't wait,' and, 'the whole world was just like you,' or something like that, but she wouldn't really talk to anybody, she just kind of sat there. We thought she was crazy, kind a felt bad for her, and Tiny and his wife gave her a ride home. You know how Tiny is. His old lady was mad he volunteered to give her a ride to Breck.

"Anyway, I got the boat; found your trailer at the marina where Joanne said you'd leave it. I got it behind my house, so come get it when you want," he waited for a few seconds, but I didn't respond. Then he said, "You alright Charlie?"

"No, not at all. I'll be alright, but today isn't a good day."

"Yeah, well trust me, the way I saw her acting at the campsite the other night, you're better off without her."

"It doesn't feel like it today."

"She was never for you," he said.

"She was my wife."

"I never trusted her."

"I spent over twenty years of my life with her. You can't tell me that."

"I remember her back then too." He hesitated for too long.

"You got something to say Edzul?"

"I never trusted her since the night she left with Smiley at the bar. When I saw him with her in the street she was calling him her seraphim," he stopped to add, "That means angel."

"I know what it means, but why is this a good time to tell me?"

"You two were hitched when I saw you next. I wasn't going to say anything, not since you looked happy, but that woman was never all there with you—not ever. I don't know no more than that. But the way she was with him that night, it wasn't no mistake, I know the man, and he was slinkin' around town for a while and don't forget, she was in that group of his. You still there?"

"Mostly."

I hung up with him promising to get the boat tomorrow.

A few hours later, I was in the jobsite trailer on the phone with a town planner when Hank pulled up in his squad car. He walked up and knocked on the door. I waved him in and rushed the town planner off the phone.

"Officer Gibs, how can I help you?"

"Heard about your wife."

"Don't you just bring the sunshine?"

"Joanne spoke to Lucy the other night on the phone." Then Hank paused and focused on me in such a way that wrinkles in his forehead pushed together in slight folds where his red hair came to rest. He still had scars from that night.

"What is it, Hank?"

He handed me a manila envelope. I took it and removed several pictures of Joanne with Smiley.

"Are you keeping tabs on her?" I said.

Again he paused but this time he took a deep breath. "We found those in Stanley Joe White's squatter's cabin in French Gulch. They were no good for the trial; he confessed, but I figured I'd hold on to 'em."

"Smiley."

"Yeah, Smiley. We found them there when we searched his place after the fire. If you look, the pictures are dated just before the fire."

"Why you showing me these?"

"I questioned Joanne about the pictures before the trial. She said they were friends. She remembered taking the pictures. Said Smiley took them with his camera. But Smiley didn't own a camera. We didn't find one in that shack, and he was *real* meticulous about how he kept his stuff. We asked him, and he said he didn't own a camera, but when I showed him the pictures, he said he lost the camera when he was hiking. The pictures don't prove anything, so we never needed to bring Joanne into court. Stanley said he lit the fire of his own accord, so there was no need to take things further. At the time, I didn't think there was any need for you to see the pictures because they don't prove anything."

"She was friends with him. I hated the bastard."

"That's what I heard too. It's just strange she's at his shack with your development in the background. And if you look, he's not the one holding the camera; someone else is there. We think it's Gwen Istofsen. I think she dates Andy. I figure maybe there's reason for suspicion and maybe not. With what's ahead of you. I mean with the divorce, you may find use for the pictures." He paused and then said, "There's something else that maybe you don't know."

"Yeah what's that?"

"The house you live in; she had you buy it?"

"You know she did."

"Well that group she belonged to financed it and built it; you bought it from them, and they earned money off it."

"I bought it from a local guy."

"Who do you think he was working for? They had trouble selling the house and . . ." he looked at me, but I didn't say a word and he continued, "We looked into their money because of Mister White's affiliation with them, and what the attorney's found was that they're all over the country from Portland, Oregon to Portland, Maine, and well funded."

"I thought the thing started in jail?"

"It's hard to tell who started what, when. But Mister Smiley isn't officially linked to anything in the group at all. There's some real interesting stuff there too, but we couldn't look beyond their money and there's plenty of that. You should see the lawyers they've got: heavy hitters. Not just pikers, but the real dedicated Washington type backed nationally, even internationally. They threatened us if we tried to link Mr. White to them. Everyone thought he was the head that founded the thing. But we couldn't get anyone to say so. There's still people looking into them on a federal level."

"For what?"

"They're a hallucinogenic religion centered around a drug, the miracle molecule, they call it, that they think will help bring about a worldwide revolution. And they have so much money, they're dangerous. I know two agents were trying to get them on drug trafficking charges as well as identity theft, extortion, forced labor, sex trafficking, money laundering, wire fraud, and obstruction of justice. And Joanne's all mixed up with the donors and the big money."

"Is she in danger?"

"Her? I think you're the one who might be in danger, Charles. They have a lot of money and political connections and are determined to protect themselves. Whatever Stanley started has taken on a whole life of its own." He paused then and added, "Just keep the photos. Sarah's a real nice girl, she's been through a lot, and she deserves to be raised right, not in any bizarre sex ritual of unification."

"What?"

"Just keep your daughter, Charles, you have enough there and there's more if you need it."

"What more?"

"There's letters from when he went to jail."

"Which time?"

"Both. But I don't have 'em. Feds do. It'll be hard as hell to get 'em. It can be done if you need. I think you got enough in your hands to keep Sarah is what I'm saying. Looking further will be painful."

"If there's letters, I want them."

"There's letters. I'll see what I can do."

I scratched the beard I had let grow the last few days and looked out the window into the rock piles. "At least I had the pleasure of knocking down his hovel. I was somewhat glad the fire didn't get it."

He smiled and left me standing with the photos and the envelope. When he walked out the door and drove away I let out a deep sigh. I looked at the pictures one more time. In the background I made out the leg of another female and the hood of a Jeep. Then I tossed the photos in a drawer and went back to work. Whenever thoughts of my wife crept into my head, I worked harder, until by the end of the day I had almost forgotten about pictures, and fires, and wives.

28

CHARLES MCKENNA

Next day, I kept the routine. The laborer who was supposed to clean up the job-site never showed, and I spent the morning sorting and cleaning the trailer, even going so far as to clean the windows and vacuum the carpets.

Friday came. I found it more difficult to keep busy and to keep Joanne out of my mind. After so many years spent with a person, it isn't overnight you forget them.

At about noon, Joanne pulled up to the trailer and, without knocking, entered. I sat at my desk. She didn't say hello; she merely came over to me.

"I want custody of Sarah."

"Nice to see you Joanne."

"Do we have to go to court?" she said bitterly.

When she said that, a slow wick of anger lit in my body, starting in my stomach and working its way upward. I reached into the drawer and tossed the pictures on the desk.

"Who are you?"

"What do these mean to me?" she said poking the images.

"They mean you won't take Sarah."

"I won't have you poisoning her with more American nonsense."

I stayed silent and looked at the pictures. She looked at them also and then picked them off the table and tossed them in my face.

"So what, your buddies at the station gave you pictures of me with Stanley. They already asked me about them. There's nothing there."

"You're not going to take Sarah from me Joanne, you won't leave me and take my daughter on whatever perverted trip you're on."

"Perverted? I can't live with you anymore, Charles. Don't you see that? Hasn't it been obvious? You live in a closet world without love. The only thing you care about is how much money you make. You don't care about me, you don't care about Sarah, you don't care about this valley. With your education you should be with us, but you're content with your own selfishness. Sarah won't be part of it."

"You can't take her," I said.

Joanne slapped my face over the desk. I looked up at her, my fists clenched tighter, but I did not raise them. Joanne slapped me again. "What do you think you have with those pictures? What do you think they prove?" Blood trickled from a small cut on my face. The silver bramble ring she started wearing must have cut me. She trembled for a moment and watched the blood, and then she looked to the pictures on the floor. "What do you think you have there?"

"I don't think I have much, but a good attorney could make a lot out of them. Like—I don't know—say, two lovers taking a picture of what they'll burn down together during their sick affair that's been going on since 1973. That looks a lot like Bill's Jeep in the background."

"You're crazy that's not Bill's jeep."

"It doesn't matter whose Jeep it is, but it's funny that the head of an organization can't get one of his minions to do his dirty work. I guess Smiley, Oh, I'm sorry, Stanley White's not so bright as you people think."

"What are you doing Charles? Do you even know? Do you? You

won't keep my daughter just because you can't stand to live alone with yourself."

"I won't let you have her."

"The pictures mean nothing, and you know it. You're a liar."

"There are no coincidences Joanne, those pictures say whatever my attorney wants them to say. If you want to see Sarah, you'll let me have her. Don't fight me, I'll do everything in my power to bury you. Try me; test me!!! Bring in the fancy lawyers that back your Human Movement or whatever it is and see if I won't lop off my nose to spite my own face. I'll haul people into court who were there in 1973 to tell what you did . . ."

"You don't know what I have on you Charles."

"I have pictures of you in front of my development with the man who burned it to the ground one week before it happened. Tell me you have pictures like that, tell me you do. And I can get your letters to Smiley in prison. Go away, Joanne. If you go, you can see your daughter whenever you want. I'll put that in writing, you just have to arrange it with Sarah first and give me a call."

"I'll take everything you have Charles, you piece of shit."

"Money, maybe, but I'll take your child."

She leaned over the table. "SHE IS NOT YOUR CHILD!" She spelled out the words slowly. "You won't take her."

"She's been my daughter her entire life, and whatever wicked things you say now or did in the past don't mean a thing to me. Sarah is mine. You're not fit to have a cat let alone a kid. If you really want we can fight it out, but the chances you'll win are slim. If you push this, we'll just see what comes up. So I can call the attorney right now, Joanne, and we can settle this here: I get full custody of Sarah. You can see her whenever you want. Like I said, arrange it with her and give me fair warning."

"I want money then."

"How much?"

"Two million, plus alimony."

"What happened to the trust from your father?"

"Don't worry about my money."

"No."

"Two million or we fight," she said.

"No."

"Don't act poor now."

"I'll give you one in cash, and the lawyers can decide what I give you for alimony."

"Don't push me, I can get more if we go to court," she said.

"Not in cash you can't."

"In everything I can."

"Then I'll see what my lawyer can do," I said.

"I'll do it then. I'll sign what you want to me to sign, but I will ruin your fucking life. It's my mission to ruin you."

"Was there ever another?"

"You won't have her. I'll be right up the road—a girl needs her mother. Before long she won't even think of you as a dad."

"Whatever you say. But," I pointed my finger in her face, "you don't leave this trailer until the attorneys come and we have everything notarized and in writing. You got it!"

She blinked several times. "I keep the pictures."

"Not on your life."

She called her snake attorney, and I called mine. I sat staring at the mountain range, and she sat in her car on the phone. Then my attorney and her attorney came and argued over the finer points and produced a draft that both of us could sign. Then they called a notary, and we signed the document and that was that. Our arrangements were made prior to our legal divorce. It took about three hours and it was done.

"I'm going to pick up Sarah today. I want to talk to her about what's going to happen."

"Fine with me," I said.

Joanne left with tears in her eyes. I believed they were real because she hated to lose. And if love is war, then she lost the battle and knew it.

My lawyer turned to me before he headed back to Boulder. "You know if she fights it later another lawyer can claim she signed under duress."

"She'd have to want to fight in a courtroom."

29

SARAH MCKENNA-HURST

M om picked me up from school. When I walked outside I found her parked next to my car in the student lot. Her hair was stringy and pulled tight behind her head, and her cheeks were wet with tears. I dropped my bag, and she got out and hugged me and brought me over to the passenger side of her car where I sat. She sat in the driver's side and we both cried.

"It will be alright," mom said, "It will all be alright honey."

"You're leaving though. You are. I know you are. Where have you been? I haven't seen you in a week mom? Why are you acting this way?"

I pulled away from her to leave the car, but she pulled me back down and rubbed my head.

"I'm getting a divorce."

"No." I already knew but to hear it stated out loud shocked me.

"It's time. You shouldn't be hurt."

"No mom."

"Two people don't just stay together anymore like they used to, and this way is natural; in real life people grow and move on. Honey, you'll see, I know you'll come to understand, even if it's difficult now; life's a journey, it's a discovery."

I started to cry, and she paused for a moment and looked at me. "Please, Sarah, this is for you. You don't live in the same world I lived in, with the same restrictive parents. All that is past now. The world moved on."

I didn't care about what she said. "It's that man. That man—Bill—You love him? He's the one, he's telling you these things, he's the one?"

"Don't be silly Sarah, Bill doesn't think like this on his own, but he understands."

"But what about me?"

"You have such a family beyond what you know, you just have to open up and live it to see it."

"But you can love dad."

"Why would I love a man that doesn't want to grow? His idea of growth is that maybe one day, if he plays by the right rules, he can finally be accepted into the big country club. Your father only wants power, that's all men like him ever want."

"Then why were you with him? Why did you have me with him? Why didn't you leave him long ago?"

She looked at me as if she wanted to say something, and then she said, "So you'd be protected. I couldn't keep you safe on my own, I was pregnant. I can't shield you from the pain, but it will teach you; the suffering will galvanize you. Don't look at Charles as your father, because you no longer need one, or a mother, you should have brothers and sisters, all unequivocally equal."

I didn't care about her speeches, I only cared that she was leaving me. Somewhere inside I thought she would change her mind and that the final wouldn't actually be final. My voice cracked. I couldn't understand, and I searched for answers in her face. I had so many questions: what would happen now when I came home from school? How would dinner work? Where would my mom be? Why was this happening? I wanted to blame that man, like he was the evil causing this; I felt that was true, I knew that was true. It wasn't her fault.

"Will you take me with you? What will I do?" I said.

"You'll stay where you are."

"But I don't want to mom, I don't want you to go. Don't go."

"I'm not going anywhere. It's only a temporary thing before your father . . . before your father understands."

30

SARAH MCKENNA-HURST

S he may not have left my dad for Bill, but she moved in with him a few weeks later. My dad was angry all the time and reduced to speechless stretches of expression where his lips curled and his teeth clenched. He hated. Not anything in particular, and it wasn't that he was mad, he just hated and was full of hatred and bitterness. Even during happy moments, the glint of hatred and killing crept back in his eyes. He made plenty of money and could amuse himself with all the toys a man could buy, but those things couldn't soothe him, and the hatred was just below the surface. He rarely bought anything, except for a big television that he watched the news casts on.

I spent time at friend's houses, but all my friends wanted to do was smoke pot, and I wasn't really into it. When I wasn't studying, I hung around Main Street in the art shops and thrift stores and around some of the restaurants. Hanging around there was more fun than spending time inside with stoners. Sometimes I saw dad downtown.

Breckenridge was fashionable and developing, or at least trying to develop, a clientele like Aspen, the very wealthy set, and some of these women showed an interest in my dad, but unless he hid his relationships very well from me, which would not have been like him, then he never reciprocated. He pretty much stuck to the schedule: work from 7:00 am to 6:00 pm, eat dinner at the Gold Pan with a beer or two 'till about 7:00 and then home to complain about the news while he helped me with my homework, and in the mornings he woke me early with breakfast before he left for work. And if I ever decide to just pop in on him, say at the Gold Pan or at work, then that is where I would find him.

As the summer changed into winter (because there is no fall here) dad rose every day at 4:30 in the morning and put wood in the stove. We didn't need the stove, we had heat like regular people, but he liked to keep the stove burning as if keeping the fire alive somehow kept him alive. Yet his bitterness increased.

One day, when I got ready to go out for the night, he got upset.

"I'm going out dad."

"When will you be home?"

"I don't know."

"God damn it, when?"

"I don't know."

"Tell Bill I said hi."

"What?"

He didn't answer me. He just looked embarrassed and turned the volume up and buried himself in news. Only the television lit the room. A beer can decorated the table. I left without saying another word. But he was like that. He was angry and sometimes boiled over, but then he wouldn't talk about it.

And as the winter settled in around Breckenridge, I spent increasingly more time with my mom. We hung out downtown on Main Street. One day, about mid January, we ate in a cowboy restaurant. The place was decorated with ropes, and saddles with six shooters, and elk's heads and cowboy hats on the walls everywhere. But I liked it, they had good steak, and a really great house salad. Mom usually didn't eat, but on this occasion I think she had a salad like I had. It was at this dinner that I told her about my plans for college. She got upset.

"Of course you want a license to steal, that's exactly what Charles has been teaching you all these years."

"Mom, what's wrong with getting an MBA, what could be wrong with me wanting to achieve something?"

"If you can't see it, then I can't tell you, but just do me a favor and don't set these plans in stone, make sure you understand the world before you rush out and join something. I'd really like it if you came to meetings with me, you can learn something there."

"I'm not going to meetings at night to see the cult."

"You're talking Charles's poison. Honey, don't take everything he says as though its truth; you have to be more skeptical than that."

"I'm skeptical of your meetings."

"I don't want to argue with you about it, it's obvious you've already made up your mind, and Charles is doing his best to take you away from me."

"He's not trying to take me from you mom, he doesn't even ever say anything about you. It's just that this whole People Group thing is weird."

"Why?

"It's just weird mom, I don't know, some of the stuff you say is frightening."

"Do you think I'm being controlled Sarah?"

"I don't know."

"Well I'm not. The last thing I want is for you to be frightened. Charles just upsets me a great deal. I don't want you to be misled."

"I love him mom."

"I know you do, I just care about you more than anything, and I want you to know the truth about the world. I don't want you to be shrouded by dogmas of the Middle Ages when there's an entire world out there if you can only see it. You could probably benefit if you came to one, that's why I ask."

"I'll have to think about it mom."

"Well do," she took a sip of water. "You should come home with me tonight."

"I don't want to sleep at Bill's house mom."

She hesitated and swallowed my comment, but a surge of anger coursed back over her face.

"Why do you do that? Why? There's nothing wrong with Bill. There's no need for you to feel strange, okay. I can't just keep paying for restaurants and hotels because you don't want to come to my house. He pulled you from a fire."

"It'll be strange mom. I don't want to; I don't feel right."

"Would you get over it already, come on, we're going to my house and you're spending the night. There is no group meeting, just friends."

"All your friends are from the meetings."

"I want to know you're sleeping under the same roof as me; I want to know what that feels like again. I shouldn't feel like I have to force you."

She made me sad, and guilty, and so I assented and followed her out of the restaurant headed to Bill's house. We walked because it was so close.

The winter snow was several feet deep and piled in banks between the sidewalk and road. There was a chill in the air, but the sky was endless blue, and the bright sun made it feel twenty degrees warmer. As we walked, we passed a long line of storefronts, some fashionable, others not. Each had displays or café tables pushed tight against the front glass. Main Street had the feeling of an open-air mall with piles of snow and Christmas lights encircling the Victorian buildings with a few newer structures peppered throughout.

We passed a store set inside a rustic mountain shack painted lime green with the trim around the display window done up in day-glow orange. Mom waved to the guy behind the counter and he waved back. A waft of deep incense wafted out.

The next set of stores was a mall made of brick that housed record and jewelry stores and an oxygen bar, where at the high altitude, nine-thousand-feet or so, flat landers could get high on the cheap with a little O2.

Through the front glass I recognized some friends from school. One of the faces belonged to the boy Mike Reilly. I had wanted to date him, but after I recovered from my burns, he was no longer in my homeroom, and then I never saw him again. He moved away, and we didn't know each other; at least we had never spoken to each other.

As I passed the open door he waved to me which was surprising because I didn't think he knew who I was. I instinctively waved back, but I hoped mom didn't see.

"Who's that?" She asked.

"Oh, just a boy."

"Anything I want to know."

"God you're nosey."

I picked up my pace. My mom followed and we passed a group fashionable people, New Yorkers, in for the ski season. As they drew near, taking up the sidewalk, narrow from snow, mom said out loud, apparently to herself but meant for their ears, "All the trash from the East Coast seems to wash in right about now."

A blond woman in a mink coat attempted to respond, but mom beat her to the punch. "Maybe for your next vacation you'll Safari in South Africa, at least the animals won't talk back and the Africans will put up with your nonsense, or maybe they won't, and they'll slit your lily white throat."

We pushed passed the woman. Mom held tight to my hand as if she didn't want to lose me. The woman stood perplexed in the street before entering a nearby store that sold sunglasses for the price, as mom said, of tuition beside a coffee shop that sold coffee for the price of sunglasses.

31

SARAH MCKENNA-HURST

"This commercial trip is too much for me," mom said as we rounded the corner and walked into Bill's barn. I hesitated at the door, but mom pulled my hand and we entered. I could hear guitar music as we passed over the threshold, but it ceased as I stepped inside. The first thing I saw was Bill carving a long thin piece of wood. The carving gave the impression that it was organic and reaching out.

"Hello," he said.

"Is that another sign?" I asked.

"No. This? No. This is a tombstone for a friend. It'll rot, but he didn't think his memory needed to last longer than the people who remembered him."

At that point I surveyed the room and noticed three others besides my mother. One of these I recognized as Gwen, my father's friend Andy's girlfriend who I had seen years before with Smiley. She seemed incredibly embarrassed that I was here. I immediately thought her outward shame had to do with how she was dressed, which was incredibly provocative. I think she saw how I felt in my facial expression, but I didn't have the chance to say anything. My mother spoke instead, also surprised to find her here and in that way, "I didn't know you would be here, Gwen?" She said with a kind of sweetness in her voice that poorly masked her agitation.

"I thought I'd have her come since Nicolas was going to be here." Bill said in nodding to one of the other men.

But as if taking a cue, the man Bill had nodded to asked, "Is this your daughter?" in slightly accented English. He had been sitting to the right of the door in a wicker chair behind Gwen in such a way as it appeared to me that she had been sitting in his lap. What stood out most about his appearance, aside from the crooked teeth he rolled his tongue back and forth over, was his skin, which was nearly as pale as the snow piled outside was white.

"Yes, this is Sarah," mom said.

He then rose and walked toward me. He was large, round, and balding, and I guessed he was in his 60s though he could have been much older than that. As he got near, I smelled alcohol on his breath. There was another man in the corner who also stood and came toward me. He was of slight build and had clear blue eyes, curly gray hair, and wore khaki slacks and a collared shirt. I thought I recognized him as a local, but I wasn't sure.

"You are beautiful like your mother," Nicolas said. I smiled and looked to mom.

"Honey, this is Nicolas," she said to me.

"Yes," he said. "Nee-ko-lass."

"Where are you from?" I asked, curious now about the accent which he had just so strangely accentuated when before it had been so very slight.

"Oh, many places. Moscow, Smolensk. I lived in many places. I have known Bill a very long time. How many years, Bill?"

But Bill didn't answer. He was deeply involved with his chisel work on the gravewood.

The other man in the room now introduced himself. He was pleasant and athletically spry. He left a guitar on the seat behind him and gently took my hand in his.

"Hi, I'm Jay," he said, as American as any American would say.

I half expected another Russian. He seemed like the descendant of roughneck outdoorsmen, now rendered slack by comfort and marijuana.

"I've known your mom a long time, I really am happy to meet you now after so many years."

"Do I know you?" I asked.

"I've met you before," Jay said. "But you were very young. I'm not in Breck often. I move a lot. I do gigs all over. I used to be on Ski Patrol here." He motioned to the acoustic guitar in the corner. "Maybe I could play you something."

"We've heard enough of your playing," Nicolas said rudely, and winked at me, his accent again nearly absent. Jay was uncomfortable and returned to his chair and guitar, and I was more confused than I had ever been. I had never expected to encounter such a weird group of people, even at my mom's house. And I think she recognized my confusion as she rather excitedly said, "Let's all sit down," and motioned to the carved chairs the group had been seated in when we entered. At the spot, a bottle of whiskey and some glasses were assembled on a rough pine table.

"You want something to drink baby, some wine?" mom said.

"Yeah, I'll have a glass of wine, mom." I answered, hoping both to calm my nerves as well as to get to know these strange people and what they were all doing together.

"Good, good, you drink." Nicolas said as my mom handed me a glass. "But you should not drink this," and he held up a glass of whiskey, "Hair on the chest," he said and I laughed as he walked to the cast iron stove a few feet away where he poked the coals for a moment and tossed in two more logs. "Very cold outside," he said, looking to Gwen who was in need of the fire more than the rest of us. He then turned his attention to Jay and added, "I admire musicians and artists, I have never been able to understand these things, I could never make art, but I admire it when it is good." I wondered where he was going.

"Oh, thank you." Jay said, blushing, "I have admired your work for some time now as well."

Work, I thought to myself, what work does this man do?

"How could you know what I have done?" Nicolas then asked, perturbed.

"But you've worked with Bill in California," Jay said.

"Bill must talk too much." Nicolas stuck his fingers in his Whiskey and flicked them toward Bill.

"I remember you emigrated when Stanley went to jail." Jay continued. "Bill told me he had a friend coming from the Soviet Union because there was no food and no more work, but you were reading about the Peoples Group there. It's heroic."

"It must have been another friend. There was no Soviet Union when I left, not for a long time, and I had plenty of food. I was never without food a day of my life." I thought that it showed. "I left because the pigs who took over the country would have killed me. They say Putin himself would like to give me polonium-210. I met Bill in Phnom Pehn."

"What's that?" I asked.

"It's Cambodia, honey, where Nixon put Bill during Vietnam."

I gathered this was an inside joke, and I didn't bother asking what else she meant.

"Not that Nixon was worse than the enemy-of-the-American-People we have now." She continued. "He was probably even better." She commented and laughed bitterly.

"We are just like you now," Nicolas added with a smile.

But I could tell by the way my mother looked at him, and then me, that she felt that this was all too weird for my comfort. For my part, I was still curious to hear more, at least it was interesting, but mom said, "I think it's time to start cooking. What do you think, honey?" I thought she was talking to me for a moment, but she looked to Bill who was lost in his work and wasn't offering her any consolation. "You see how passionate he is with his work?" She said as if to recover.

"I'll help you cook, Joanne."

"I don't mind cooking for people who appreciate it, Jay," she replied, but I wasn't sure if she was referring to my dad, or to Bill, or maybe to both.

Nicolas then jumped into the conversation with his own topic;

by this point I was nearly ready to laugh out loud, "He has to be passionate about his work," he said, "if he wants his money. Look, see how he carves for his money?" Bill looked up but didn't smile. "I know, you say it's no better, even worse, that I must run a cleaning service." And with those words, Nicolas turned his attention back to Jay. "They pay you money to play your guitar, no?" I could see mom was getting angry, and Gwen had practically disappeared.

"Yes." Jay responded to Nicolas in a hesitant way.

"What type of girls do you meet?"

"All different types really."

"You probably like the little Russian girls that come to Brecken-ridge to clean houses, no? Yes, yes, I see it. They seem so scared and so white, but in the bed they have no fear." Jay blushed. "See, you blush, I wonder where you found your Russian mistress, did she clean your condominium? She's not one of mine, I would know. No, Joanne, I'm serious. They are better than Mexicans are they not? Please, please, do not get angry. You are musician," he said and I realized then that he was drunk, "This is what you do. The more money you make the better girls you get. Right, now you can have Russian cleaning girls, better than Mexicans, but not so good as American women. Maybe you like the black ones."

"Nicolas," mom said. "That's enough. Gwen take the bottle of whisky from him." And Gwen did exactly as mom asked. "We have trout for dinner, Jay, and I think we have apple pie, Nicolas. Maybe you can help me, Jay?" Her calm, but direct demeanor defused the room. The men all seemed to fear upsetting her, maybe they knew her temper, and Gwen seemed in the habit of doing what she was told.

But Nicolas was easily distracted, and aggravated, and as he looked out the window into the street he saw some children running down the hill from the new parking garages that had gone up where Shamus's bar used to be. "Stupid people. Stupid stupid. They run from store to store . . ."

"We're going to have dinner, now, Nicholas!" Mom said, and that was the end of whatever rant he was about to go on. If he didn't like the way she had spoken to him, he didn't show it. But I added, because I couldn't help it, "I thought it was just getting good, mom." No one laughed, of course, and I thought from how she looked at me that my mom might kill me.

32

SARAH MCKENNA-HURST

J ay and Bill went with my mom to prepare dinner. At my mom's request, Nicholas remained outside by himself.

Inside, my mom assigned tasks and in short order dinner was complete. We ate, and then had dessert. It was somewhere around ten o'clock, or later when we finished pie and coffee, but I couldn't be sure because there were no clocks in the house. At that point we went into the stuffy living area and sat on the couches. Gwen remained in the kitchen to clean up.

They began to talk again, but their talk had bored me. I leaned my head back on the cushion.

"Are you tired, honey?" mom asked.

"No."

"I have a room ready for you."

"No, I'm going home to sleep," I said.

"No, don't worry honey. I've been waiting for you to stay. Don't be silly."

I agreed. The men said goodnight, and mom brought me up the narrow staircase to a cramped room on the second floor with a small window looking on the mountains. When I saw the room I wanted to go home. It smelled of dust and age.

"I love the view from this room," mom said. "I know it's not your plush pillow top mattress but you can handle it."

She pulled back the bedding and handed me the television remote. I gave her a hug and then put of the PJs she gave me and climbed into bed. The mattress was worse than what prisoners slept on. I imagined a miner slept on it a hundred years ago, but I refrained from commenting. She sat down in a chair next to the door.

"Do you need anything else?"

"I'm fine mom."

She hugged me and squeezed me, "I love you," and left the room.

I turned on the television; its noise covered the noise that came up the stairs and helped to take my mind off the smell of old in the air. I eased into bed and rolled around before finding a comfortable position, which was not easy.

Sometime later, I awoke confused and unsure.

The television was off. I felt an immediate shock of insecurity. Who had done it? I should have gone home. On the nightstand nearest the door, on the opposite side of the bed from where I had left it, I found the controller and flicked on the television for light, which gave me a certain sense of relief, but I still didn't like that someone had come in and shut the television off; it felt invasive. As my eyes adjusted to the TV light, what really bothered me was that the chair by the door had been pulled up to the foot of the bed. I was sure that it hadn't been there before. And I was sure of something else as well: someone had watched me while I slept. I was aware of it then, and they were talking to me—babbling almost.

I took a deep breath and put my feet on the floor and left them there a moment, taunting my fear and whatever childish nightmare lay under the bed. I then stood and looked around the room.

The room looked dingy under the static light from the television; it was old, with a wood floor, two nightstands and a bureau with a television thrown on top of it. Mom had the room cleaned for me, and had done a good job, but there was still a layer of old and anti-quated on everything that could never be removed.

I reached to the table and turned on and old lamp. When the darkness was pushed back to the corners of the room, I walked to the bedroom door and out into the hallway looking for the bathroom, but I couldn't find one. I found only another dilapidated bedroom, and a sticky door that led up to the attic. When I pulled that door open a gust of foul, descended onto me like a falling avalanche. I shut the door quickly, but it wouldn't close, and I thought I heard a floor board creak above me and that was all I could take and I quickly backed away and headed for the stairs.

On the way down I heard the sound of a guitar and laughter out by the barn. I walked through the kitchen to the backdoor and saw the light on there. Curiosity compelled me, and I slipped on my shearling boots without socks and my coat and headed onto the shoveled path to the barn.

At the door to the barn I heard Nicolas laugh, and then my mother. Jay continued playing his folksy guitar. Beneath the guitar's low melody, Jay sang some repeated verse, which I couldn't make out. I reached out, opened the door, and entered. Jay sat to the right of the door by the wood stove. Nicolas sat behind him wearing only tight white underwear and a t-shirt, barefooted, with Gwen in his lap. Across from them, Bill sat beside my mom on a log bench. Her legs were draped over his waist, and she was wearing a red bathrobe and smoking a joint. The odd gravewood stood up behind them like an old time god.

"Please close the door. It is very cold outside," Nicolas said when he saw me.

The guitar stopped and Jay looked up. Bill watched, and my mom put the joint into the ashtray and walked toward me in a deliberate manner that had a theatricality which I attributed to the fact that she wasn't sober but trying to appear like she was. My eyes moved from Bill, who watched me hawkishly; to Jay, who stopped playing his tune but was still rhythmically stroking the strings as if he didn't know what else to do; to Nicolas, who now stood over the fire now and pushed the coals around with his poker grumbling to himself. The backs of his legs had big purple veins running this way and that, and I cried.

"It's okay honey," mom said slowly. The way cynical teachers speak to rambunctious children. She drew me in. I pulled away from her. Her eyes widened.

"This is disgusting mom."

"What, no it's okay honey. Nicolas spilled a glass of Whiskey in his lap . . ."

"I'm surprised that Gwen didn't lap it up for him, maybe you could've helped."

I barely uttered the word "helped" when she slapped me sharply across the cheek, but when she hit me, I wasn't sad, and I wasn't afraid. I was angry. I slapped her back across her face. She grabbed her cheek in total surprise. A tear came down her face and dangled on her chin before splashing to the floor. I had never hit either of my parents before, never even contemplated the reality of such a thing, and now that I had, I waited for a response; as if somehow the guiding force of the universe would step out of thin air and set things back the way they were supposed to be, but since my mom had violated her motherly contract, maybe the universe didn't care.

"You would hit your own mother; what kind of child are you?"

"You aren't my mother; you'd rather be in a cult than a family. Who are these people? And where's Smiley? He completes the circle. Is he in the shadows? The attic? This is what you left us for?"

"I didn't leave you . . ." but she held what she wanted to say. "Honey, just relax, there's nothing wrong," she said in the same tone as before.

She put her hands on my shoulders, but I pushed them away—I was just so mad. I was crying now and breathing fast.

"Please, Sarah, it's okay."

She put her hands on my back now because I hunched over to cry. "Don't worry honey, we'll go upstairs and go to be bed."

I felt cheated and lied to. I ran out the door. "You're a liar"

I ran onto the shoveled path between snow banks, but the path led back to the house, and so I climbed up the snow bank to get into the driveway. At the top, I slipped and fell down the other side. I stood up covered in snow and saw Nicolas's head peering over the snow bank.

"What is this?" Nicolas said. Jay watched through the barn window. Behind him, Bill held my mom whose head was down. I jumped through the snowdrifts on the lawn and through the banks at the side of the driveway and finally out into the road toward home. I was freezing cold as I ran down the street. Snow was in my boots and had worked its way up my pajama pant legs and onto the skin grafts above my knees.

When I reached home, I ran up the long set of wooden stairs that led to the front door and grabbed the doorknob, praying it was unlocked and that I didn't have to wake dad. It was, and I rushed inside and stood next to the fire that he kept perpetually stoked. I was happy for his eccentricities because they were predictable. The fire warmed me.

"Some entrance," dad said from the couch where he watched a muted television. I was startled because I didn't see him. "You didn't call," he said.

I nearly burst out crying when he switched on the light. He noticed that I had snow in my hair and I was wearing a coat over my pajamas. He jumped off the couch.

"Who did this to you?" he said, "Who, some boy, who is he. Tell me!"

But I couldn't say a word. I just fell into his chest and cried and cried. He held onto me tightly next to the stove. After a moment he pulled away from me to grab a chair from the kitchen that he carried beside the fire.

"Sit," he said. "Now, what happened?"

"I stayed at mom's."

"At Bill's?" he said.

"At Bill's. And I just got scared in the bed mom had me in, and I came downstairs and some guy was playing the guitar and another guy was in his underwear."

"What. What happened?"

"I just ran home. No dad, where are you going, don't go over there, you can't go over there."

"They can't be acting like freaks with you sleeping over. I know he saved you, but I've known Bill long enough to know he's a strange guy."

"Dad, nothing happened. I won't go there anymore, I don't want to, you don't need to, I think mom's upset enough."

He threw his coat back onto the rack and went and sat on the couch and thought for a moment. Beside him the television churned out today's news silently with subtitles at the bottom of the screen.

"Were you watching the news?" I asked.

"I was waiting for you. You didn't call. I was worried."

A report from earlier this afternoon came onto the television. Amy Shiller reported an avalanche that occurred down by Denver.

"Yes—Amy—what—can—you—tell—us?" the words scrolled across the screen.

Amy's hair was perfect, and she pushed her lips together as if to give the screen a kiss. She wore tight blue ski parka and thin gloves; she may as well have been a news bunny rather than a reporter, although she seemed to hold my dad's attention.

"Here at Loveland Pass Colorado, site of a large avalanche earlier killing two. Heroic rescuers are still looking in the snow and debris as we speak . . . "

I stopped reading. It was now two-thirty in the morning. The news then switched from a report in Oklahoma where a mother left her infant in a garbage can, to a report about a brave and nuanced a politician and then showed a car bomb explode. I wasn't really sure why dad bothered watching at all, and I was about to ask him when the phone rang.

"She's here, yeah, okay," and then he hung up the phone. "Your mother was checking on you."

33

SARAH MCKENNA-HURST

In the morning, dad was out in the driveway washing his truck like he loved to do on weekends. The sun was out and he plowed the snow out of the way so he could work. He hosed off the truck and quickly dried it to avoid forming icicles.

Mom pulled in the driveway and parked away from his truck. I was up in the big window above the driveway and saw her car. At first I didn't recognize her because she wasn't in the big BMW she usually drove. She was in a Toyota. I didn't recognize her until she got out and shouted. I went to the door at the top of the outside stairs and listened.

She was so angry, she was rabid. I had never seen her so vicious before.

"You finally got your way, Charles. No, you finally did; you turned my daughter against me."

"What are you talking about? You're delusional. I never even uttered a bad word against you."

"You've always worked against me and now you've won. Congratulations, you won, alright . . . ALRIGHT . . . ALRIGHT!" After she screamed and stood tall puffing her chest out. She looked like she would pounce on him. People driving by stopped to see what happened.

"You're crazy," dad said.

"Don't ever call me that . . .EVER!"

She bent down and threw a handful of gravel and ice against his truck. The little rocks pinged and scratched against the paint and my dad took a few steps forward like he was going to punch her.

"Daddy no," I shouted from the stairs, and mom looked up through the cracked door.

"That's all he cares about." She said

"Get out of here lunatic!"

She bent down at the edge of the driveway and picked up a soft-ball-sized rock lodged in the snow bank and hoisted it over her head.

"Don't throw that!"

She cocked her arms back and threw it through the rear window of his pick-up; his pride and joy. The window smashed and shards rattled around the bed of the truck and onto the driveway. He ran at her. I pushed the door open and ran down the stairs. When he reached her, he retracted his fist and bumped her instead. She fell to the ground, slushy from the mixture of snow and hose water, and screamed. He stood over her with a crazed look in his eye, and she got to her feet as quickly as an opponent in a death match.

"I'm not scared of you bully. You big bull, what, hit me, bully. HIT ME!"

"Forget your medication today?"

She pushed him backward and then spit in his direction and walked to her compact car. She turned when she reached the car. "You're lower than dirt. You poisoned my daughter. You poisoned her!"

"You need help," he said, "Really and truly you do."

"I have nothing. I have nothing. You took it from me. You taught her and she took it from me. I have nothing stoping me."

"Mom," I said.

"Don't hurt me with that word."

"Joanne, calm down. You're scaring Sarah."

She got into the car in such a rage that I thought she might die of a heart attack.

I felt sorry for her then, and embarrassed for how I had acted the previous night, but it wasn't my fault that I saw them doing whatever they were doing in Bill's barn. The whole thing was bizarre. I didn't know she was on the verge of mental breakdown.

I collapsed to the driveway in a heap and sobbed hopelessly for my mom. It was all lost, everything was different now, I just got used to the idea of not living with her and now I no longer knew her. Dad picked me up from the driveway, dusted me off and carried me back up the stairs into the house where he put me on the couch.

"I'm sorry that happened, and I'm sorry you had to see it," he said.

Then he was silent, and I think he was silent for weeks, even months afterward. Before that moment he stewed in anger, now he went beyond disappointed anger and into a realm of silence.

He began attending a local church regularly.

TODAY

34

CHARLES MCKENNA

I t was 4:30 in the afternoon and nearly dark. I finished work for the day and left my neighborhood in French Gulch. Driving my truck through the cluster of one hundred and forty, nearly all finished houses, I made a final visual survey of the neighborhood to ease my mind, but my mind was not easily calmed today. I shifted my thoughts from Joanne, who had been gone almost six years, to a shapeless fear of impending doom.

As I drove down, I passed Sheriff Hank, who had recently bought one of the small blue houses with a farmer's porch in front. He was at the end of his driveway digging out the snow pushed there by the plows. I slowed as I approached and rolled my window down.

"You headed down the Gold Pan?" he asked.

"Yup."

He jammed his shovel into a pile of slush at the end of his drive-way. "I'll see you when I'm done here . . . . I swear the guy that drives that plow pushes snow in my driveway 'cause he knows I'm a cop."

"I'll make him stop for a get-out-of-jail-free card," I said.

"Get arrested first, then we'll talk."

I pulled foreword several feet. "You must like digging."

Hank smiled. I drove away. I made a final stop to check and see if the storage trailer was locked before I left for the day. You never can tell what's going to get lost, stolen or even what's going to explode on a jobsite, and if you're the one responsible then you can never be too careful. Even after I pulled out of the neighborhood, I ran down a checklist of what could go wrong, who could get killed, and how much money it would cost.

I was badly in need of a drink now; probably more like three or four, and then I could unwind with idle chatter at the Gold Pan.

The day was beautiful, bright, and full of promise, and warm enough that the December snow melted and dripped water into the streets. The runoff made it difficult to keep my new truck clean, and I had just washed it so I veered around puddles as I drove to the bar.

Sarah made fun of me for how often I washed my truck. After Joanne left me, and then eventually Bill for the West Coast, I built a garage on my house with drains and a heated floor to wash the truck inside during the winter. The garage was expensive. Sarah thought I was senile. She showed friends the garage like it was an oddity. "Look. See what my father built so he can wash his truck in winter?" But Sarah wasn't seeing me now, not after the episode we had.

I arrived at the Gold Pan and parked by the curb on Main Street.

Andy was still the bartender, and when a man holds a social position like that in a small town for a long period of time, he tends to know the gossip.

"I hear your daughter's back in town?" He said when he saw me.

"Yup," I said, "She's living with a friend up in Blue River. Could I get a Budweiser?"

For beer selection, the Gold Pan also offered local homemade brews, but I stuck to the commercial crap because it was predictable and sometimes the local stuff made me sweat.

Andy poured me a glass from the tap. "She didn't want to live with dad, huh?"

Questions like that made me wonder why I still came here.

"Some kids actually *do* move out of their parent's house," I said. His parents owned the bar and he lived upstairs.

He seemed hurt. I kept talking. "She's taking a year off before she goes for an MBA. Said she always wanted to bum around and ski for a year, now she's got the money."

"That should be nice for her."

"We'll see. I'm glad to have her back. She's up with her boyfriend, Mike Reilly, he's semi local; moved here from New York when he was fourteen and jumped back and forth between here and the east; still sounds like an East Coaster though; you may know his parents."

"His mother's an architect and his dad drinks all day." Like a bartender, he knew all the relevant facts

"Well, he's a good kid anyway," I said.

"How old's Sarah now?"

"Twenty-four."

He poured himself a glass of water and draped the bar rag over his shoulder. "Bet that makes you feel like an old man."

"We get old, what the hell am I gonna' do, cry?"

"You could," he said. "How long has she been back now?"

"Off and on since the summer."

"You still haven't talked to her since Christmas?"

"We've talked."

"She just hasn't visited you?"

I took a sip of beer and again wondered why I came here.

Bill walked in and sat at the end of the bar. I nodded at him and he nodded back. He had stopped coming in here for a few years after he and Joanne got together. For that time, I came every single day, sometimes because I looked for fight, but mostly because it was my routine.

A few years ago, I think after Joanne left him, Bill resumed frequent trips to the Gold Pan for dinner and whatever else he got from it. I no longer cared though. He was old and lonely and so was I. Besides, what was I going to do? We weren't in high school, and I never believed he actively tried to take Joanne from me; it's just what happened. He was one of her fans. She had many. I am sure he was the most convenient man to move to.

Joanne left me because that's what she wanted to do; God knows she left him too. She was a runaway wife. She ran from me to Bill; then she ran from Bill to the West Coast.

Andy brought Bill a glass of water. He sipped it and looked over at me. I always felt him watch me.

"You got something to say Bill?" I was wound tight tonight.

He thought for a second. "No."

I pointed to my glass, and Andy refilled it. "I wonder what the hell you think when you sit over there?"

He rubbed his hand on the edge of the bar. "I often wonder the same thing."

Edzul walked in the front door. "You at it again?" He looked at me. "I thought you were cutting back?"

"I got to thinking about lawyers and lawsuits and losing everything. Then I talked to Bill and forgot which way was up."

"Don't talk to Bill then," Edzul said.

Bill looked away. He seemed angry. Edzul sat beside me. Andy wiped the bar in front of him. "You drinking?"

"Why else would I be here?"

The bell over the door rang again and RJ walked in. He worked up at French Gulch on the heating and air-conditioning systems. I introduced him to Edzul and after a few beers, Edzul reminisced.

"Hell," RJ said, "I'd a loved to a seen that. They really took over the town like-at?"

"I couldn't stop em'," Edzul said, "Some guys started beating on old Sheriff Dodge and Hank. I never saw anything like it. We got blamed for it. It was the time though. Things were crazy then, nobody had any sense, but that's the way it was."

"You aint lying," RJ said.

Edzul brought his glass down hard on the bar. "Dodge was a good man though. He was a Sheriff, but he was a good man."

"Who? The Sheriff they all beat?" RJ asked.

"Yeah. He died a few years ago. Great old man."

Bill stared at Edzul.

"I liked that old buzzard. And Bill went down and broke him out of jail and strung the guy up that put him there."

"That wasn't me."

"Oh, yeah?" Edzul inquired. "Dodge thought different. Told me a few years ago. Said you broke him out and caught Smiley coming back down the trail. You telling me the old man was lying?"

"What happened, happened."

"Some of the boys was gonna' get you after that. But Smiley wouldn't let 'em. He wouldn't let anything happen to you. Did you know that? Before he went to jail back then, he told everybody that you were marked to be somebody with him. Then he went real weird. He was always whacked out, but he got spooky after that night. He stopped talkin' for a while, but not really, 'cause some of the boys'd talk for him. I don't know what he was waitin' for, but people listened to him. I mean people you wouldn't expect: he had the mailman turned on and the bartender; people like that, but it only lasted a month, maybe two, and and then the MP's came and worked over the whole room just to get at him, and he sat there. It wasn't normal, and I never forget, but I also remember that he thought he was meant to be hung like he was, and that you shouldn't feel any heat over it. No one understood, but that's the way he wanted it." Edzul leaned back to see Bill more clearly behind my back. "I always wanted to know what happened that night?"

"I don't want to talk about it."

Edzul leaned forward and sipped his beer. "Dodge was a good man."

"Charles met his ex-wife that day," Andy said.

"I would have been better off staying home."

35

CHARLES MCKENNA

"I'm gonna' head out Charles." Edzul said, "I'll see you, alright."

"I think I got a little more time here before I head out."

"Good luck," Edzul said as he left.

"Well." Andy thought for a second. "You want another drink Charles?"

"No, I'm fine. I'm done drinking." I stood from the table and returned to my barstool. "Sarah thinks I should."

"I'm not trying to lose a customer," Andy said, "but if you're trying to quit, then maybe coming down here's not the best idea."

Bill sat in the corner like a stone. He may as well have collected moss. He had stayed hours longer than I ever remember him doing, and now that he had heard his name he said, "Cutting back?"

"I think I'm going to start. You're here a little late."

"Just biding my time. Sarah's in town this week?"

"She is, but I haven't seen her. Not since last winter. Well, you were here."

I turned back to the bar. Nearly a year had passed, and I was still stung by how angry Sarah was last winter.

"You still haven't talked to Sarah?" Bill said.

I didn't answer and thought over what she said to me last winter again and again:

———————

SHE WAS BACK from school on winter break and headed into her final semester. We planned to have dinner after I got off work. She cooked, but I forgot and went about my normal routine and drove down to the Gold Pan.

I was in the bar for an hour thinking about my parents. My mother died a few years ago, and my father followed shortly behind her. Their funerals were months apart back in Boston.

I asked for a beer. Andy gave me flat swill. I was a regular local; that swill was for tourists, not me. If I didn't say anything, he'd feed it to me all night.

"Your beer is flat," I said. My life was like déjà vu, and bad beer was a central figure.

"You're a whiny one tonight. I'll change it over master," Andy said.

I was reflective that night, and there was more than beer on my mind. "I'd be doing the same thing in Boston," I said.

"What about Boston."

"If I never moved here, I'd be sitting in some bar in Boston just like I'm sitting in a bar in Breckenridge. People are a little different that's all."

"I think your daughter's coming in."

Andy pointed to Sarah who walked in. She was angry and tired from the five-hour flight and hour and a half drive to Breckenridge in a rent-a-car. Her hair was slightly out of place and she had bags under her eyes. She moved with that assured grace that her mother had. The men turned to watch her as she walked in.

"I figured this is where you've been hiding."

What was I to say? It was months since I last saw her, and I forgot to go to my own home to eat dinner with her. I had no defense.

"Ah," I stumbled and she took the opportunity to pounce.

"Ah . . . that's what I'll put on your tombstone. I already have the design made, it's very nice. Bill might even carve it for you."

Bill looked up when she said that.

"You're mad at me. I . . ." But I was cut off.

"I would be if I thought it bothered you. I just wish you loved me more than booze. You're a drunk, and you lied to me. You've never lied to me before, but now you have and I don't know how I can forget that dad."

Everyone, especially Bill, paid deep attention to us. Their eyes were turned away but their ears were fixedly pointed toward us. One woman who sat with her poor boyfriend at a table was so intrigued that she completely ignored him and watched our fight.

"Can we leave here?" Sarah asked.

"I'll pay the tab."

"Hurry up, we were already supposed to have dinner an hour ago." She walked out the door and waited for me on the curb.

The door had barely closed behind me when Sarah started in:

"How can you forget about me? I haven't seen you all semester and you forget I'm cooking dinner and go to a bar instead dad, God," she had tears in her eyes and I felt bad. "Maybe I shouldn't expect so much."

"I'm sorry."

"You are sorry. The only thing you want is this stupid bar, and I hate it, I hate it. I thought I would come back here and have my dad, that's all, and I cooked dinner at the house and . . ." She choked up and then quickly pulled herself together. I walked toward her, but she pulled away from me.

"I've never forgotten you before."

"That's not the point, dad. You're drinking yourself to death. You don't even have a girlfriend, or girlfriends; I would at least think that was normal, you just work and drink. I think it's your major food source. I don't remember you like this."

Sarah had tears in her eyes. I could always blame her mother for the pain Sarah felt, but it was my fault now. I walked toward her. She pulled away from me again.

"Dad, I don't want to see you tonight. I don't want to see you any night that you go to this bar."

Her words stung—as I get old, the painful moments don't hurt so much at the point of impact as they ache and throb over time. But it hadn't been enough to get me away from the Gold Pan.

36

SARAH MCKENNA-HURST

H e forgot me. And it wasn't like we had some huge family that took care of itself with grandmothers and uncles. No—we were mostly alone. I was mostly alone. My mom was seldom if ever heard from. The last time she wrote me, she was in Oregon living with a group of people she said were all close friends (whatever that meant) but it didn't help me. She said she was attending the Newlife Temple, which was part of The Peoples Group, but who cared.

I came home from the airport while he was at work and cooked dinner and waited, but he forgot. When I realized he forgot me I actually felt nauseous. After I got over feeling sick and alone and depressed, I got angry and confronted him, but that didn't do anything. When I left him outside the bar, I felt so cold, almost cold in my bones. I couldn't shake the cold feelings I felt. I was just so sad. The feelings I had went deeper than words. The feelings I had were of irrelevance, and if you've ever actually felt irrelevant, then you know the sense of anguish where it almost feels like the sun stopped shining, but only for you, everyone else continues as usual in the daylight.

The night he forgot me, I was too alone to be alone. Main Street was full of bars, and the ski season had begun so they were packed.

There were enough bars in Breckenridge that choosing one was difficult. I settled on a place where the parking was close to the rear exit so that when I left, I didn't have far to walk.

Inside, the lights were low and people had a good time. I hovered by the door not really sure whether or not I wanted to remain but an icy wind sent me deeper.

The bartender asked me what I wanted, and I thought for a moment.

"I need something to calm me down," I said.

"We can accommodate," he said knowingly in a way that I disliked.

He made a drink I don't remember the name of. The first sip was like the raising of the white flag. I was not a drinker, and I hated that my dad drank.

The drink the bartender made actually tasted alright, aside from the alcohol flavor, and I took another sip as Tommy, a boy I knew from High School, came up next to me. He was happy to see me. In school he thought he was so cool. He was always with the right people, or at least they thought they were the right people. God, what happened to him now? I wonder if he knew. He looked the same; just a few years older with the same ski jacket he had senior year. He came with the gravity of the school cafeteria where he had thought he was a prince. In some ways, and on special occasions, the barroom probably had that feel for him. "Been a long time," he said.

And I remembered then that he had once made fun of my hands in high school. He didn't know I heard what he said.

He said, "Did you see how pizza hands tried to hide those things in her jacket?" and no one protested. That meant that I was pizza hands to them. I cried for a month after that. I wrote to my mom that week. I had not spoken to her since her explosion. I sent the letter to Bill's house and she responded immediately from California. I was surprised I got a reply from her at all. But it was colder than I would have liked. If anything it was distant.

"I saw your father last night," Tommy added, apparently under the impression this would help his cause. "We were at The Gold Pan drinking. He's over there a lot you know. He's a really cool old man. Where's he from originally?"

I sighed and said, "Boston."

"Never lost the accent?"

"I guess not."

He thought I was an easy target because of my hands. He even seemed to think that he was stooping when he hit on me. "I got some smoke if you want, or whatever," he said.

I'm surprised he couldn't read that I hated him, but then again, I wasn't that surprised. And when I was just about to tell him to get away from me, a man stepped in front of Tommy.

"You look like you're in pain," he said to me.

"Mike Reilly?" I said.

"Hey, I was talking to her."

"She doesn't seem to care."

I smiled. Tommy sank back into his beer without a fuss. He pretended not to know Mike. His loss was more than a momentary loss of face however; it was a true defeat the coming of which was predestined from high school. I assumed that his life would only degenerate from there, and he would soon take on the weather worn features of the native bar fly.

Mike asked me what I was drinking and then ordered me another and for himself a coke. "Just a coke," he said.

"I haven't seen you in years," I said.

"I know, it's actually weird, but when I came to Breck last week I wondered if I'd see you."

I took a sip of my drink. "That's a pretty weak line."

"Not a line."

"Other girls go for that kind of stuff?"

He sat in the stool Tommy vacated. "I haven't had much time for girls."

The bartender handed out drinks, and Mike took his coke and sipped it. His hair was black like coal and his eyes were so brown they almost matched his hair.

I've never known such a feeling as when I looked at him under the cheap lights of the bar. Not love, but something like it. Or maybe it was because I always felt that I knew him; I felt that way without any real reason, but that didn't matter because I'd felt it since high school.

And how could it have been love or something like it? It sounded so stupid. I disliked the notion of love at first sight because it was so much like what dad used to tell mom. He loved her the instant they met. He thought they were meant to be together. He believed their union, despite mom's disbelief, was divinely inspired; as if their relationship were a sign, or whatever is implied in divine inspiration or, like dad called it, a providential arrangement, which mom always hated to hear, but he said it anyway.

"It does happen," dad said. But could it be true? The question that was more painful for me was, if it were true, and Mike and I were somehow *arranged* to be in love, then what if we were *arranged* to be broken apart as well? Like mom and dad were. I don't think I could handle that pain.

The booze must have been too much for me; all of this was too much for me. I couldn't love Mike because I didn't know him. I wanted to go home now.

"I want to leave," I said.

"Can I walk you to your car?"

I thought a moment for suspense. "Of course you can."

My heart beat rapidly, and I wanted him to walk me down the aisle. I felt disgusting. I would not drink again. I'd be pregnant in a year if I did.

He walked me to my car with his hand at my back. The parking lot was crusted with snow. I opened my car door and slipped on the ice. Mike caught me and took my keys away.

"Let me drive you to your door."

"No, really, I don't need you to."

He held my hand. "Please. You're in no shape to drive, and you really can't afford to get arrested."

"It was the ice."

"I will drive."

I pulled away from him. "I live close. I'll walk home then."

"I'll walk with you, let me walk with you, I would really like to."

I cried.

"Are you all right? What's wrong?" he said.

"It's not you. This is so stupid. I don't have anywhere to go."

"Doesn't your father live in town?"

"I just came back from school today, and we fought, and now I don't want to go home, I can't really. I was going to go to a hotel or something. I'm sorry. This is really stupid."

"Don't be," he said, "There's no problem, there are plenty of places to stay. We'll just find you a room on Main Street, something nice, you don't need to worry. I'll pay for it."

"No, no, I have plenty of money, you don't need to pay for it."

"I want to."

"That's alright Mike, really."

We walked up Main Street. Tourists were everywhere and many were dunk. A man with a ten-gallon hat smiled at me, and a woman with bad shoes and teeth scowled at me.

Mike saw her and laughed. "Women are vicious," he said.

"Like men are better."

"We fight and it's usually over. Girls fight and there's a life long death grudge."

"I didn't even know that woman. I don't know why she looked at me like that."

"She hates beautiful women. She probably sits at home shouting terrible things at pretty girls on TV."

"You're flirting."

He stepped back. "It was an accident."

"That's no way to win my heart."

"I didn't mean it was an accident like I don't want to flirt with you."

"So you are flirting with me, or you want to, but you haven't tried yet?"

He puffed his chest out. "You're beautiful. Is that deliberate enough?"

"Very."

We stood in the street in front of the hotel.

"Are we having a moment?" I said, "Because the hotel is right there, and I wouldn't want to interrupt it."

"I think you just did."

"Oh, silly me."

We walked inside the hotel. It was a big place; the lobby was made to look like a log cabin with rustic furniture and antlers on the chandeliers. When I finished at the desk, I walked to Mike who sat on a sofa by a large fieldstone fireplace in the lobby.

"Thanks for everything, but I think I'm going to bed now, it's kind of been a rough night."

"Have you lived here your whole life?"

"I have," I hesitated for a moment and wondered whether I should sit and talk or rush away to bed. I decided to stay. The atmosphere in the lobby was quaint, comfortable and romantic, and the attraction I had to Mike was magnetic and powerful. He looked into the fire, and I sat and filled him in on all the pieces of my life that he had missed so far. I must have babbled, but I swear that he cared.

" . . . My dad moved here in the seventies and met my mom and I came along in '81. They divorced though, a long time ago, and now she lives in Oregon, I think. She's part of some cult or something out there. Well, not really, who knows what she's doing; by now who knows?"

"My father is a little like that, but his problem isn't joining cults unless you call AA a cult."

He stopped talking and stared at me, "You all right?" He asked. "You keep looking away."

I had been looking away because a thought had struck me.

"No. I mean, my mom and I fought a few months ago."

"About what?"

"She told me something I didn't want to hear."

"What did she say?"

"It doesn't matter."

"It shouldn't bother you then."

"It matters, but not like she wants it to. I just wish my dad wouldn't drink though."

"Was it about him?"

"Let it go."

We got quiet. Then I asked him why he left junior year, and he told me he got accepted to some prep school in Connecticut, and after that he went to the Marines and to college, but he didn't want to talk about himself. It wasn't that he had anything to hide; he was just more interested in me.

At one point I yawned and leaned my head back.

Mike leaned forward. "I didn't mean to keep you up. I know you wanted to sleep hours ago."

"Don't worry, I'm happy we talked."

I went up to my room to sleep, but before I went, he kissed my cheek. I kissed his lips, and then I went to bed.

37

CHARLES MCKENNA

"Joanne," I said.

"What," Andy said.

"Bill?" I said, and Bill turned to me, "I always wanted to know why Joanne left you. I mean, I know why she left me, but why did she leave you?"

"Charles it's late," Andy said.

"It is late; I've been curious about this for years. You just never stayed late enough for me to remember to ask you."

"She left me because she moved on, I was a stopover."

"A facilitator," I said.

"If you want to call it that."

"Well, you were good at your job."

"Here Charles, have a beer," Andy said.

"I told you earlier, I'm not drinking anymore." I knocked the glass over and it spilled on the bar.

"You're really not going to drink anymore?" Andy said. He put a bowl of peanuts in front of me and mopped up the bar with a towel.

Bill watched me. He had never stayed this late before. He watched me put the peanuts in my mouth.

"Get Bill some peanuts too, he looks hungry."

"No thanks. I'm fine."

Andy walked away to do something in the kitchen.

I don't know where Sarah stayed the night she yelled at me. She didn't come home, and I didn't see her again. I haven't seen her since, but she didn't disappear completely like Joanne had. Sarah went back to New York City for her final semester. She called and wrote letters, but our relationship was no longer the same, it was strained. Our relationship was different since she was accepted to college back in New York.

When she first went off to college, I gave her a sizeable bank account and access to funds in her name. I knew she was responsible and wouldn't squander the money. She was even wise enough to invest some for profit. This summer she profited enough to travel around the country with her boyfriend Mike Reilly. Now that her travels were over, they moved into a place up valley from me. Still, after our fight, she did not bother to come by and see me.

When she wrote that she was dating Mike and that Mike was a Marine, I told her to think twice about dating a man who had time to serve in the military during an actual war. I thought he was honorable to join when the Towers fell, but I worried for Sarah if she lost him. My worries fell on deaf ears. She never replied to my letter. I just didn't want to see her hurt, but maybe that was foolish of me. She was an adult and had every right to be hurt.

RJ made a reappearance.

"I figured you'd still be here drinkin'," he said to me.

"I quit drinking."

"Could have fooled me."

"I quit about an hour ago."

"I just came in to say goodbye to ya'. Tomorrow, boss." I nodded and he left.

"On that note," I said, "I'm heading out too."

"Be careful," Andy said.

Bill nodded and looked back at the bar. Why did he stay so late? I waved goodbye to Andy and walked to my truck.

Outside the air was cold. I saw my breath in the moonlight. The snow was piled high between the curb and sidewalk, and the mountains were large and bright with a strange purple luminescence. Inside my truck, the leather seat creaked from the cold as I sat. I turned the key and fired the engine and the cabin lit up with digital readouts. The monitor in the middle of the dashboard booted up and showed my position on GPS. When I backed the truck up, the monitor showed what was behind me, just in case I couldn't see in my mirror. On Main Street, the first vehicle I passed was a parked Breckenridge police Land Cruiser. I waved to the policeman inside, and he waved back. He seemed vaguely familiar, but before I could remember his name, I was home.

I parked in my driveway because I had my motorcycle in the middle of the garage floor to work on it. I didn't feel like moving the bike tonight. I was sober now. A car drove by on the street, and I focused on it. My daughter was in the passenger seat lit by the green glow of the car's instrument panel. That Marine from the east drove. He was taking her somewhere. I made eye contact for a moment and then he broke it, Sarah didn't notice me at all. She didn't even look in my direction, the direction of her home. The car moved out of sight. It was as if I didn't exist.

I walked into my kitchen and slammed my keys on the table. My house was dark but I didn't bother turning the lights on and so I stood in the kitchen and looked at the mountains. I remembered when Sarah still loved me; I remembered when Joanne was still around. I was all alone now, and looked up at my ceiling and asked God questions. I needed a rope, something to pull myself out of this with.

I looked at my cell phone on the table. The ringer was off, and there was a message listed on the front screen that diverted my attention for a moment. "New Message." The phone said when I tapped the voicemail icon. "Message received at Five-O-Two P-M."

I looked at my watch and saw that it was after midnight.

The message began with static. Then a female voice cleared. Someone hesitated.

Joanne spoke. I didn't know what to make of it. My stomach knotted, and I grabbed a stool from the kitchen and sat.

"I've been thinking of you. I know I ruined everything, but I was under influences at the time, and I feel free now. I want to apologize to you in person. I want to see Sarah as well and apologize to her. I would just feel so much better inside if I could apologize to you face to face, but if you're going to ignore me then I have to use the phone. Maybe you haven't ignored me, did you receive my letter?"

What letter? When we first parted, I always expected she would resurface but after years and years my hope subsided.

Her message continued:

"Well if you didn't get my letter, then you will soon because I sent you one. It talks about all the things I never said because I was too emotionally backed up to know. I'm so sorry Charles, I'm so sorry about everything, about Sarah and about us, about how I left. I can't apologize for what I've done, and I can't take it back. I would if I could. I'm sorry."

She didn't sound like herself: she apologized. What a rotten, rotten woman. I wished her message fell on deaf ears. The message continued and I tried to deaden myself to her, but I couldn't. I felt low, but I also felt that my prayer had been answered, and Joanne was the rope I could pull myself from this funk with. Not that we would be together—that would be impossible—but I could know closure and maybe suture my wound.

"I know you're mad at me. I would be too if roles were reversed, but please, hear me out. Just listen. I wish I could do this in person, I wish that you were here right now or that I was there, and that I could just talk to you like we used to talk."

It seemed she was acting. Every pause and word sounded rehearsed; although, apologizing would have been so foreign to her that she would have needed practice. I listened to the rest of the message. It ended with her phone number, and when I heard it, I grabbed a pen and pad.

After I took the number, I struggled over whether I should call her or not. Then I remembered that she sent a letter. I just needed to check my P.O. Box, as the mail didn't come to my house, which I had twenty-four hour access to.

I decided to go to the Post Office which just a few blocks over. What else was I going to do? I should at least hear her out?

I should have erased her message. It was insane like everything else connected with her, but her voice was like air for my asphyxiation.

I left my house and drove over to the brick building that housed a liquor store and Post Office.

I used my key and walked in through the glass doors. The Post Office portion of the building was closed and partitioned off with a steel cage that hung from the ceiling. I walked passed the cage and around a concrete-block wall behind which were boxes in rows. On the opposite wall there was a long desk, and trash barrels where you could sort your mail.

The fluorescents hummed a dull tune of dim purplish light, which reflected strangely off the aluminum P.O. boxes and gave me the childish sense that I was in a horror novel.

I opened my box and searched the mail, but found nothing from Joanne. I searched the stack again and found a letter marked with my wife's name and return address in Oregon. I felt youthful when I saw it and grasped the letter in my hands and tore it open and read it under the dim light. When I finished, I walked to my truck and re-read the letter.

Charles,

FOR YEARS I tried to put you out of my head, but I can't. The memory of you always sneaks back. I move from place to place, and still the memory of how I left follows me. I was influenced and misguided then, and I hurt for how we ended. It has taken me all this time to learn how important you were, but now that I have, I am consumed. I know you don't want to hear from me, and I understand. I am sorry. I love you. I want to see you again. I need to see you, if it's only just once.

WITH LOVE

. . .

Joanne

I was angry that it took her so long to realize what she did and how she was influenced.

When I got home, I read the letter again and listened to the message to compare the two. It was hard not to call her right away. I didn't want her to think I was desperate, and so I sat down and tried to watch TV to forget, but I couldn't forget her, the thought of her consumed my mind. God, I still loved her like the day I met her. I hated her.

I heard a truck out in the street. The tires crunched the gravel. I looked out the window, and brake lights headed away, and just then my phone rang.

"Hello."

"Hi."

I knew her voice.

"It's me," she said.

"I know."

"How are you?"

"Alive." I said.

We passed the pleasantries and talked about the weather, and where she was living, and how she was doing, and about Sarah, and then she said,

"I've been thinking about you Charles. I had to call. I didn't want to for a while. I was afraid you would reject me. I'm sorry about what I did to you, I really am. You are a good man. You were right. I was a mess. I run it all through my head, and I know how you must feel; I just want to see you again. I have wanted to see you for so long now."

"I wasn't expecting that," I said.

"I know. I'm sorry and if you don't want to see me, I understand."

"It's hard to forget someone like that."

"No, it's more than that. It's just, I want to be with you, I don't know, maybe it's silly but I really want to be near you again. I miss how sweet you are. I miss it. I didn't know that it was important."

"That what was important?"

"How good you are. But it's more than that: you're stable. With the way we divorced, I understand that you never want to see me again, I really can understand that, but it took me all this time to see what was important in life and escape some influences. Part of me believes I had to be away from you to realize just how important you are. I never realized how much you did for me on a spiritual level. I don't know that I'm looking for a reconciliation, I don't know what I'm looking for at all, but I know that I have to see you again before I die, if it's just one more time, I need to see your eyes. It must sound so silly after six years."

"I understand." Chances were she was out of her mind, but I had to give her the benefit of the doubt. All of those years as family did account for something.

"You wouldn't mind seeing me? Oh. It makes me so happy that you would say that."

"I was thinking about you tonight."

"Oh really. That's so weird. Somehow I knew that you'd be awake. I'm glad you answered. I can come out there you know. I can get a flight for pretty cheap and be there next week if you don't mind."

"That fast?"

"I know, I'm sorry." It wasn't in her nature to apologize and I wondered what happened to humble her.

"I've been thinking about you and kind of fantasizing," she went on, "And I've been checking the flights out there. It sounds silly I know, and I had no way at all to know you'd agree. I can also get a flight Wednesday and stay at a hotel if that's not too soon."

"In two days?"

"I really want to get there. If I didn't get in touch with you, I was going to just come and surprise you. I know it sounds crazy. And I'm not saying we should get back together, but I just have to see you. You're all I think about now. You embody so many things for me. Just once more is all I need."

"You really do want to see me?"

"You have no idea."

A voice inside me wanted to reject her, but that voice was low now.

"I just have to buy the tickets and check to see if the flight still has seats. You're for sure you want to do this because I don't want to come if you don't want me too?" she said.

"Just tell me when and where."

"You'll get me?"

"I will."

We arranged it all and then hung up. I walked to the faucet and poured a glass of water and for a moment watched the ripples formed by my shaking hand. I hadn't felt alive in years, and now I felt alive because of the woman that caused me so much pain— because of the woman who divorced me. I felt alive again for the first time in years because of Joanne.

38

SARAH MCKENNA-HURST

"We should have stopped and said something to your father," Mike said

"It's nearly midnight. I don't know . . . it's weird."

"Still, he is your father, and he saw you in the car, I know he did."

"Stop, he didn't see me in the car. I'll go see him tomorrow. I've been meaning to see him anyway. I just, I don't know, it's hard, I'm afraid of him a little. Not that he hits me, but he spiraled down low and he's depressing. It's scary for me to see him like that. He's been that way ever since my mom left."

"She left you too."

"It hurt him more."

Mike steered the car through the intersection where Main Street ends and becomes Highway Nine. We drove south out of Breckenridge toward the small town of Blue River, just a few miles away. Tonight the road was well lit by the moon, and we wound our way through the alpine forest toward home in a small valley off the road. It was a single story, and consisted of a kitchen, a large family area, a dinning area, two bedrooms and a bath. The approach to the house wound through a swamp created by a beaver dam, and then through a grove of aspens and finally ended in an open pasture surrounded by naked peaks and blocked in by a sheer cliff.

Our house was low and covered by snow. The walls were rough-hewn and irregular, and tanned deep brown. By the peak, the black spout of a chimney pipe stood above all else, and on the ground the piles of snow that slid off the green aluminum roof stood nearly six feet tall. The driveway ended beneath a carport beside which a pile of split wood for the stove was piled.

Traveling was fun but quickly lost its allure, and I wanted to settle down, at least for the rest of the winter and relax before I went for my MBA. I'd like to see the Mediterranean in the springtime, Rome or North Africa, and we had plans to do all that, but for the time being I wanted to remain where we were. No more planes, no more long drives, and no more restless nights in unfamiliar hotel beds. Mike didn't travel well. He got cranky in airports and in new places. The Marines pushed him a lot, and I think he tried to avoid that feeling whenever he wasn't wearing the uniform. We decided that we wouldn't travel any more. For the winter we would remain nestled in our mountains until the spring came and through the summer and then back to New York for school.

I thought of dad as Mike parked our car. Mike brought an armload of wood with him, and after he stoked the stove he turned it down for the night. We got dressed for bed. I didn't want him to see without my long pajamas, and I made him go into the bathroom. He went reluctantly. "I think you're beautiful," he said, "And nothing I see will change my opinion."

"Just leave me alone about it Mike."

He remained in the bathroom. I heard the faucet, and then he said, "You should go see your dad."

"I'll call him in the morning."

Mike was brushing his teeth and spit in the sink. "You guys are weird. I don't know why you don't go and see him."

"He hasn't called me in a while either, you know."

"Both of you are playing."

We went to sleep without saying another word. Mike snored and I slept terribly.

In the morning my phone rang and the caller ID said: daddy.

"It's my dad," I said as I held the phone up.

"I told you he saw us last night." Mike stood to get dressed on the other side of the bed. "Well, answer it!" He said.

"Hi dad. I was going to call you today so we could have dinner. I know we haven't seen each other yet."

"That's fine," he said. "Don't worry; you just needed space. But I called because I have some news you need to hear."

For some reason when he said that my hair stood and I felt a burst of anxiety. "What?"

"Your mother called me. She's coming here Wednesday."

"But that's tomorrow, what happened. I thought you hated each other. I thought she would never come here to see you. I mean, why would she, it's been so long and the way she left? Dad, do you want to see her?"

"I don't know. She's coming anyway."

"I don't want to see her. It's too strange."

"I think you should."

"I don't think I will."

"I thought you guys talked to each other a lot?"

"She hasn't spoken to me since I was accepted to business school when she told me. . ."

"What?"

"I don't want to see her."

"I think you should." He repeated.

I hung up the phone.

"Why did you do that?" Mike said.

"My mom is coming here tomorrow and *he* wants me to see her, to see them together."

"You're going to run from her? You can't run."

"I'm not running."

The phone rang. Again it showed the word "daddy", and now instead of anger a deep sinking feeling overcame me. I pushed the talk button on the cell-phone, but I didn't say hello. My dad talked. "Sarah. You should be angry, but you should also see her."

"It's so sudden dad. It's just insane. Who knows what she's been doing."

Mike walked over and sat beside me on the bed and rubbed my back. I pushed him away, and he got up and did push ups on his fists.

"What's wrong with her dad? She hasn't talked to you in years, and she stopped talking to me. Why now, why? She just can't do this and have her way and do whatever she wants to. It just . . . It has something to do with The Peoples Group. Some of them got busted for sex trafficking and forced labor. That's slavery. They're crazy, and she's probably the craziest one!"

"I know. I even heard they were trafficking people over the border for sex slavery. But I can't imagine she would ever have been involved in that. I've known her since the 70s. If she says she's not with them anymore I've got to believe her."

"She needs money then."

"I'd be willing to bet she doesn't, she came into a small fortune when her parents died."

"I never saw any of it."

"I think she was embarrassed by it."

"This whole thing is weird."

Dad cleared his throat. "When I spoke with her last night, I was angry. I didn't know what to feel. She said she had a plane ticket, and I told her I'd pick her up. She wants to make amends. That's all. When you break things, it always comes back to you, and when you get old the pain you brought wears on you."

"I doubt that's true for her."

"I owe her at least this much, Sarah."

"You don't owe her anything."

"I was married to her for two decades."

"All the more reason to be mad at her dad."

"Sarah. I'm going to see her. If you don't want to, no one can make you. But you should at least have dinner with her. We don't get to pick our parents, but they're still out parents."

"Oh, why do you have to be so sensible. Fine," I said. Mike smiled from across the room and went back to push ups.

"Her flight arrives at one-thirty. I'm going to pick her up. We should be back up here by three-thirty. You want to meet us at the house?"

"Come to my place? I'll cook an early supper. I'll have it ready for four-thirty."

"That'll be good Sarah."

"Wait." I felt so sad.

"What?" He nearly seemed happy.

Mike walked away and I said, "I love you, dad. You . . . She's not worth picking up."

"Don't say that."

"She . . . She's not even worth your consideration, dad. I'm sorry. She never deserved you."

"Well, that's not how I feel."

"No. She never, ever deserved to even walk on the same ground with you dad. I love you."

"I love you, too."

"You're my father, she's just a surrogate."

"Sarah, don't be so harsh."

"I'll be nice to her if you want me too, dad, at least until she hurts you, and then I'll stop pretending."

"She wouldn't come here for that."

"Maybe."

When I put the phone down Mike said, "You're really going to see her? How long has it been?"

"Not long enough."

Outside the wind blew snow around in swirls and the cliffs sparkled from the frozen waterfall that clung to the rock face. In the summer the waterfall was a trickle, but in winter, the freezing started with a few drips and grew into a massive downward flow of ice that broke off pieces of the rocks it clung to and shattered trees in the valley below.

39

CHARLES MCKENNA

J oanne's flight didn't arrive until one-thirty in the afternoon, but I couldn't sleep. I woke at 4:00 am and tried to go back to sleep, but by 5:00 I had taken a shower, and by 6:30 I was on the road to I-70 headed east for Joanne. Sitting around waiting to leave wasn't an option. I hadn't been to Denver in months, and I needed to do some shopping. I needed a new TV.

It was dark when I reached I-70, but the distant horizon was red and I soon drove into the rising sun. This morning had the feeling of limitless beauty and cruelty. Over the next hilltop was either the most spectacular valley or broken and frozen death. Every morning in the Rockies had this feeling: the feeling of endless promise and sudden death simultaneously—maybe that's what beauty is.

A few years ago, a woman came to town with her husband to ski, but his heart couldn't handle the extra stress of high altitude, and he died on the side of a ski trail, his face contorted into a macabre expression of agony. His sad widow returned a few years later to face the fear she built up regarding the Mountains. At a bar on the second night of her four-day trip, she said to me after a few glasses of wine and several cigarettes:

"I knew he was going to die that morning," she paused and

looked into her wine, "I don't know why I knew. There was a feeling all that week. I remember looking at him waiting in line for the chair lift and thinking 'this will be the last time I see him.' It was like the mountains needed a sacrifice."

I know the feeling she described. I had come to know the face of an unforgiving God in the Rockies.

I descended toward Denver, headed perfectly east, and drove into the Eisenhower Tunnel. It had been bored straight through a granite mountain and extended from the western side of the Continental Divide to the eastern. After the tunnel, the mountains opened; to my right ran the old scenic route that climbed over snowy Loveland Pass and back to Breckenridge.

After the tunnel, I caught my first glimpse of the city and the endless great plains. They were golden brown and snowless, and the massive half sun loomed on the horizon like a bright two-dimensional theatre prop.

I drove into the sun for half an hour and more. Denver was close. On my left was a long barbed wire fence that enclosed a grassy hillside and a sign that read "Buffalo Bill's Ranch". Some large crows stood on top of the sign, and a herd of buffalo stood by the roadside. I continued on past the herd that had been imported from the Bronx Zoo when buffalo were nearly exterminated in the West.

Traffic picked up as I reached the city. Cars swarmed around my truck, and we slowed and slowed until we stopped. I took the first exit.

The retail stores were open and ready to serve customers. GPS directed me to an electronics store. I browsed for a while and then bought a massive TV, on sale, of course.

"You want it in the bed," the guy who brought it to my truck asked.

"No. It may snow, I want it in the backseat."

"It won't fit."

"It will."

After a few minutes, they got the TV into the back seat like I said they could do.

"Here." I tipped them and then put a seatbelt around the TV. I left the store parking lot and drove over and filled my tank so I didn't have to bother later when I picked up Joanne. The truck took nearly $120 to fill.

After a quick bite to eat, I headed back to I-70. Traffic dissipated and I had smooth sailing all the way through the prairie to the airport, which was a large white tent with several peaks meant to mirror the mountains. I had time this morning and drove out of my way to compare the tent's imitation mountain peaks against the real ones in the west. The place looked like a circus, and I wondered why they couldn't just make normal buildings anymore.

I then parked in the lot as close to the big top as I could get and entered the building trying to understand the architecture. I became even more perplexed as I passed a demented mural of a scimitar wielding storm trooper wearing a gas mask holding an AK-47 towering over two shattered buildings beneath a rainbow alongside other peculiar figure. I was beyond confused. The mural prepared me for what came next, a security station where a fat, poorly shaven guard with an ill fitted brown uniform eyed me as though I were a terrorist. Throngs of people, young and old, ran back and forth on the floor of the airport, and he eyed every one of us with a disgust that only comes when you hate yourself.

Every style of human life walked about the airport. There were so many people that I felt dizzy. I looked for a bar.

40

CHARLES MCKENNA

I set myself up in the bar nearest the baggage claim and positioned my seat so that I could see Joanne when she walked out of the subway that came from her terminal. The bartender cleaned the counter around me.

"You drinkin'?" he asked.

"No," I said, "How about a root beer?"

The root beer would calm me down. A television was on. The sound was low. It murmured. Wednesday morning news coverage is normally light and fluffy. This morning it was not. The coverage showed people moving about in city streets in a panic, it looked like New York or maybe Washington. Out of the hum of low volume, I picked up screams and the panicked cadence of the reporter reporting. But I couldn't tell what tragic event had happened or exactly where, and I passed it out of my mind.

The bartender refilled my root beer without asking. Then he leaned against the mirror behind the bar. He wanted to say something. A white towel hung low out of the back pocket of his black slacks. His knuckles were scarred, and he twiddled his thumbs for a moment and watched me. I haven't met many tongue-tied bartenders. He was looking at me and wanted something.

"You mind if I change the channel?" he said.

"No."

He changed the channel to a twenty-four hour sports station. Someone just won a game where a ball is chased and thrown and points are scored. I had liked to play football once, but rooting for other men wasn't my thing.

A flood of people suddenly came through the doorway where the train from the terminals unloaded. I left the bar. People walked off this way and that beneath the big top, and I looked for Joanne. As the crowd thinned, a very large woman walked up with bags in every direction, and behind her, as skinny as a rail with stringy gray hair cropped to the ears, was Joanne. She didn't recognize me at first and then she did.

"Hi," she said. "Hi, wow, you've changed. No, but I like it, I do." She turned and surveyed the airport as though she waited for someone else. I was confused. Then she turned back to me.

"Are you happy I came?" she asked.

"Of course," I said, "It's just a bit strange."

"I know, I know."

Her hair was longer than short, badly cut and gray, while her face was deeply wrinkled from worry or overexposure, and she wore a flowing purple skirt that hung to her socks and sandals. She also had a bleached hemp bracelet that I noticed only when it rubbed against my neck and nearly cut me while she hugged me. It felt like she ground it into me.

"Ow."

"Oh I'm sorry," she said. "My bracelet left a mark."

There was a moment of awkwardness where neither of us knew what to do and we stood in the center of the moving mass together but separate and alone in the world. A man with a red security badge in a baggage cart blew his horn and waved us out of his way. Joanne moved far out to the side, but I stood still and let him go around me. There was no real reason for him to be blowing his horn the way he was other than to exercise the little power he had in the airport. On his way past, he eyed me, and I saw tags on the luggage behind him marked with the names of airports all over the world. All the international baggage landed here and needed to be sorted. Apparently there was a problem down below with the handling system and the airports inner workings had spilled onto the surface level. Some people were frantic and excited, and the lines coiled back out of the gates. All the airport employees were angry, and the people were anxious about getting to their final destination, but were being held up for reasons I did not know at the time.

"You look good," Joanne said to me.

She hugged me again and kissed my cheek, and then she looked in my eyes. I thought she would say she loved me. "Can we get out of here," she said, "I'm really eager to get to the mountains as fast as possible."

"Yeah, of course."

"Where are you parked?" she said.

"You don't have any luggage?"

"No."

"Just that handbag?"

"That's all I need. I'm not staying long."

I told her where I parked, and she sped off in the direction I pointed. Years ago, when we were together, she was often annoyed by how fast I walked. She used to ask if I was in a race with myself. "We live all the way up here, this isn't the big city, there's no need to run."

Now, she ran out in front of me and looked back from time to time to see if I still followed her. When I increased my pace, she did the same, and I was always a step behind. It bothered me, but for the moment I held my tongue. I didn't want to get angry yet.

"I really want to get out of here. This place is a zoo. I can't believe there are so many people here now, it's almost like the coasts vomited their unwanteds into the middle of the country," she looked over her shoulder at me.

Her hair had been cut unevenly in the back, and she placed a weathered green baseball hat on her head before we went out under the sun. I continued following. We walked into a jumble of asphalt and New Jersey barriers, and I yelled at her to point her in the right direction. "No, that garage!"

She walked fast in the direction I pointed and weaved through traffic and then didn't bother to wait for me to cross the street until she entered the garage. She only turned back when she realized that she didn't know where my truck was. She stopped like a statue at the head of the crosswalk, irritated, waiting for me to catch up.

Instead of yelling at her, I said, "I like that color on you, it's a deep purple."

"Thank you, the dye comes from crushed snails in the Mediterranean, it's ancient. I have a friend that spent some time there. The blue on the collar and at the bottom is also taken from the same snail. It's for special occasions."

"Ceremonial?" I said, half joking.

"You could say that."

She turned quickly and walked off in the direction I pointed. An old SUV growled past us in the garage and spewed dark smoke from the tailpipe. Joanne cursed the man driving.

While she mumbled angry curses we arrived at my truck.

"You got a new one?" she said.

"You broke the window on the old truck."

"Couldn't get it fixed?"

"I didn't like that truck anymore. I like this one better. There's more room in the back seat and a screen in the dashboard. I supposedly have a TV tuner but I've never used it. This is actually my second truck since the one with the broken window, I tried a Japanese truck for a while, but I got sick of it."

"You certainly have no shortage of toys."

I opened the back door for her to put her bag in. I forgot about the huge television on the seat strapped in with seat belts.

"You're full of surprises, Charles," she said. "Funny that you don't wear your own seatbelt, but your TV certainly does."

"I was always responsible."

She pushed her handbag in around the television box and then closed the door.

"Can we go? I really can't stand this garage anymore. The plane and the airport, it's too much."

"Yeah, we can go, just relax!"

I pulled out onto the highway.

"Don't go straight, take that exit, it's at least ten minutes faster," she said.

"I like the view of the mountains from this direction."

She turned to me. "That's ten minutes."

I drove on passed the exit she pointed to. She was angry.

"Are you in a hurry?" I asked.

"I just want to get there, I want to get out of this city, it's such a desert of sprawling houses. They're all so awful. It won't matter soon anyway . . ." But she trailed off and looked silently out the window. For the next few minutes she shook her right leg up and down like an overly active teenage boy. I expected to see her bite her nails, but they were so short there was nothing left to bite. She probably finished biting them on the airplane.

"Is that GPS?" she asked.

"Yeah."

I watched her. She pushed the screen on the dashboard until a map came up that showed our current location moving through the mountains. "There are so many roads now. They're like black veins. I can't believe how quickly this place changed."

"It was the fastest growing state in the country for a while."

"It used to be special to me."

"It's still special to me," I said.

"Sarah cooked us dinner." I said, but she didn't respond. I then asked, "How come you stopped talking to Sarah?"

"She said that?"

"She said that when she got into business school you stopped talking to her."

"I love my daughter Charles, more than you could ever know . . ." She let her sentence hang and then die.

"She has a serious boyfriend now," I said. "Do you remember Mike Reilly?"

"No."

"When she was in the hospital it was the boy she talked about."

"I *do* remember that boy, but I thought he moved."

"He's back. I don't know the whole story. He's a Marine."

"A Marine. I've never understood that. She tries to hurt me with the things she does," Joanne said and fidgeted with the radio.

"Not everything she does is to hurt you."

"You're just as oblivious as the day I left."

"Maybe this wasn't such a good idea."

"I get to see my daughter. If it's too much for you to handle, I'll rent a car. Just drop me at my hotel. Don't put that angry face on, it doesn't work on me anymore."

We were out of the foothills now and climbing steadily into the mountains on I-70. Despite the company, the drive was beautiful. The distance between Denver and Breckenridge gave the illusion of escape, but as we drove into the mountains it became clear there was no escape. I drove sixty-five miles an hour and as cars passed us Joanne told me to speed up. "Speed up, why won't you speed up?" she said.

"The road has too many turns."

"You'll never change."

"For Christ sake, Joanne, what the hell's the matter with you?"

"For Christ sake yourself Charles, I want to get there."

She played with the screen in the dashboard until it displayed the truck's current gas mileage. "You're only getting six miles to the gallon. I don't think it will hurt too much to go a little faster."

I held on and kept going the speed I liked. Suddenly, cars passed me on all sides and at every rate of speed. Joanne looked at me with disgust. "You're going so slow people in the slow lane are passing you."

Cars raced up the mountain. A Camero and a new Mustang passed me at the same time on either side at over a hundred miles an hour. I was angry.

"I wonder what they get for mileage," I said.

Joanne rolled her eyes. The muscle cars weren't the only cars speeding up the mountain. In a minute a convoy was behind us, racing west on I-70.

"Speed up," Joanne said.

"What's going on, damn it?"

A red pickup truck attempted to pass me in the slow lane. I swerved to block his path. He slammed on his brakes to avoid me and veered into the other lane. When he came alongside my left his passenger pointed a small gun out the window. I touched the brakes and slowed so that he went ahead of me. For a moment he lingered, then he stuck his finger out the window and moved on.

"What is this, 1973? I hate when people pass me in the slow lane."

"Seems like a good reason to kill us, Charles."

I jammed the accelerator to the floor and we steadily accelerated to a hundred. We jerked forward, and I swerved to avoid a car that went slower than I was.

"You're always so herky jerky when you drive," she half smiled.

"Shut up and sit there."

"This really is just a wasteful American truck. Now we're only getting two miles to the gallon. Look," she said and pointed to the readout on the dashboard screen. The engine noise filled the cabin.

"Just look at the scenery. You'll be in your hotel soon. This was a mistake."

She looked at me and sneered.

We were on the last ascent before Eisenhower Tunnel and had gained enough altitude that the scenery took on the crumbling, elevated look of the Rocky Mountains, with snow piled in high banks on the roadside. The trees changed and were smaller here with knobs of frozen ice plastered to the tops like salt pillars. I pushed on, and we drove through a waft of cloud pressed low against the highway. My truck groaned under the pressure that the grade, altitude and speed put on the engine. At this altitude, there was less oxygen, and the truck had to work harder than at lower altitudes.

Joanne was a bundle of nerves beside me. I could feel her anxiety.

The anger she felt toward me now was visible. We rounded the last bend before Eisenhower Tunnel. The Camero and the Ford shot through the hole and disappeared into the blackness. Other cars, and the pickup truck with the gun followed into the tunnel.

Suddenly, the gates at the entrance to the Eisenhower Tunnel moved and armed officers darted into the highway behind cruisers flashing lights. Orange plow trucks pulled in front of them. The plows were on and pointed toward traffic. They blocked us now. No one would pass.

Above the tunnel the mountain shot up against the sky. The mountain served as the gateway to Summit County and my home, and without going under or over them, there was no way into Breckenridge.

"What's going on?" I said.

"It was all over the news on the plane ride in," she said. "You didn't hear?"

"Hear what?"

41

SARAH MCKENNA-HURST

"Turn on the news now! You have to turn on the news. Something awful happened. I'll be right home. I've got to go," Mike said on the phone.

"But what happened?"

The phone was dead.

Mike was on his way home from the ski shop where he worked part time for a friend. I got off the phone and watched the news channels in High Definition. I sat on our couch as snow fell outside.

On every channel people ran, screaming and driving for their lives. People were stuck on bridges in New York, and I pitied them. I recognized the landmarks that made up my home for four years, but the city was not the same. A soundless helicopter view swept up the city from the Empire State building north. Looking down at them, the city's buildings stood erect like corn stalks, and between the buildings, the ground was so densely packed that the roads seemed paved with automobiles and people.

The helicopter flew up the middle of Manhattan, and I felt dizzy from the three dimensional experience. The camera panned left to show the West Side Highway and then right to the FDR. Both were parking lots. The camera straightened out and caught a glimpse of a roof top sign written on a bed sheet that said, "Is this the end?" with an immense question mark after the statement. Another rooftop sign read, "**We Are Here**". The silent view on the TV showed another helicopter hovering over the Brooklyn Bridge, which was covered by people.

The news footage switched to a split screen and showed the George Washington Bridge also inundated, as well as the entrance to the Lincoln Tunnel. Pedestrians were entering the tunnel on foot to escape the city. At the top of the screen on a blue background in red letters were the words **"FLIGHT FROM EPIDEMIC"** and **"LIVE COVERAGE."**

A news anchor on one station said, "We have been reporting this story since it began earlier this afternoon."

These poor people tried to get out of the city, but were bottle necked in and trapped on the bridges and tunnels. Cars weren't moving on the highways; rather, there was a perpetual traffic jam of humans that streamed off the island of Manhattan. I changed channels and soon understood that it wasn't only New York, it was also Washington, Boston, Chicago, Dallas, and Los Angeles; people attempted to flee almost every major population center and, wherever the highway systems were overloaded, people fled on foot.

Chaos and anarchy ruled, especially on the news stations that constantly switched from pictures of one city to another and showed frantic scenes with equally frantic reporters.

I changed stations, but it seemed that news reporting lost sight of its primary goal and instead of giving the over-all picture, reporters feverishly described the action in "the streets." After what seemed like half an hour of coverage, an excited male reporter who stood in the center of the George Washington Bridge among the throngs of people began his news report:

"I am here on the George Washington Bridge where people are walking out of upper Manhattan. Some have abandoned cars in the grid locked traffic on I-95 and are now walking westward trying their best to get out of New York over the Hudson River and into New Jersey, but who knows what awaits them there."

The anchor broke in, "Can you explain for those who have not heard what has caused this mass migration all over the country, the news is so fluid that we hear conflicting reports at this desk, is there anything you can add?"

"From what we have been told here, and what we have seen, this whole story started at around 3:30 pm, eastern standard time, when it was reported that a man intentionally infected with Small Pox boarded a flight in Portland, Oregon. That plane was quarantined on the ground at JFK, and officials here won't release the man's name but have stated that a plane did land here from Portland and there were fears of a contamination risk from that plane."

"Do you know if the entire plane was put under quarantine or if only the man in question was?"

"I do not have that information here at this time, but as this story grew here in New York, we began to see people flee the city, first in a steady trickle and then in the flood you can see behind me now. It seems most people who are attempting to escape the city are commuters trying to get home. It's just that everyone left all at once, and even worse, night will fall here soon in Manhattan."

"Thank you, Tod. We now go live to Brent Fitchburg outside of JFK in New York. Brent:"

"Thank you, Joe. Officials here stated that in an apparent coordinated attack, other flights out of Portland may have contained passengers infected by Small Pox, and that around two hours ago police raided a house outside of Portland, Oregon, where a man was apparently dead from the virus. Police are not releasing the man's name but we have been told that he was a Russian immigrant who lived in Colorado legally for over a decade and recently returned from a trip to the Ukraine. We are also told that all officers who went into the house have been quarantined as well, and that those earlier flight records are being searched to learn the names of the passengers and find if anyone fell ill. The fear with small pox is that the people have not been vaccinated for the virus since its eradication and that the population is more susceptible to that virus than at any time in the last two millennia."

"Excuse me Brent, but we have to leave you to pick up the Mayor of New York who is speaking live."

The coverage then switched to the Mayor of New York City who was asked:

"We have gotten word that road blocks have been posted outside Denver to keep the infection there from spreading out of that hub, do you have a similar plan for New York?"

"No such plan exists because no such plan would work in New York. We have set up a quarantine around the airport."

"I'm sorry, will people be allowed to leave the airport?"

"No, the airport has been closed off."

"Why is that different from what Denver is doing?"

"I don't know what Denver is doing, but in New York, we cannot quarantine large portions of the city. The suggestion that we should close off Long Island, or Manhattan from the Bronx and New Jersey, is absurd. To close off five or ten million people when at this point we have only one confirmed case of the disease doesn't make sense. What has happened and is happening is that acting on information from the FBI, and the Portland police department regarding a passenger on flight 222, that flight was moved to a repair hangar where it was thoroughly tested by the Center for Disease Control, and all passengers were quarantined inside a tent in another hangar. A passenger by the name of John Megiddo was arrested and placed in a separate tent under suspicion of willfully spreading a contagious disease. He is the only suspect at this time in New York."

"How did you know he was the passenger?"

"His name was found on an itinerary in the Portland apartment raided earlier this afternoon. From what I am told, the apartment was used as a communal living space for The Peoples Group. And that is all I know at this time."

When he said the "The People Group" my nervous system nearly stopped functioning, and I could hardly focus on the television before me. Several minutes passed before I regained composure. The news jumped around from city to city and similar reports were given. The terror alert was raised from yellow to red and there was mass panic throughout. I searched every news station for some mention of my mom's name. More than likely, it was only a matter of time.

I tried dad's cell phone again, but he was out of service. I turned from the television and looked out the window. There was a car coming up my drive, and I stood to see who it was. A crumby old pickup with rust spots on the door was headed toward the house. I felt nervous. The truck pulled up and a balding white man with blue jeans, a ponytail and a hard walk stepped out. He flicked a cigarette into the snow, walked to my door and knocked. He hadn't seen me yet. I thought about hiding but decided against it. The front door creaked a little when it opened.

"Can I help you?"

"Sarah McKenna?"

"I am."

"I have a letter that a man wants you to have."

"It couldn't have been sent in the mail?"

"They read his mail."

"Who?"

"The correction's officers."

"Who sent this letter?

"Read it."

He held the letter out for me to take. I stepped back, and he pushed the envelope through the doorway.

"Here."

I grabbed the letter, and he walked back to his truck, but he didn't leave.

I pulled the card from its envelope.

I told you that I would never hurt you. I will never hurt you. Your mother is wrong about you. Not everything is an absolute. She misunderstands you. You will be among those who remake the world when this is over. The man in your driveway will not allow her near you.

42

CHARLES MCKENNA

E isenhower Tunnel was closed. I hit the brakes and brought the truck to a stop.

"What is this?"

Joanne didn't reply. Her eyes were closed and she hummed and meditated to herself.

"Joanne?"

"It was all over the news on the plane ride in. I was happy we landed, they were talking about a weaponized Small Pox outbreak."

"Who was talking?" I said.

A bead of sweat trickled down her forehead. "The news, but it was in New York, and the reporters didn't have facts about what happened. That was a few hours ago."

"Why didn't you say something?"

"I thought it was just the East Coast."

"You should have said something, what the hell is the matter with you?"

We were one of the first vehicles stopped by the roadblock. The barricade was impenetrable and a wall of cold granite mountain shot straight up behind it. Other cars came fast after us. I punched the steering wheel and Joanne leaned away. She looked out my window.

"Quick," she said. "Drive through the break in the median."

"Where?"

"Right there. You see. We can jump down one exit to Loveland Pass. There's less cops. It's just a scenic route."

She was right. Several officers ran toward us with orange cones and headed for the small break in the median strip that was used as a turn around. A helicopter hovered over head.

I pushed the gas to the floor and the rear wheels squealed and spun and then gripped and we shot off left through the opening in the concrete barrier. The car beside us made the same move and so did the car behind them.

We now headed east toward Denver on I-70 as we approached old Route 6, which was the original road over the Continental Divide and into Summit County. Route 6 saw little traffic since the Eisenhower Tunnel was constructed; it was now primarily used to bring hazardous materials through the mountains to avoid the tunnel.

I took the right hand turn onto Route 6 and passed a sign that said, "Continental Divide, 6 miles; Breckenridge, 24 miles." The car behind me caught up and tried to pass me, but I put my foot to the floor and the big V-8 under the GMC's hood roared. We pulled away from the small car and into a long gentle left hand turn. The road straightened. To our right was a steep, rocky hillside that the road wrapped around like a snake around a frozen tree. Then the road took a hard right hand turn around a jutting cliff into a high alpine valley. Around the bend, we drove into a snow-covered valley that was blindingly white from the reflection of the setting sun off the snow. The road straightened and I brought the truck to one hundred miles an hour as it began to snow.

We climbed the eastern slope of the Continental Divide at a high rate of speed. Joanne was silent.

After a series of S shaped corners, we hit a switchback where the road turned over itself like a hairpin. There I slowed to twenty miles an hour, but the tires still screeched on the road just wet with snow.

When the route straightened, I pushed the peddle to the floor again and soon we reached tree line and were surrounded by an empty desert of snow.

We headed up the last uphill climb on the eastern side of the Divide. A snowflake falling on this side would eventually melt and make its way into the Atlantic, but once over the Divide our doings would drip down to the Pacific. I could see the divide sign ahead at the crest.

The truck crested the hill and caught air on the final bump. The engine raced. We lurched to the side when we landed. To the right on the high side of the road, a narrow grove of short pine trees ran next to turnout for the scenic overlook where the large brown and gold sign proclaimed:

Loveland Pass
Elevation 11,990 feet
Continental Divide
Pacific Atlantic

HAVING CRESTED THE HILL, I saw beyond the sign. Several orange barrels with flashing red lights blocked the road. Beyond the barrels, two navy blue and gold police cars parked nose to nose blocked the road, and two officers dressed in sharp brown uniforms stood out in front of the cars with their rifles point at us. I slammed on the brakes and the truck came to a stop alongside the Continental Divide sign while the orange barrels stood between us and the police in a no man's land. Just ahead of me, and beside the sign, stood the opening for the scenic overlook.

I stopped while the car from earlier pulled right alongside me. Above, an officer shouted into a bullhorn from the roadblock and told us to turn around. I recognized Hank's voice over the bullhorn and stepped out of my truck. I saw his face from where I stood. The young officer standing beside Hank aimed his rifle at me. He looked frightened and eager to kill.

"Charles, just get back in your truck. We have orders, and they go for you as well. Now turn around and head back down the mountain."

As he spoke, cars and trucks packed the road behind us. High snow banks locked us in on both sides and within a few minutes the road back to the eastern slope where it dropped away was blocked. A big old boat of a Ford pickup truck now pulled up around the traffic. The truck traveled up the narrow breakdown lane with its right tire in the snow bank and drove ahead and stopped by the orange barrels. Hank shouted at the driver to turn around.

I stepped back into the truck. Joanne's eyes were closed again, and she meditated and hummed to herself.

I grabbed the knob and turned the radio on. Every station gave the news, and we picked up the feed in the middle of some press conference where a Colorado official explained why the roads were closed. He said that Denver received reliable intelligence that a person or persons infected with Small Pox flew into Denver this afternoon.

" . . . The City of Denver is the target of terrorist attack. In the interest of National Security we have been advised by the federal government to close off all routes leaving the city of Denver. We face the risk of a national epidemic and until we can learn more about the identity of those who may be infected with Small Pox, all routes leaving Denver will be closed. The information we have been given is that earlier this afternoon at approximately 1:00 pm Mountain time a flight . . . "

Gunshots rang out.

I ducked down to avoid being killed. The pickup truck that had come up the breakdown lane tried to pull through the orange barrels near the police cars. Hank fired into the truck and it stopped; smoke poured from its hood. I was surprised to see Andy open the door and climb out of the smoking pick up truck.

The other officer fired another shot into the ground by the truck's front tire, and Andy wheeled around and ran back toward us. When he reached the front of my truck he stood still, caught his breath and looked back to the roadblock. I didn't know whether I should call him to my window or not. He was frenzied. I looked to Joanne whose eyes were closed, her short gray hair hung limp and frazzled about her forehead, and she had deep lines in her cheeks.

"Are you paying attention to this?" I said.

She was sweating, and I turned the heat down. I touched her and she opened her eyes.

"I know what's happening. Who's that man in front of the truck?"

"That's Andy, I don't know what he's doing there, but stay awake for God's sake people are shooting."

"Would you like me to shoot back?" she closed her eyes again.

I rolled down the window to cool the truck off. Outside the air was frigid. With the window down, I heard Andy's feet grinding the snow now accumulating on the road. We were parked on the west side of the divide, near the crest of a ridge. To my left, the ridge descended down into a valley where the road ahead continued into Breckenridge; to the right, behind the sign and north, the ridge rose about 400 yards to the peak of the mountain.

"Andy, what's going on, take it easy."

"We don't have to take this. There's only two deputies up there, and there are plenty enough people down here to take em'."

"That's Hank up there." I said.

"We don't have to stand for this."

"Where the hell are you coming from anyway, don't you work Wednesdays Andy?"

He thought for a second. "I went to see my girlfriend, she lives in Columbine."

"What about Gwen?"

"We don't have to stand for this Charles, we're Americans." His eyes were wild. He was scared.

When he said that, I watched Edzul's pickup truck unload a group of men (his carpenters) behind the police cars above. Hank pointed and shouted and the men followed his command. Edzul parked and walked to the safe side of the roadblock and stared at my truck for a minute; then he and Hank spoke. Bill's Jeep pulled up, and Bill stepped out with a wooden Kalashnikov rifle and a long clip of bullets. Hank nodded to Bill, and Bill leaned back on the bumper of his Jeep with his rifle pointed up on his shoulder watching me.

It looked like Hank had been forced to recruit men from the Gold Pan. If roles were reversed, I might have been inspired to come myself. Instead, I was on the wrong side of the law with Andy and my angry ex.

Andy repeated himself, "We don't have to take this. Are you just going to sit here?"

"What do you propose we do?"

He removed and replaced the black baseball cap on his head so many times that the bald spot there grew before my eyes. "We've got to do something." His eyes darted back and forth.

"You're a bartender. We'll just sit tight is what we'll do. There's no reason to go crazy and get hurt. We don't need to worry about getting infected here, and whenever they figure out what's going on, we'll be the first ones through."

He looked at me and Joanne and got angry. "They can't treat us like cattle Charles. By the people for the people; what a lie"

"Either way, they've got the guns, and we can't go anywhere."

Joanne suddenly perked up. "That's all we are to the statisticians and number crunchers on Wall Street and in Washington; we're a liability to the rest of the country and we've been cut off. Denver is just a write off, get used to it, now the heartland isn't safe and everyone will be afraid."

"Joanne will help me!" Andy said.

"No, she won't help you." I rolled the window up in his face, and he grabbed the handle to open the door. It was locked. When he saw that, he banged on the window until I thought it was going to break. He was spooked. I didn't want him near me. I reached into the glove compartment and pulled out my gun. I grabbed the magazine and slapped it into the gun and chambered a round and pointed it into his face through the glass. When he saw it, he blinked a number of times and moved to the front of the truck, I turned on my headlights, which irritated him, and he shouted, "You're like the Jews that went along with Hitler."

After he finished his tirade, Joanne laughed and then closed her eyes again.

"Looks like all your buddies are on the roadblock," she said. "Maybe if you give Hank a beer he'll let you and Andy through."

I ignored her and watched Andy walk back up to my window.

"What am I supposed to do out here, freeze?" he said.

"Light a fire, that should keep you warm."

He was angry and turned and walked around and tried to recruit people from the other cars. I didn't know what he said to them, but his arms flailed about, and his face turned red, but no one helped him.

43

CHARLES MCKENNA

A ndy walked in front of my truck again, but this time he didn't stay. Instead, he approached the roadblock.

"This ought to be good," I said.

Edzul pointed to the no-mans land where Andy walked by the orange cones and kept on going. As he got close to the police cars Hank shouted, and one of the men fired into the air. The concussion made me flinch but Andy stayed on course and continued to his truck.

Hank was livid. "Turn around. Turn around now," he shouted through his bullhorn.

Andy got to the back of his truck and turned around to look at the traffic jam. I still thought he would get shot. He turned back and lifted the window on the aluminum top that covered his pickup bed, and from within, produced a chainsaw and canister of gasoline. He then walked to the scenic overlook where he proceeded to cut down several trees until he had felled about twelve small (maybe seven foot tall) pines. Other people came out of their vehicles and helped pull the trees into a large pile by the Continental Divide sign. While this took place, two news vans pulled up behind the roadblock, and a reporter with cameramen got out and shot pictures.

"This is interesting now," I said.

"It couldn't get any better," Joanne said.

At that moment, there was a whoosh from the gasoline and a black plume of smoke mixed with a red ball of fire. Joanne put her window down and the heat pressed our faces and lit the trucks cabin in orange light. The fire seemed to give people an excuse to step out of their vehicles and stretch.

After a few minutes, Hank pointed to the man beside him and then pointed to Andy's truck parked by the roadblock and shouted out commands. When he finished giving orders, the officer ran to Andy's truck and got inside. He was inside for a few seconds, and then he pushed the truck at the door. Andy's truck rolled away and into a snow bank on the high side of the road.

"Fire's like a male aphrodisiac," Joanne said. "There's no difference between any of these people here, just one's on the west side of the orange cones and the other one's on the east side of the cones."

"And one side has guns."

"All of you have guns," she said.

I ignored her and watched the men behind me pull grills out of their pickup trucks along with coolers full of meat and other food. The people set up the grills on the turnout by the Continental Divide sign but many feet away from the fire. Apparently, when they had heard about the infection, people packed the contents of their freezers into coolers and headed into the mountains for safety.

44

CHARLES MCKENNA

The fire fully engulfed the pile of pine trees, and the damp wood and pine needles popped and sparkled. The sun hung low on the cloudless sky and to the west, the horizon was drawn with the broken lines of a distant mountain range. It was near full dark.

"Pretty soon the people keeping the road block will also start a barbeque. It's only natural." Joanne said with her head turned away to look out the window.

She watched what happened the way a critic watches a play.

"They're like boys in the parking lot of a football game, only they get to drive big trucks and light big fires. You know what it's like, you used to play that silly game; now they can carry guns."

"Hopefully somebody gets to use those guns on the evil bastards that caused all this," she looked straight ahead at the blockade, I continued, "They said on the radio that it wasn't even Muslims that did it, I'm surprised at that; murder seems to be one of their Ten Commandments. Guess these are domestic sickos."

She was struck with anger. "I don't believe there are any truly bad people, there are only reasons that people don't understand," she said looking ahead.

"Except men like me right. Keep talking like that. I'm glad I came to pick you up. I've gotten closure."

"Likewise," she said, "You're a relic. You do realize that, don't you? You're a burden that America has to get beyond in order for the rebirth to occur."

I would have replied, but I noticed a man crouched against my rear tire holding a short rifle.

"What the hell is that guy doing?" I said, "There's a guy sliding up the side of the truck with a gun."

"I can see him," she said, "He's playing Cowboys and Indians; exactly like you'd be doing if I weren't here."

I turned from the mirror to look at her. She had hate in her eyes, which seemed all too normal to her. I looked ahead up to the roadblock and saw that Hank had his rifle trained on my windshield. Just then, I saw the crest of the man's head as he slinked forward beside my truck.

"You should get out your gun and go play cowboy too."

"Will you shut up!"

I slammed my truck door into the gunman. He fell over several feet away from the truck. His gun tumbled away and into the snow. He got to his feet, enraged and lunged for the gun. Hank shouted from above, while Edzul and others crowded around the police cars with guns raised.

"Look at this motley crew," Joanne said, "They probably all have hard-ons."

I closed my truck door.

"LEAVE THE GUN." Hank's voice boomed through the bullhorn. "DON'T TOUCH THE GUN."

The man didn't listen. He picked up his rifle from the ground and fired one round in the direction of the roadblock. Edzul's carpenters seemed most eager and accurate. The instant the man fired, their shots came back in return. His body vibrated. The crack of the shots echoed off the mountainside and back to the truck. His gun fell to the ground, and he stood upright as though a steel rod replaced his spine. Then he walked sharply and fell off the road at the point where plows pushed snow, and skiers descended to be picked up on the road to Breckenridge. I put my window down and heard the muffled sound his body made as it impacted the snow below. Everyone around was silent and watched what happened. The breeze picked up and then died and some of the men moved about on the roadblock.

The mountain slope that the man fell onto faced southeast which caused frequent cycles of freeze and thaw. After his body hit, there was a pause and then came a loud crack and a rumble growing deeper. My mirrors vibrated. I stepped out of my truck and ran to the edge of the road. Over the edge, the snow surface fractured ten feet deep and cracked audibly like a whip. The mountainside slid to the ground, and the snow boiled and frothed like a living mass with large hunks of icy snow peppered by sharded hunks of granite mixed up in the froth and tide of avalanche. For a flash of an instant, I saw the dead man's body come to the surface. Then his body was pummeled and broken by the large hunks of ice and stone. He disappeared in time for the avalanche to crash onto the road in the valley below.

The only access to the town of Breckenridge from here was now indefinitely closed.

The men on the roadblock watched the avalanche and shifted about as the reality of what happened sank in. Edzul turned to Hank with a frown and they talked between themselves. Hank pointed to something on the road below, Edzul simply shook his head, and Bill sat back on the hood of the Jeep with his Kalashnikov and relaxed. I walked over to my truck and stepped in.

Joanne looked at me. "You killed that man, do you feel big?"

"Stop, I didn't kill that man. I got him away from my truck so we didn't get shot."

"However you want to look at it. Maybe now your friends will accept you at the roadblock. You should go ask them." She leaned forward and occupied herself with the dashboard screen, "I thought you said you got television on this thing?"

I didn't bother to answer her, and she continued fiddling with the screen until she picked up the Denver news.

"Don't you want to listen to the news," she said. "We haven't really been listening; you don't really know what's going on?" She turned the volume knob and the sound of a somber male news voice filled the cab:

"There are not nearly enough Small Pox vaccinations for everyone in the country. This begs the question, why didn't someone fix this sooner?" The anchor was speaking to an expert on a panel of experts. The expert said, "And because it was eradicated in the world, it makes the population that much more susceptible. And if it's true what we hear, that this is a stronger and biologically modified version of the disease from back in the cold war, then America may be in deep trouble."

"Are you saying this is part of the cold war?"

"I am saying that the threats didn't go away, they multiplied." Joanne switched channels and another news anchor said, "The number of arrests is so far six across the country. Starting with John Megiddo on flight 222 earlier today at JFK in New York, then just a few hours ago the arrest of two in Portland Oregon along with a Russian man who died of the disease outside of that city. We are told his name was Nicolas Stopovich and he left Russia in 1999 with a visa that some believe was fast tracked. Stopovich may have been infected by unaccounted for weaponized Small Pox as late as one week ago on a return trip when he left Azerbaijan for Rome and then Atlanta and finally Seattle. The suspects are all under questioning as we speak and officials overseas seek anyone that may have seen this man. We just don't know at this point whether Stopovich was infected in the former Soviet Union or, with the exception of John Megiddo on flight 222, if Small Pox has been reintroduced to the United States population at all."

I looked from the screen to Joanne and said, "Lucky you weren't on one of those flights."

"Luck had nothing to do with it," she reached out her trembling hand and turned the volume down in the truck.

"What are you talking about?" I said.

"You're as oblivious to the world as you've always been. You're asleep to everything."

"Would you shut up with that?" I turned to her.

"We are going to bring about a rebirth for our mother Gaya."

"What's your problem?" I said.

"Hit me. It won't help you, but you might feel better for a while."

"We're in the right place for me to hit you."

"You would if you thought you wouldn't get in trouble. You always were a coward. But inside you're a murderer. Aren't you a murderer? Come on, you know you are. Like every American, you would murder for gold, for money for whatever you think you need."

"Sorry, I didn't inherit a trust fund."

She clutched my wrist. "I learned to talk to greed heads by living with you. We have generations of greed heads like you. You are not special."

"How 'bout I throw you in the road and you can stand there with Andy and roast marshmallows."

"Why don't you kill me, I already killed you." She leaned toward me in a taunt.

I slapped her face hard, and she faked crying and laughed.

"You only know how to solve problems with violence. You're just a pig like your friends on the roadblock; a fascist. Beat me down. It won't help you. You're dead already. You're all dead—your order. Do you know? Can you see? Do you know you've ruined our mother? You can't be allowed to live. You think you can hide in your private community; your racist town in an illusion mountain citadel and suck everyone dry. But that's why it was important to get you here. We stopped you. I killed you . . . Nicolas swabbed the culture there for you . . . We killed you. Go ahead and murder me now, isn't that what you'll do, can't you feel the murder."

I put my hand to the abrasion, "What?" Then I looked down at the screen in the dashboard. Joanne's smiling picture stared back at me on the local news. She was dressed in the same purple and blue dress that she told me was dyed with crushed snails and wore the same filthy necklace that now dangled from her aging wrinkled neck.

Her name ran atop the screen. Talking-suits talked about her in conjunction with The Peoples Group, but I couldn't hear them. The screen spilt between her and her other conspirators. I looked from the screen to her. She smiled gleefully beside me. A rush of hate came over me.

She saw it. "See, I told you that you would murder."

I leaned toward her with my teeth gritted. "You're insane!"

"I'm perfectly sane. We may be the only perfectly sane people left. And this is what must be done in order for Mother Nature to live; in order for the People to live as they were born to: without the constructed bonds of slavery. America's a lie that ruins everything, but She'll revive it: like the ashes of a burnt field make it fertile, or the Black Plague cleared backward Europe for the Renaissance: She'll bring the new renaissance. There needs to be such a catalyst in order for the change to come.

"Man's too proud for humankind to come. You think Mother Earth is yours to exploit at your will. But you're wrong. You think the land is yours to exploit as you will and the animals are yours to murder. But you won't be allowed to. You can't. Mother Nature is god and man won't treat her as he will. He'll be taught respect for her. He'll be brought to heel. In her womb is all life. In her fluid breaths all life. And you forget that she can cut the cord; she can abort the child that will grow to rape her; she can choke the arrogant boy within her with her germ. Who do you think you are? Who could you ever think you were?"

"What we were created to be."

She laughed, hysterically, and I thought of Sarah, and of how Joanne sought to kill her also.

"You'd murder your own daughter?" I said.

She looked at me, "You ruined her, but she wasn't yours. I never had one of your babies I let live."

"You killed my babies!"

"You're not fit to pass your seed. Your boy choked in my womb. Does that shock you? And the daughter you perverted is not yours. Her real father knew she'd be safe under your roof because in your world he could not protect her—he sacrificed her. You killed her."

"You killed my son!!!"

"He had no right to live polluted by your paternity."

I had no words to speak, only hate. I was dizzy. My vision shrank. I saw red.

Joanne continued, "Bill told me what you needed to hear and when I should call so you'd be receptive. I could hardly bring myself to leave the message and write the letter, it made my skin crawl, but it worked. Here I am. You're so weak, you couldn't even say no when it went against every bone in your body to reconcile with me, and you're supposed to be educated. You're disposable."

I grabbed her by the collar and dragged her onto the center console. I was euphoric with hate. She struggled then went limp and blew in my face. She turned her head left to right and exhaled all over me. "Have some more."

"Family used to have value."

"But you don't have one."

"Is Bill her father you lunatic?"

"Bill's not her father, Stanley White's the father, didn't you know that, couldn't you see it all those years? He was the greatest event in my life, I never knew anything like him, and I never will. It took me years to understand. What I did before others. It was what I hadn't done before. He liberated me—and you . . . you." She scoffed. "It was immaculate; it opened me up and freed me from the chains I'd been bound under since I was born—to think that act should be owned by Dark Age constructs. I could never deny what he did for me. But even much later when he made me pregnant I couldn't admit what *he* was. He was in me no mater what vows I took or what I did to escape. I was always running from my mother's fears, like virginity was something to be honored. But he was my true husband from nature, my priest for Mother Nature. We were her children in Love. Her gods on earth. He showed his loyalty by burning your vanity, and they imprisoned him for the love of her, but I kept hope, and Sarah was his daughter, she was his, and she had his potential, but you ruined her. All she knows now is Jesus, Death and Money."

I squeezed her until she shut up and threw her into the seat against the passenger door. Her head banged off the glass. She whimpered and held her head in pain.

In a moment she regained her evil. "You're shaking," she said.

"You came to kill my daughter?"

"She's not yours. She never was."

"She always was."

"I took care of her when she was burned. You perverted her. She prays at the church of the dollar beside you."

"But you've failed."

"Have I?"

"You're a murderer," I said.

"I'm a renewer. A catalyst. We're a feature of Her cycle."

"You never evolved past your twenties,"

"Rich or poor, the disease is perfect: it doesn't discriminate. It's the catharsis which prepares growth."

45

CHARLES MCKENNA

I didn't want to look at her anymore. I wanted nothing to do with her. She was pathetic. I needed air. I needed fresh air, not what she polluted. Outside there was air— outside away from the lunatic. She had returned the part of me she stole when we first met. It was black and malignant. I wondered if it always was.

I stepped out of the truck. The sun was gone. The only light came from the bonfire of fresh pine trees and the headlights off the traffic. The sky was filled with a billion stars and as many possibilities. I looked back through my open truck door at the dashboard screen while Joanne rambled her idiocy. On the screen there was a man in a red prison jump suit with long blond hair and a beard cropped to look like philosophers of old. He smiled in his interview. A caption read, "Father of The Peoples Group," but he was saying, "It was not me. It was her."

I slammed shut the door and walked in front of my truck's headlights and over to the group of men by the bonfire. I stumbled and looked back. Joanne had the window down.

"Are you alright, buddy?" a man by the bonfire asked me.

"No," I said. "It's her. I just picked her up from the airport."

"What?"

"Are you deaf? That woman is infected, she's one of them!" I shouted.

"What you talking about," a man holding a shotgun asked me.

"If you don't believe look, her picture's everywhere. It's her."

The mob continued moving toward me but some of them put their heads down to look at their phones their faces aglow with the devices. I turned and headed off toward the roadblock, but as I went I heard Joanne say, "I told you that you would murder me. The messenger is always killed," as the mob now came toward her. I wanted to kill her myself.

"Don't move any closer. Get away from that truck!" Hank yelled through the bullhorn. The officer beside him fired a shot that stopped the mob in its tracks.

I walked toward the orange cones. The fire lighted me for all to see and I continued forward not sure what I would do. Every eye was on me as I moved in the no-mans land between tribes. Another shot came from the roadblock, and the people in the mob turned their heads to watch me get killed. I looked over my shoulder and saw them assemble.

"Charles. Turn around. Walk back!" Hank yelled.

As I walked up beside one of the orange road barrels, Bill fired a shot with the Kalashnikov that ruptured the light on top of the orange barrel beside me. I felt strange when the light exploded. I knew Bill would kill me.

I took off running to the side of the road with the mountain in my eyes. Several shots hit the snowy pavement around me, and I dove over the snow bank at the edge of the roadside by Andy's truck.

"Don't kill him for Christ's sake!" Hank shouted from the road-block. "Stop shooting damn it!"

I ran down the ditch that was made between the bank and the hillside. When I reached the spine of the ridge behind the Continental Divide sign I raised my head and looked back to the road-block and the mob. The bonfire was far left of me, and the mob was between where I crouched and my truck. Bill swept the snowy mountainside with a spotlight attached to his Jeep searching for me. When he saw my head he fired.

"Stop firing Bill!" Hank shouted

Edzul fired a shot at Bill but missed, and Bill turned and shot Edzul dead. His body hit the pavement. Hank yelled and raised his rifle, but Bill fired shots into the police cars where Hank and the men dove for their lives away from Bill's gunfire. A cameraman was crouched behind Bill's Jeep, leaning out with a large black camera so he could film.

I ran as fast as I've ever run. At any other location on the mountain I would have been stuck in yards of deep snow, but the ridge line on which I ran was exposed to a constant wind, and the trail was either hard packed from skier foot traffic or was gravel.

46

SARAH MCKENNA-HURST

"What's going on?" Mike said. He just walked in. "There's a man in the driveway in a truck. I knocked, but he pretended he couldn't hear me. I was going to break his window and find out who he was, but then I figured he was a friend your father sent to watch out for you."

"He is," I said absentmindedly while watching the news. Then I said, "My mom's on the news."

There was an awful picture of my mom on TV in some dress with a foolish grin across her face that went from cheek to cheek.

"This is apparently a taped recording from the group," the anchor said and then began a recording of my mom in front of a light purple canvas. She looked dead into the camera without the slightest show of emotion. She had no heart, which was evident in her soulless spoken word and cadence. She said:

"We have sent people to four major cities. This is the most immoral nation in history. The world cannot continue as it has, there needs to be a pruning of the tree so that other branches can grow. . ." Then the message became garbled and the internet transmission blurred. The newscast switched away and the anchor apologized and finished by reading parts of the transcript.

The anchor then gave information on how mom was suspected of leaving a house where Nicolas Stopovich died of Small Pox. Her picture came back up on screen. Then his again; I remembered his fat, stupid face. They switched back to mom's picture.

"This is Terror Mom," the anchorman said.

"I'm sorry," Mike said when he heard that.

I expected to see a news van in my driveway to interview me. I wondered if the man in the truck out there would let them in. I heard the questions run through my head, "What is it like to be Terror Mom's daughter?" "Did you know this was coming?"

The picture switched from the news desk graphics and now showed live footage of Loveland Pass. The camera zoomed onto my dad's truck where mom sat with her face turned to an angry mob of people.

"We are pretty certain that this is Joanne Hurst, Terror Mom," the reporter said. The camera focused in tight onto her face in the window of dad's truck. She looked like an unkempt broken old starlet in the eye of the paparazzi.

Then the camera panned left and swept over the bonfire and fell on the mountain ridge on the way to the peak. In the distance a light moved up the side of the mountain.

The reporter at the roadblock began hysterically reporting, "A man has just run from that truck. There has been chaos here. The man attempted to flee and was shot at from the roadblock. The man shooting turned and shot a person protecting the roadblock. Things are not good here." She spoke in breathless reporter-english. "Amy Schiller of our own News 3 team followed behind them. We think the man being chased is the former husband of Terror Mom, Charles McKenna, but we do not at this time know the identity of the man who fired at the people on the roadblock. But Amy has followed behind them in the treacherous conditions and as you can see it is very difficult to bring a camera up such a steep incline. In some spots I am told the mountain there reaches almost thirty degrees, and you can just imagine what it's like to lug a camera up that mountain in the middle of the night." The reporter was reporting on the other reporter reporting, and I wondered who this event was about.

"News 3 exclusive," the anchor said. There were a series of cluttered reports and I thought I heard some fast talking women call my mom the TM, but I wasn't sure. The coverage changed again and came back to Loveland.

The camera zoomed onto the mountainside. I saw red hair on the man who chased my dad.

Someone shouted off camera. Then the camera panned from showing the mountainside where my father ascended and swept back over the bonfire and showed the traffic jam. There, mom yelled at the crowd that assembled near the truck.

Men pointed guns at her, but they were afraid and stayed back. She yelled, but the camera couldn't pick up her words. The camera bounced and moved from the roadblock where it was stationed and went toward my mom at the traffic jam. Her voice was nearly audible. She walked away from dad's truck then until she was between the camera and the bonfire casting a large black shadow under the firelight. The mob of people inched closer and she moved near the flames. The cameraman had gotten close enough now that he picked up what she said. "Is that really her?" one of the mob shouted.

Several people stooped their necks to look into their smartphones. One man looked up and said, "That's her." Followed by others. "She's wearing the same dress as in the picture."

He pointed to his phone. There was general agreement among them that my mom was Terror Mom. One of the men drew back and took aim with his rifle but thought better of shooting as another man took a picture.

My mom stared at the crowd.

"Kill her, kill her," they said," kill her, kill her."

The shouts got louder. Someone threw a can of beer that splattered her dress and face. The camera turned and caught the police running from the roadblock to put a stop to what was about to happen, but when they reached the end of mom's shadow they stopped; likely afraid of her infection. I recognized Hank. He had a rifle and aimed it at the crowd.

"Lay down your guns. Lay them down. Now. No one is going to kill anyone tonight," Hank said.

"What kind of a mother are you anyway?" someone shouted.

"What kind of child are you?" she asked and took a step toward the crowd that took a step away from her. "Are you all afraid? You have all those guns, but you're all cowards."

She stepped forward again but this time the audience remained where it was.

"Joanne," Hank said. "Stay calm."

"I am calm."

"Aren't you going to do anything to her," a man in the crowd shouted.

"Get her," someone said.

"What will you do Hank?" mom taunted.

"Shut up and get back. Joanne, you're under arrest."

"Come arrest me."

He tossed handcuffs that fell to the snowy ground beside her sandals. "Put those on Joanne."

"Come and put them on me. Are you afraid too?"

"Just shoot her. Shoot her or we will."

"You won't do anything," Hank said. "Now put down your weapons or I'll shoot you. Drop them."

"You can't stop us."

Hank fired a shot in the air. "I'll try."

"Kill her."

"Murder me then," mom said. "You're all murderers, look at you with your guns. You mass murder culture. I'm the beginning and you're the end." She turned from the crowd and walked to the fire. "These flames are purer than your filthy hands. I'll release myself if you won't."

The man behind the camera said, "Oh my God, oh my God."

The snow fell a little harder than before. My mom picked up the can of gasoline and poured it over her head, showering in the gasoline.

"Joanne!" Hank screamed, but he was frozen.

She was ten feet from the fire, looking at the crowd, then she turned to the camera with gasoline dripping down her face and clothes.

"I am the American Dream," she said and rushed into the flames. Her body exploded from the gasoline and disappeared behind a wall of fire.

Phone cameras flashed in the background.

"Oh my God," I said.

Mike turned off the television.

"Oh my God oh my God." I said.

I cried and shivered, and Mike covered me. He didn't speak, he merely held me.

"Turn it back on," I said.

"No, you don't need to see anymore."

"My dad is running up the mountain, and Bill is chasing him."

47

CHARLES MCKENNA

I ran. My lungs burned from exertion. I passed a two-thousand-year-old broad bristlecone pine tree. The oldest of its kind was some 4,000 years old, known as Abram's Tree. I thought of taking shelter beneath its ancient branches, but I couldn't, I had to keep running. I had to reach the top of the mountain and meet fate. I was not out of rope yet.

Bill was behind me holding his rifle and running up the ridge toward me. From time to time he fired, but he wasn't aiming to kill me. No. He toyed with me. He could have shot me long ago, I was sure of it, but he hadn't. Down on the roadside he tried to shoot me, there was no doubt, but as we ran onto the ridge it was apparent he was waiting for something else. I wondered what. Behind him the cameraman gained on us.

A few minutes more and I reached the top. My lungs ached and burned, and my right thigh went into spasm. I collected myself and stood looking out to the world. To the east, I looked over the massive traffic jam that covered I-70. I traced the traffic through the deep valleys by the light of the headlights. Any other night, and the distant valleys would have been invisible in the darkness. Stars twinkled above. The universe around was closing in and time felt slow.

My eyes had a strange sort of focus tonight, a focus caused by pain and revelation. I looked to the west and thought I saw the high-water mark of the West, but it was just the light off the reflection of the camera.

Bill ran closer with his rifle. I shouted, and sat and then stood and turned to see him behind me. He stood several feet away; his rifle pointed at my heart. I stepped toward him out of anger, and he fired a shot that whizzed by my head.

"Don't move Charles, or I'll kill you."

"Joanne's gone now," I said.

"She achieved her goal."

"Achieve *yours* then. I don't want to wait."

"You give up quickly,"

I laughed. In truth, I wanted to live more than anything, but I would never beg for life. I'd rather he just shot me and got it over with, but now that he was so close, I had a chance. When he was far away, with his assault rifle and an endless supply of bullets, he had all the advantage in the world. Now, at close range, I had opportunity; especially if he was going to stand and look at me. I had every intention of killing him. But what was he waiting for?

Anger welled inside me. "We both lost the woman we loved, didn't we?" I said, "Were you two going to celebrate, smoke a little dope, watch the world die, that sort of thing?"

He walked closer. "You never understood. There was something there, something real."

"Beautiful thing that must have been?"

"You've got a lot of anger Charles. . . it won't help you though."

I took a step toward him.

"Don't move like that," he said. "I wouldn't want to kill you before the camera's here."

"I didn't know this was a movie."

"If it's not on TV," he cocked his head at an angle, "it's not real."

"What kind of Kool Aid you drink?"

"I just see the progress of history."

"Did Smiley show it to you? Now you'll kill everyone."

"He loves the world too much to kill *everyone*."

"Of course he does." I said.

He smirked, "No. He put the bug in her ear and retired to a cell, and Joanne followed through like we knew she would. She's the heart and soul of The Peoples Group."

"And you're just a soldier, you execute commands."

Bill stepped to the side. "Power is what you can do. Power is what can't be taken from you. Power is truth, and it's not yours anymore."

"Is that so?" I breathed heavily from the altitude. We faced each other moving parallel on the mountaintop.

"I'd be angry too if I lived so long in a dream, Charles. Your daughter's not even your own." He looked pleased. "You're the father she never looked for."

"She never had to."

"But she's not yours."

"Is this the first you think I heard?"

"Doesn't change the fact."

"She always was my daughter." When I said that, he lost his composure and was livid.

"You don't deserve to live anymore." He said.

Suddenly, the cameraman and reporter burst over the last hump of mountain and stood flat-footed before us. They lost track of where they were in the heavy snow and were startled to be so close. We stood as if on points of a triangle. The reporter breathlessly talked into her microphone. The voice of an anchorman screeched out of a hidden speaker mounted on the cameraman beside her.

"We believe New 3 reporter Amy Schiller is following Terror Mom's husband, Charles McKenna, and Peoples Group conspirator, Bill Saxon," the anchor said through the speaker before the cameraman was able to turn the volume down.

Bill turned to acknowledge the news team. The wind picked up and snow fell. There was a gust of wind and the snow turned into whiteout. Then the light from the camera lit the snowflakes. I couldn't see more than ten feet. I took a few steps in the direction of the light. A shot was fired. Then another. I reached behind me.

48

SARAH MCKENNA-HURST

The camera zoomed to dad's face. He was angry. Snow fell. In the distance were lights from the traffic jam below. The moon hung huge over everything. The reporter pointed to Bill. The screen split; on one half of the screen there was a picture of Bill taken a few years ago side by side with his living image. The anchor said that he was one of the conspirators. He helped put the plot in motion.

Snow fell harder now; almost to the point where the camera couldn't pick up what happened. My dad backed slightly away and the snow increased until we couldn't see anything. It was a blizzard, a near whiteout. The camera's nearly blind.

"What's happening?" I said.

Suddenly there were gunshots on television that lit up the falling snowflakes along with Bill's face. Another gunshot followed and the reporter fell, her blood splattering the camera lens, leaving red streaks to smear some of the screen. The cameraman's hand rose to wipe the lens. He kept filming all the while.

Bill came close to the picture and crouched on the mountaintop. I couldn't see my dad. Bill was right in front of the lens scanning the mountain. His hair blew in the wind. His face looked pale and cruel.

"What's happening?" I said to Mike.

Bill fired another shot into the whirling blizzard. The flash was bright and affected the camera for a moment. The screen turned blank and white. When the image returned, dad rushed into the picture from behind the camera. Bill couldn't react quickly enough. His rifle pointed forward as dad tackled him from the side. There was a dull thud as bodies collided. Bill grunted when dad's shoulder struck him in the ribs, and the rifle skidded off into the freshly fallen snow and disappeared beyond the camera's range. Bill toppled onto his back, and dad fell several feet away. Both rose instantly. Bill pulled a knife. Dad held his handgun outstretched with both hands, and they stood looking at each other.

One lunge and Bill was on top of my dad with the knife.

There were more flashes right before the camera. FLASH—flash-flash. The flashes were quick and tight together. The sound of the three shots distorted in my speakers. The screen went white for a second and returned with Bill bloody on the ground writhing for a moment and dead the next. The white snow was covered red with blood.

Dad turned and faced the camera. The camera angle shifted to film him in different light.

He looked straight at the lens with anger in his eyes. "I'm sick of your camera." He said and raised his handgun. The camera then dropped to the ground, and the picture vibrated as the frame caught the cameraman's feet running off. Just then there was a flash concurrent with the crack of a gunshot and the screen went blank for a second and then switched quickly back over to the news desk where a bewildered looking anchor stuttered out some words: "Obviously, he's a crazed man to shoot a camera."

The newscast shifted to the camera that had just witnessed my mom's self-immolation. The scene at the traffic jam was somber and the reporter was questioning the people who witnessed what happened moments ago.

"Excuse me sir." The reporter said to a man in a Ford F-250. For a second the camera couldn't hear their words, and then the sound returned as she talked at him. "We are being told that this strain of the virus has the ability to infect one third of the population, and kill a third of that, another third will become blind?"

The camera switched again to the helicopter view where they caught my dad walking west away from the road block and into the wilderness.

"Daddy," I said, but he couldn't hear me now. "Daddy." And I cried. Mike moved to hold me. I knew what he was doing. I watched my dad walk into the wilderness to freeze to death. But he didn't keep walking. Instead he stopped and looked up at the helicopter with its spotlight; right into the camera in the swirl of snow. He seemed to be considering something. In a moment he walked back to the peak. The helicopter spun its rotors making circles in the snow that erased dad's footprints. At the top he paused again; gun still in hand. The commentator was speechless. Dad looked up at the helicopter one more time and then walked back to the roadblock on the divide.

"Dad." I said and cried out of happiness.

THANK YOU FOR READING

If you enjoyed the book and would like to see more of this author's work please go to the Chris Moore Author Page on Amazon. Feel free to leave a review.

amazon.com/author/chrismoore